WUTHERING

FRIGHTS

Also by HP Mallory:

THE JOLIE WILKINS SERIES:

Fire Burn and Cauldron Bubble
Toil and Trouble
Be Witched (Novella)
Witchful Thinking
The Witch Is Back
Something Witchy This Way Comes

THE DULCIE O'NEIL SERIES:

To Kill A Warlock
A Tale Of Two Goblins
Great Hexpectations
Wuthering Frights

WUTHERING

FRIGHTS

Book 4 of the Dulcie O'Neil series

HP Mallory

WUTHERING FRIGHTS

by

H.P. Mallory

I dedicate this book to myself seventeen years ago when I decided I wanted to become a writer and then wondered if I actually had enough talent to make it happen...

You did it.

Acknowledgements:

To my fabulous mother:
Thank you for all your help.

To my editor, Teri, at www.editingfairy.com:
Thank you for the clean up!

To my husband:
Thank you for all your love and support.

To my son, Finn: I love you.

To the winner of my "become a character in my
next book" contest, Christina Sabbiondo:
I hope you enjoy seeing yourself in print!

And to my past contest winners: Dia Robinson,
Caressa Brandenburg and Alexandra Fields
Garrity: I hope you enjoy your return in this
book!

O N E

It is said that during times of immense fear, shock or heartache, your body does weird things. And I'm here to say it's true. Why? Because I endured all three of those emotions as I stood in front of the Head of the Netherworld, a double-dealing bastard who'd been importing illegal potions from the Netherworld to Earth for Hades-only-knew-how-long. And in dealing with the feelings of fear, shock and heartache, my knees went wobbly and I had to stabilize myself against the bookshelf standing next to me. Afraid I might accidentally blow a hole into the floor, I rested my Op 7 handgun, similar to a Glock 31, on the shelf. Why had my knees suddenly become the consistency of jelly? And why was I now finding it difficult to breathe? Because the bastard standing before me had just informed me that he was my father.

It was almost as if the doors to my brain had blown open in a hurricane because I was bombarded with thoughts and memories—memories of a time long ago, nine years long ago, when my mother was still alive.

My mother ...

In general, I tried to shield myself from thoughts of my mother because those thoughts invariably led to feelings of darkness and depression that would clutch my insides until I could barely breathe. My mother had been killed by a goblin nine years ago, which is why I'd decided to become a Regulator (think, law enforcement agent) for the Association of Netherworld Creatures (ANC) in Splendor, California.

I felt my eyes narrow as I glanced up at the man who called himself my father. It wasn't that I doubted him—I

1

couldn't. If our last names weren't illustrative enough of our shared lineage, the similarity of our faces was—I had my father's emerald green eyes, both in shape and color as well as his high cheekbones. And my mane of honey blond hair seemed borrowed from the man standing just before me, although his hair was now generously sprinkled with grey. But while I was a fairy, my father was an elf. 'Course, he'd failed to mention his elfin ancestry when he'd introduced himself to me as "Melchior O'Neil, your father." But, as a fairy, I possess the ability to detect bloodlines of everyone I meet, his included.

Family likeness aside, it was time I asked a few questions of my own and got some closure on some subjects I'd always wondered about. I'd practically abandoned my search for the answers seeing as how my mother was dead and prior to this moment, I'd never met my father.

"My mother said you left us, that she came to California because she was pregnant with me and you ran off," I managed to say in a constricted, sore voice.

My father nodded but that small smile he'd been wearing since he'd admitted to our familial connections was still in place and still just as infuriating. "Yes, I imagined your mother would say something of the sort." He shook his head like he was amused, like I'd just told him some funny little anecdote about when I was a kid. "That Marjorie ..."

"Then it isn't true?" I demanded, hating the sound of her name on his tongue. And that was when it was pretty clear that I hated him. I felt my hands fist at my sides and glanced down at the floor as I forced myself to count to five. An outburst would do me no good at this point. No, I had to maintain my cool while I figured out how to get myself out of this mess. Glancing down, I suddenly remembered I was wearing nothing but my bra and jeans. In the process of breaking into the Head of the Netherworld's office, I'd lost my shirt.

Lost a shirt but gained a father ...

"No, it isn't true," my father announced and then turned to face the third person in the room who I could honestly say I'd completely forgotten about since I'd realized Melchior was my father. Quillan, who I'd mistaken for the Head of the Netherworld when I'd broken in and found him occupying my father's chair, was really Melchior's henchman, his right-hand man. And Quillan was also my ex-boss and ex—close friend. But that was a long and convoluted story.

Quillan remained silent and I found it strange that Melchior bothered to glance at him. Did he think Quill might have something to say about the mess known as my family? Instead, my old man looked at me and shook his head slowly.

"I never left your mother. She left me."

I nodded as everything suddenly became crystal clear. My mother hadn't wanted to raise her child in the Netherworld, which was basically a combat zone and completely unsafe. More than that, though, I'm sure she didn't want to raise a child with this asshole, Melchior—someone who was, for all intents and purposes, a crime boss. He was making a killing off the black market in the illegal potions trade and was so high up the proverbial ladder, he was untouchable.

"Smart woman," I said in the same tight voice.

Melchior said nothing but eyed me with no expression of sadness in his eyes at all—like it was no skin off his teeth that my mother had left him to raise me all by herself, like he could have given a rat's ass that he'd never had a connection with his daughter. As soon as that thought entered my mind, his demeanor changed, as if he'd clued into my feelings and wanted to prove me wrong.

"You look just like her," he said in a haunted tone, something that sounded barren and void. It was as though he was suddenly sad that he'd missed out on all those years, like he was bummed he hadn't been there to potty train me, teach me to ride a bike, or tell me how beautiful I looked on prom night.

"Lucky for me," I answered, my lips tight.

He chuckled then and shook his head, eyeing Quillan again almost as if he were embarrassed that Quillan was still sitting there. Then my father faced me and seemed to study me as if he were about to draw a detailed portrait of me. "Your mother was a beautiful woman and you are just as lovely." He paused, as if waiting for me to say, "Ah, gee, thanks, Dad," but when I remained silent, he continued. "Though she had none of your fire."

That was when I realized the entire time I was making small talk with this jerk, Knight was still imprisoned, subjected to the beatings of the ruthless guards and probably worried that any minute could be his last. The main prison of the Netherworld was no vacation, not by a long shot.

I turned to face Quillan, no longer interested in playing the game of family charades with Melchior. "Get Caressa on the phone," I said in a voice that warned him not to argue with me. "And put her on speaker."

Quillan started to shake his head at the same time that he looked at my father. "Dulce, Caressa can't know you're here."

I nodded. "She won't know I'm here—I won't say a word. I just want to make sure you're really going to call her and that you aren't trying to pull a fast one over on me." I took a deep breath. "And don't call me Dulce. My name is Dulcie," I finished with as much bravado as I could muster.

"Have you always been so suspicious?" Melchior asked me, his eyebrow raised in an amused sort of way.

I glared at him. "Yes, which is why I've survived this long."

My father said nothing more but turned and nodded at Quillan as if to say putting Caressa on speakerphone was okay. Caressa Brandenburg was the only respectable, high-ranking ANC employee I'd encountered so far in the

Netherworld. I knew she'd make damn sure Knight was out of High Prison and on his way back to Earth as soon as Quillan gave her the go ahead. Yep, Caressa was an angel of mercy, as far as I was concerned.

I watched as Quillan faced the rotary phone which looked like it was straight out of the sixties and any hopes I had of getting Caressa on speaker phone flew out the window. That was the weird part about the Netherworld—it was almost like a third world country, no modern conveniences. When I'd first met Knight, he'd described the Netherworld as existing in the same spatial plane as Earth. He'd said it was like a cake with layers, the Netherworld being one layer and Earth the layer just above. So even though I was currently in the Netherworld, I was also in the twenty-first century, yet you'd never know it by looking around.

"No speakerphone?" I asked, irritated.

Quillan frowned. "Not everything is as it appears, Dulcie."

He started dialing when my father interrupted him. "Before you dial Caressa," Melchior started as he gave me a nonchalant smile. My heartbeat pounded inside me as if it were still trying to deal with the bewilderment I'd been experiencing for the last ten minutes.

"Yeah?" Quillan asked. He paused with his index finger pointing aimlessly in the air as he faced my father.

"Then you agree to everything I've laid out for you, Dulcie?" Melchior asked me. His lips were tight and his expression stern.

I swallowed hard as I remembered the bargain I'd made—that I would resume my place as a Regulator for the ANC located in Splendor, California, and Knight would again be my boss. Only this time, I'd also be working for Melchior to make sure his illegal potions made it to Splendor so they could hit the streets and be sold on the black market to thugs, addicts and ... kids. I felt bile climbing up my throat and had to swallow it back down. The only reason I'd agreed to such terms was to save Knightley Vander's life. At the moment, that was all that mattered to me. I promised myself to think of a long-term solution later; but for now, I just had to save Knight.

Knight headed the ANC Splendor branch and he was a good, honest and loyal guy. For reasons unknown to me, he'd been kicked out of the Netherworld and forced to Earth. But when he'd taken the rap for me by pleading guilty to a mistake I'd made, he'd found himself back in the Netherworld. And back in the Netherworld, Knight had been exactly where Melchior wanted him. It was becoming increasingly clear that my father had always wanted Knight Vander dead.

"Yes, as I told you before," I started and faced my father. "If working for you means saving Knight's life, I'll agree to it." I paused. "But that's the only reason I'm agreeing to it. Otherwise I would have told you to go fu ..."

Melchior nodded and interrupted me with a chuckle as he faced Quillan. "Very well," he said and I watched Quillan start dialing the rotary phone again.

I narrowed my eyes at my father, wanting some answers of my own. "What did Knight ever do to you that made you so intent on getting rid of him?"

My father seemed surprised by the question, and his eyebrows lifted. "If the Loki hasn't informed you, then neither shall I."

By Loki, he was referring to Knight—Knight was a Loki, a soldier of the Netherworld forged by the fires of Hades, the god of the Netherworld. As to whether Hades had ever existed was anyone's guess. It wasn't like anyone I knew had ever met him—it was just one of those stories that some people believed and others didn't. Sort of like Santa Claus ... well, if you're seven years old.

But back to the fact that my father wasn't going to enlighten me about the issues between my Loki and him ... I guessed I was just SOL.

"Brandenburg, please," Quillan said into the mouthpiece as he faced me and waited for Caressa to pick up. He glanced at my current state of undress and frowned. Then he started unbuttoning his long-sleeved shirt, pulling it down his arms and placing it on the desk. He yanked his white undershirt over his head and the sight of Quillan's beautiful upper body made me look away.

As an elf, Quillan is tall and regal looking with wavy blond hair and hazel eyes. He's definitely a looker and as I mentioned earlier, he was my former boss. Throughout our time together at the ANC in Splendor, I had a crush on him and we even shared a kiss or two. Once I learned he was working for the bad guys, however, I completely clipped him. Sometime after that, I came very close to arresting him. I even had him in the sights of my Op 7 but was unable to pull the trigger, and Quillan escaped. It was all my fault, but Knight took the rap.

Quillan glanced at me and balling up his T-shirt, tossed it over. I caught it midair and nodded my head quickly to say thanks. Pulling the shirt over my head, I smoothed it down around my lithe, five foot one frame and found it fit me like a dress. Well, T-shirt dress or not, it was better than standing there with my boobs hanging out of my bra.

"What do you want, Beaurigard?" Caressa's voice rang out and I could only wonder how they managed to rig up the rotary phone into a speakerphone. Must have been magic.

Quillan cleared his throat, apparently ill at ease with the fact that Caressa obviously didn't think much of him. But Caressa must have known he was Melchior's wingman, right? Hmm, the more I thought about it, the more I wondered exactly how much Caressa did know about all the ins and outs of the Netherworld and the illegal potions industry. I mean, how could she be such a highly ranked official and not know?

"I'm calling about Knightley Vander," Quillan answered.

There was a moment or two of silence on the other end. "Why?" Caressa asked and her voice held much less boldness this time. She was obviously worried about Knight.

"He is to be released immediately," Quillan ordered.

I heard Caressa exhale deeply. "I will see to it personally," she answered and I felt tears well in my eyes, knowing Knight was now safe. Well, as soon as he was in Caressa's custody, he would be safe. Caressa and Knight had worked together when Knight still lived in the Netherworld and they'd become good friends. Really, Caressa had been the only friend Knight had in this godforsaken place.

"You are to accompany him to the portal on Albany Street and he is never to return to the Netherworld," Quillan continued. "If he asks you any questions, Caressa, don't answer. As far as you're concerned, all you were ordered to do was release him. End of story."

"So why the sudden change?" Caressa asked.

Quillan eyed Melchior and my father shook his head as Quillan wrapped the phone cord around his fingers. When he spoke, his voice was hard. "Not something you need to know."

"Okay," Caressa said impatiently. "I gotta go." Before Quillan could respond, she hung up and the blaring of the dial tone rang out through the room.

I was finally leaving the Netherworld and although I'd accomplished my mission, and obtained Knight's release, I couldn't say I felt good. Instead, there was a new cloud hanging over my head—one that kept insisting I'd foolishly sold my soul to the devil. I, Dulcie O'Neil, someone dedicated to fighting crime, had caved and was now one of the bad guys. The thought made me sick every time it crossed my mind.

"How long have you been working for him?" I asked Quillan as he escorted me from ANC headquarters to his company car. It was an old Ford something or other that looked circa 1970. "What is this?" I asked, glancing down at the car, suddenly irritated that it felt like I was stuck in a rerun of Grease.

"A 1961 Ford Galaxy Town Victoria," he answered almost sadly. Then he rolled his eyes in an indifferent sort of way, adding, "I fucking hate it." It wasn't lost on me that he really wasn't talking about the car.

"How long have you been working for my father?" I asked again, immediately regretting the brief change of topic. I needed to focus on the facts from here on out, not sideline myself with frivolity. The time for small talk was long gone. Quill opened my door and I seated myself as I watched him close it and then walk around to the driver's side. He opened the door and settled himself before looking over at me.

"The whole time I've known you."

That would be nine years now, since my mother had died. My stomach dropped all the way to my feet. Quillan had been double dealing from the first time I'd stepped foot through the double doors of the ANC headquarters and asked how one became a Regulator. Throughout our entire acquaintance, he'd been pretending to be something he wasn't. But I couldn't focus on that anymore. What I needed to concentrate on was what the hell I was going to do about the mess I was now in. Because staying in this mess wasn't an option.

"But how long have you been working for my father in total?" I asked, rephrasing the question.

Quillan started the car and it hummed loudly, sounding only a hiccup away from stalling. "Nearly fifteen years." He put the car in drive as we started out of the parking lot. I wasn't sure what time it was, but the nascent blue of early morning was just starting to tickle the horizon, pushing the navy blue cloak of night aside.

Something occurred to me and echoed through my entire being. "Did you know I was his daughter when you hired me?" I asked hollowly, wondering if that was the reason I was offered the position of Junior Regulator in the first place. I hoped the answer was no, because if I felt proud about anything, it was how good I was at my job. And furthermore, I absolutely detested the concept that I was given special treatment merely because I was the daughter of the Head of the Netherworld.

"Yes, I've always known," Quillan answered, but refused to look at me. He glanced to his right and left briefly before starting down the street. "Your father kept strict surveillance over you your entire life." He paused and then added, "You are his only child."

I shook my head and felt a knot starting in my stomach. I couldn't even concentrate on the fact that my father had been aware of my comings and goings all along—it seemed almost meaningless in its immense depth. Instead, I merely catalogued it in my already overwhelmed mind for future exploration. At this point, I was still wondering how much my father had done to promote me in the ANC. I faced Quillan's profile. "Did he tell you to hire me?"

"Dulcie ..." Quillan started and offered me a discouraging look.

"Did he tell you to hire me?" I demanded again, my voice slightly more emphatic.

Quillan merely nodded as I dropped my gaze to my lap and tried to staunch the tide of disappointment that was currently filling me.

"But that doesn't take away from what a good Regulator you are, Dulcie. You are the best; and I'm not just saying that because of who your father is."

"Save it," I said, looking out the window and exhaling deeply. The streetlights reflected against the dark pavement and I let my eyes fasten onto the yellow lines of the road.

"I know this isn't easy for you, Dulcie," he started.

"No, it isn't easy for me," I interrupted him, turning to face him. "It goes against everything I believe in, everything I stand for!"

"And he's worth it?" Quillan threw back at me, his eyes narrowed and burning with something that resembled jealousy.

I sighed and relaxed in the pleather seat. "Yes, he's worth it," I said, because it was the truth. In all honesty, I would have given my own life to save Knight's.

Quillan just nodded, falling quiet for a few more minutes as my mind raced. It was almost as if I didn't believe, or couldn't believe that I'd actually agreed to any of this. It was like I was living a nightmare, hoping that any second I'd wake up and find out none of this was actually real and that I was the same Dulcie I always had been. But try as I might, I couldn't wake up, because this wasn't just a figment of my imagination. It was as real as I was.

"I'll be with you every step of the way, Dulcie," Quillan said in a soft voice, sighing deeply. "You won't have to go it alone." He cleared his throat. "I'll protect you."

I gulped, realizing he was trying to make this as easy on me as he could. Even though Quillan had been double-dealing all along, in his own awkward and limited way, he had been and still was trying to be a good friend to me. I could see as much in his eyes. "There has to be something we can do, Quill," I started, shaking my head as I searched

11

for a way out. I just couldn't give up yet—not before I'd exhausted all plausible escape routes.

He shook his head as he started up an on-ramp to what looked like a freeway. "Don't even think about it," he said sharply. "Your father isn't just the Head of the ANC, Dulcie, he basically owns the Netherworld. His word is law. He's not only the top of the pyramid, but the pyramid belongs to him."

I swallowed hard and forced thoughts of mutiny from my mind. Well, for now at any rate. For now I'd just have to play by my father's rules. I was about to start a life in crime and there was nothing I could do about it, short of seeing Knight die. And even if my father polished Knight off, I was sure he wouldn't just let me go back to my old life. Not now, not when I knew as much as I did. Yep, Knight's assassination would undoubtedly be followed with mine.

"I know you're overwhelmed right now, Dulce," Quill said and glanced over at me with an encouraging smile. "But it gets easier, I promise."

"Does it?" I asked with raw anger in my tone. I shook my head. "How can you wake up in the morning and face yourself, Quill? How can you live from day to day knowing what you're doing?"

He nodded and his eyes were heavy. "You just learn to cope."

And that was when I realized this wasn't a walk in the park for Quillan. Yes, he'd had nearly fifteen years to come to terms with it, but deep down, I knew Quillan wasn't a bad person. Now more than ever before it was obvious that Quillan hadn't chosen this life, but it had been forced on him all the same. Prior to this moment, I'd figured he'd just shacked up with the bad guys out of greed, but I'd been very wrong. Quillan had been bullied into this life as much as I had.

"What did he hold over your head?" I asked, my voice soft.

"What do you mean?" he asked.

"Why did you agree to work for my father?"

He was quiet for a few seconds and his eyes seemed suddenly hollow, drained, his lips tight.

"You don't have to tell me if you don't want to," I said, worried I was forcing him to relive memories painful to him.

"No," he said immediately. "I want to tell you but I'm just not sure what to say. It wasn't the same as what he did to you...with Vander. For me...it just sort of happened." He took a deep breath. "I started working for the ANC when I was very young and worked my way up to the top pretty quickly. I got a name for myself as a very good Regulator and when Melchior invited me to the Netherworld for some honorary award or some bullshit, I bought into it. Of course when I got there, what he offered me was something I wanted no part of."

"But you must have realized there was no going back?" I asked. "He must have told you what was going on?"

Quill glanced at me and nodded, sighing deeply. "I knew too much at that point so it was just a matter of connecting A with B. If I didn't agree to work for him, he would've had me killed. It was an easy decision."

"I'm sorry, Quill," I said softly, hating my father.

He eyed me with surprise. "Sorry?"

"I'm sorry he did this to you."

Quillan sighed and just nodded as if he understood what I was saying, but had no words for me. And, really, he was right. The past was history and he'd had fifteen years, plenty of time to come to terms with it.

He pulled off the freeway and we started down a long, dark road that snaked between a forest of oak trees. When the road did a hairpin loop, nearly backing up on itself, Quillan pulled over onto the dirt shoulder and turned the car off. With the loud humming now silent, I could hear the gentle chirping of night insects and I felt my entire being deflate. This was it—I was headed home to open a new chapter of my life—a chapter I didn't want to begin.

"Is this where the portal is located?" I asked dryly.

Quillan nodded and opened his door. "I'll make sure you get home okay," he said, offering me a sweet smile. I said nothing, but opened my door and stepped outside, inhaling the clean, early morning air. Then I remembered that the Netherworld was somewhat prehistoric, considering the flying, bat-like creatures that patrolled the skies like pterodactyls, scavenging for unfortunate creatures on which to feed.

"What about the flying monsters, Quill?" I asked as I looked at the sky nervously.

Quill shrugged. "We're pretty safe out here. They tend to hover around residential areas where the eating is regular. There's nothing out here."

Feeling slightly relieved, I followed him from the Ford into the cover of the oak grove. He stopped walking once he was parallel with the nearest oak tree and then glanced down at his wrist like he was checking the time.

"What are you doing?" I asked.

"Checking my compass," he answered. He walked three steps to the right, then two steps directly in front of him, then turned ninety degrees to the left. "Yep, got it," he said softly and then ran his hand back and forth in the air in front of him. "Don't come too close," he warned me.

I waved him away with my hand and frowned. "I could get sucked in," I finished for him, not missing his expression of surprise. "I know, Bram already told me." Bram was a vampire and a pseudo-friend of mine. He'd also served as my guide to the Netherworld.

Quillan nodded and didn't seem surprised. That was when I remembered that Bram had told me he'd contacted Quill to let him know that I was rotting in a Netherworld prison for failing to apprehend him. And speaking of Bram,

I hoped he'd discovered that I'd been released and returned to Splendor. At any rate, tonight I planned to pay Bram a visit to his nightclub, No Regrets, just to make sure he knew I'd returned from the Netherworld. I figured it was the least I could do considering the huge favor he'd done for me in taking me there.

"Well, let's not waste any more time," Quillan said, glancing over at me with a sad smile. I took a step nearer, but he held me back with an outstretched arm. "Do you know how to get through one of these?" he checked.

I just nodded. I'd learned the rules of portal crossing with Bram.

"Okay, you'll have about three seconds once I cross over," Quillan continued. I nodded again and watched him simply lift his leg and sort of catapult himself forward. Then he merely disappeared into the air as if he'd never been there. Remembering the three-second rule, I leapt forward and threw one leg into the air where Quillan had just disappeared. The air was always denser in a portal, like a gel—balmy and wet. It was like being in a wind tunnel for all of one second. I kept my eyes clamped shut and tried to fight the feelings of nausea.

Landing on my butt, I glanced around myself, trying to figure out where I was. Looking to my left, I noticed Quillan standing there with a smile and an outstretched hand. I took it and stood up, taking a deep breath as I realized I was truly out of the hellhole known as the Netherworld and back in good ol' Splendor, California.

TWO

    After we arrived in Splendor, with the portal spitting us out in the absolute worst part of town—by the loading docks where the smell of rotting fish was pervasive—Quillan led me to a spare car. He kept it in a storage facility near an unoccupied warehouse. It was the perfect backdrop for suspicious activities. The portal we'd just come from was Quillan's mode of travel to and from the Netherworld, so the spare car was used for the express purpose of portal travel.

    After about twenty minutes of being on the road, I found myself back in my unremarkable apartment all alone. As soon as I walked through my front door, I took a shower. I hadn't had one in Hades only knew how long and the urge to wash as much of the Netherworld out of my hair and off my skin was the only thing to occupy my mind. Well, that wasn't exactly true. Thoughts of Knight were first and foremost in my head as I wondered where he was and if he'd made it home yet. Being released from High Prison wasn't as simple as being escorted out and slipping through the portal back to Splendor. There would be reams of paperwork both Caressa and Knight would have to wade through, so he'd be lucky if he made it home by the evening.

    And of course I wanted nothing more than to throw my arms around him and reassure myself that he really was out of the Netherworld and safe. But the more I thought about it, the more I realized things between Knight and me were going to have to be different from now on. I mean, I couldn't willingly continue in a relationship with him anymore, knowing I was hiding such a huge secret. I couldn't look him in the eye, while I rammed the proverbial knife in his back.

Yes, I did consider the possibility that I should just tell him what happened—how I was backed into a corner and agreed to work for my father. Well, first I'd have to tell him who my father was. And I had to imagine that in itself might jeopardize things between us, considering he hated my father. But I soon realized thinking along these lines was a waste of time anyway because of Melchior's words—that if Knight ever found out I was working for my father, it would mean the end of Knight's life. I wasn't about to take those odds. And knowing Knight, he'd fight for what was right and end up right back in the Netherworld and there wouldn't be anything I could do to help him. Nope, any way I looked at it ... this time, I was stuck.

Of one thing I was certain though, I would have to break things off with Knight but I'd also beg to be reinstated as a Regulator so I could get back into the ANC to act as the eyes and ears for Melchior. In so doing, I'd tell Knight I couldn't work for and date him at the same time—it was a conflict of interest.

I felt my heart break even as I considered the whole concept of never being intimate with Knight again, but I wouldn't allow myself to wallow in my own self pity. I'd made my bed and I'd have lie in it. All that mattered was that Knight was no longer in High Prison, at the mercy of my father, and for now, safe. And it wasn't like I'd never see him again. Quite the opposite—we'd be working together, which meant I'd see him every day—that dazzlingly handsome smile and those gorgeous blue eyes. I'd hear his hearty chuckle and have to remind myself that no matter what happened, Knight was still alive. And that would have to be enough for me ...

I stepped out of the shower and wrapped myself in my robe, sliding my feet into my dog head slippers and padded into the living room. My stomach gurgled with hunger, but somehow I couldn't bring myself to eat. The thought was completely unappealing. Instead, I threw myself on the small sofa and didn't move for the next thirty minutes, at least. It was almost as if I was incapable of shifting position. I could have gone to retrieve my dog from an old coworker and friend, Trey (a hobgoblin who'd been watching my dog, Blue, while I was in the Netherworld). And I still had to pay a visit to Bram to let him know I was safe and sound ... At the moment, however, I couldn't bring myself to do much more than sit on my couch and zone out on the television which wasn't even turned on. Not that it mattered because there was no way I could have paid attention to anything on it. But then, thinking I was being a bad friend, I picked up my cell phone and texted my best friend, Sam. I wrote:

Hi Sam, I'm home and safe.

Let's catch up tomorrow because I'm exhausted and not in the mood to talk.

Love you, Dulce.

Thinking I should do the same for my other good friend, Dia Robinson, who worked for the ANC in the bordering province of Moon, and whose help I'd recruited while I was in the Netherworld, I pulled up her information and texted her something similar to what I'd just texted Sam.

Then I put the phone down and resumed staring at the grey of the television screen while my mind raced. I had to figure out a story for Knight. Why? Because he was too smart not to question his release as well as my own. And the worst thing I could do was go into that situation unprepared. So I forced myself to remember everything that had happened before I broke into my father's building. I forced myself to remember the way Knight and I had left things.

We'd been sitting together in High Prison when Caressa announced that I was to be set free, per orders from above. It was pretty obvious that Melchior had been responsible for my release, probably once he'd realized his "prized" daughter was rotting away in a Netherworld prison, awaiting her death sentence. At the time though, I had no clue Melchior was responsible and neither did Knight. Well,

Knight didn't know Melchior had anything to do with me ... as far as I knew anyway. So on that point, I'd just play it cool ... I'd say I'd been released for reasons unbeknownst to me, that it was as much a surprise to me as to Knight. What it amounted to, really, was that I'd have to become a good actress. I could not, under any circumstances, blow my cover, or it would mean Knight's life.

I was prohibited from further planning my cover-up when the sound of someone's fist against my front door broke through the silence. I felt my heart ricochet into my throat and I stood up, feeling wobbly as I did so, since I hadn't had a good meal in days. I walked to the door and got up on my tiptoes to see through the peephole.

Knight.

I felt my palms go clammy as my body reacted of its own accord and I flung the door open. I didn't know what to say or do and ended up doing nothing. I just stood there staring at him. And he did the same thing. Neither of us said a word, but just gazed at one another as if we hadn't seen each other in twenty years. I felt my heart pounding in my chest, my breathing just as obvious.

"You," I started, but the words caught in my throat, dying on my tongue. He was just as beautiful as he'd always been—so tall he nearly took up my entire doorway and almost just as broad. His dark hair was longish, owing to his time in prison. His eyes were the same crystalline azure I remembered, contrasting against the healthy tan of his skin. Knight is by far the most handsome man I've ever seen and even though he still had dirt and bruises distracting from the sculpted planes of his face, he was simply breathtaking.

"I was released," he said quickly, shrugging in as much wonder as he said it.

I realized then that I had to act surprised. As far as he knew, I'd been released, but I shouldn't have known he'd been. "You were?" I started again, having a difficult time finding my voice. I cleared my throat, surprised that seeing him was so tough for me. "You're here," I finished, my voice cracking as tears flooded my eyes.

Knight didn't say anything. He simply nodded and offered me a warm smile, his plump lips revealing large, white teeth. I swallowed hard and glanced down at my feet for a second or two, willing the tears to subside. I didn't want to cry—no, this was supposed to be a happy moment. I returned my gaze to his striking face and felt my heart begin to race again. There was just something about him, something I couldn't place.

Did he know? Could he know?

"Knight," I started, but before I could finish my statement, he suddenly wrapped his arms around me and pushing me backward into my house. He didn't say anything, but once he entered my living room, he kicked the door closed behind him, his eyes never leaving mine. He placed his hands on either side of my waist and lifted me up as my dog slippers dropped off my feet. I felt my breath catch while he carried me a few steps before reaching the wall. But it wasn't as if the wall had gotten in his way, he was aiming for it. He pushed me against it, still holding me maybe two feet off the ground, so we were eye level. He gazed at me for a few seconds and then his mouth found my lips, his tongue wrapped around mine. It was a raw kiss, drenched in impatience and determination. As I ran my hands through his hair and shoved my tongue inside his mouth, I realized I shared the same need, the same feelings of insatiable hunger that had to be filled immediately.

Even though I'd just spent the better half of my afternoon convincing myself that I had to break things off with Knight, that it wasn't fair to him to pursue our relationship, I couldn't even think along those lines now. No, now those were like remote thoughts that had washed up on a distant shore. Instead, all I could think about was that I needed Knight. I needed him in a way I'd never needed him before. I couldn't stop myself from folding my legs around his middle. I couldn't stop my tongue from meeting his or from biting his lower lip. And I definitely couldn't stop the moan that escaped my lips when he started grinding himself against me. I could feel his erection straining behind his pants.

That was when I promised myself that tomorrow things would be different. Tomorrow would begin the rest of my godforsaken life. But for today, I would live in the moment. For today, I would pretend that nothing was wrong, that there was no Netherworld, no Melchior O'Neil—today it was just Knight and me.

"I want to see you," I whispered, wanting only to revel in the glory of his naked chest, to run my hands over the swells of the muscles of his shoulders and back. He chuckled slightly and using the wall as leverage, pinned himself against me, keeping me in place with his knee below my butt. He allowed me to help him pull his T-shirt up and over his head. When he was naked from the waist up, I eyed him greedily. Even though there were cuts and bruises all over him, he was glorious to behold.

"I need to be inside you now," Knight said in a tight voice as he toyed with the tie around my robe, then dropped it from my shoulders until I was completely naked. "I can't wait, Dulcie."

I just nodded, not only understanding his need, but sharing it. Continuing to rely on his knee to stabilize me against the wall, he palmed my right breast, rolling my nipple between his fingers as my breathing sped up. He dropped my breast and his hand traveled south down my body, crossing the threshold of my thigh and pausing just between my legs. When I felt his fingers on me, I jumped slightly and then closed my eyes, throwing my head back against the wall as I felt his fingers caress me from top to bottom, flicking my sensitive nub.

"Open your eyes," he demanded as he pushed a finger inside me and I bucked again, opening my eyes to find his fastened on mine, glowing with a whiteness that hinted to the fact that his body had selected mine as his mate.

I felt something cold erupt inside me at the thought that I was going to have to end things between us, but I forced it to retreat from my mind as I focused on the feel of his fingers sliding in and out of my wetness. We would have today. We would have this moment and I wasn't going to let anything get in the way of that.

"I want you," I whimpered. "So badly."

Knight didn't say anything, but reached down and I heard the sound of him unzipping his fly and then the shuffle of his pants as he slid them down his legs. Supporting my body against the wall, he pushed himself between my legs until I could feel the swollen tip of him at my entrance. I tried to prepare myself for his plunge, remembering how large he was, but when I felt him slide into me, my breath caught all the same.

"Are you okay?" he asked, eyeing me with sincere concern.

I nodded adamantly and reached around him, palming his tight butt and pushing him forward, into me. "Stop talking," I whispered as he chuckled and thrust himself until he was deeply ensconced inside me. I arched against him and moaned as he started his rhythm, pushing into me and pulling out repeatedly. He pinched my nipples and looked down, watching himself going in and out. Watching him watching me, I felt something blossom inside me and I clenched my eyes tightly, allowing the orgasm to seize me. I screamed out with the force of it and dug my nails into Knight's back, trying to pull him all the way into me, wanting him buried to the hilt. He pushed into me even harder and faster as my legs began to shake, my entire body shuddering with another orgasm.

That was the difference between having sex with Knight and having sex with anyone else—it was as if his body could control mine—he dictated when I'd have an orgasm and how many. I'd never been able to come this many times with other partners—this was just another of Knight's Loki abilities.

"Dulce," he groaned as he started pushing inside me harder and quicker. I wasn't sure how much more I could take. Then he sighed loudly and moments later, simply collapsed against me, his head resting on my breast. He pulled out of me and set me on the ground again, being careful to support me when it seemed I might keel over.

"How did you get out?" I asked, remembering myself and the part I had to play.

Knight took a deep breath and walked away from me, shrugging as he did so. I could see the tension in his upper back and I didn't even have to feel his shoulders to know he had knots between them. He clasped his hands behind his head, handcuffed-style, and then turned around to face me again, completely awe-inspiring in his nudity.

"I don't know," he said simply as he shook his head. "Caressa said they just didn't have enough to go on and that putting me to death would have caused a public outrage."

Well, it wasn't a great reason, but it also wasn't like Caressa had had much time to come up with a flawless alibi. I took the few steps that separated us and threw my arms around him, needing to be close to him, needing to feel the heat of his skin against me.

"I'm gross, Dulce," he said as he tried to push me away. "I need a shower."

I smiled at him and allowed him his space. "It didn't seem to bother you earlier."

He nodded and returned the smile. "As soon as I saw you, I knew I wouldn't be able to control myself." Then he shook his head as if he were surprised by the fact that he'd just pushed me up against the wall and pounded the hell out of me. "You have a way about you, Dulcie."

I smiled but said nothing, merely pointed to my bathroom. "Go take a shower and I'll see what I have in the kitchen. I'm sure you're starving."

He nodded and grinned boyishly before disappearing into my bathroom. Once I heard the shower start, I turned to the subject of food. Opening my cabinets, I spotted some Jif peanut butter and bread, an open box of Triscuits and a few cans of Progresso soup. Hoping the fridge had more to offer, I opened it, but wasn't impressed. A carton of milk, long past its date of expiration, loomed ominously so I shut the fridge with a sigh. Reaching for the peanut butter and the bread, I figured I'd make Knight a sandwich to tide him over while I ordered a pizza for us.

Ten minutes later, Knight was out of the shower and I'd ordered "the works" pizza and made him a sandwich. He walked into my living room with a towel wrapped around his middle and I was suddenly overcome with feelings of depression as I realized this little charade wasn't going to last longer than today. That thought settled in my stomach like an anvil. Why? Because I wanted to play this game of house with Knight. I suddenly loved the idea of him plodding into my living room, leaving wet footprints in his wake while asking me what was for dinner every night.

I felt tears threaten again and swallowed them down angrily. That scenario was never going to happen and the sooner I realized it, the better.

"Here," I said, handing him the peanut butter sandwich. I watched him smile in thanks and take a seat at my kitchen table. "I ordered pizza."

"Is everything okay, Dulce?" he asked, eyeing me curiously as he palmed the sandwich and glanced at it thoughtfully before facing me again. "You don't seem yourself."

I took a deep breath and realized my depressing thoughts were coloring my mood. I watched him take a bite of the sandwich, a huge bite to where only one half of it remained, and told myself to snap out of it. Today was the last day I was allowing myself to have with Knight, and as such, I needed to enjoy it wholeheartedly. "I'm sorry," I started and exhaled deeply as I watched him cram the last bit of sandwich in his mouth. "I'm just still in shock, I guess. I just ... never thought you'd be standing here, that they would have released you."

He tilted his head and raised his brows as if he, too, were surprised. "Neither did I." Then he propped his hands on either of his thighs and faced me with a crease in his forehead. "What happened after you left prison?"

I swallowed hard, realizing my lies would start now. The time for telling the truth was long past and I had to inwardly take a big breath to prepare myself for what I was about to do. In general, I prided myself on my honesty. Well, things were about to change. "Nothing really. Caressa took me to the portal and after lots of paperwork, she sent me on my way."

"Which portal?" he asked, looking at his plate, picking at the crumbs that littered it and bringing them to his mouth. He was obviously still hungry.

I swallowed harder, hoping my answers wouldn't come back to bite me later. "Um, the one at the airport. The same one Bram took me through when we arrived in the Netherworld." I tried to sound confident. "Why, which one did Caressa take you to?"

He shrugged. "The same one." Then he eyed me squarely. "I never said Caressa escorted me."

I felt my stomach drop for the nth time and tried to act nonchalant, unconcerned. "Well I figured as much, since she accompanied me to the portal."

Knight just nodded as if he bought my indifference and I sighed inwardly with relief, but before I could change the subject, Knight was at it again. "So did Caressa just drop you off? Or did she see to it that you arrived safely in Splendor?"

That was a quick decision I'd have to make, and given the fact that I didn't think Caressa liked me much, I opted for, "She just dropped me off."

Knight nodded, but was interrupted from further questioning me when the doorbell rang. Knight stood up to answer it and when he pulled out his wallet, I figured it was the pizza delivery guy. He thanked the man and brought the pizza inside, laying it on the table while I tried to replay everything we'd just discussed to ask myself if I'd made a mistake in any of my lies. I didn't think I had.

"Plates?" Knight asked.

I reached inside the cupboard closest to me and offered him a paper one. In general I liked paper as it was easier to clean up. I detested doing dishes. He smiled in thanks and took the plate, placing a generous piece of pizza on it and handed it to me. I accepted it and started picking off the things I didn't like until I was left with a piece of plain cheese pizza.

"Why did you order all that stuff on it if you won't eat it?" he asked with a smile.

I shrugged. "I thought you'd appreciate it fully loaded."

We continued to make small talk for the next twenty minutes, after which time, Knight had polished off the entire pizza, minus my one slice. I'd made it about halfway through mine. It seemed there was something in the air that I couldn't put my finger on, but neither Knight nor I had said much after the pizza arrived. I'd been overwhelmed with thoughts regarding whether or not Knight suspected I was involved in his release somehow, but as to his silence, I couldn't guess.

He stood up and carried the empty cardboard pizza box to my recycling bin, forcing it to fit, then faced me with a smile. "I have to get back to my place, Dulce," he said. "I need to do laundry, get myself situated for tomorrow."

I guessed he meant he was going into the office tomorrow. "Okay," I started.

"Do you want to come by later? We can get a movie, relax, try to put all of this behind us?"

I wanted to desperately, but I knew I shouldn't. I shook my head and didn't miss the disappointment in his eyes. "I'm just a little overwhelmed at the moment with everything that's happened," I said softly. "I feel like I need some alone time. That and I need to pick up my dog."

Knight nodded and started toward me, grasping each of my shoulders in his large hands. "Okay, I understand. If you want company, you know who to call." Then he bent down and kissed me on the lips while my heart broke.

THREE

When I opened my front door, my eyes fell on a manila package lying on my doormat. Sighing deeply as I figured the package couldn't contain anything good (I mean, I hadn't ordered anything so it wasn't like I was expecting it), I leaned down and picked it up. Not only was there no return address, but there was no address, period. It had just been left blank. Yep, this was definitely something ominous but I tore open the seal, all the same. Inside I found a white piece of paper folded in half. I opened it and read:

D, This is for when I need to get in touch with you. More later.

Quillan hadn't signed his name, but he didn't have to—I knew his handwriting as well as my own. I further searched inside the package and retrieved a cell phone. It wasn't anything high-tech or sporty. It just looked like a run-of-the-mill, old school cell phone. I had to imagine it was pre-paid and therefore untraceable. So now I really was on call for my father, twenty four/seven.

Great. Just great.

Jamming the phone into my purse, I plodded toward my only means of transportation, my motorcycle, a Suzuki DL 650. Well, that wasn't totally true. Recently, Knight had gifted me with a much faster and nicer motorcycle, but I couldn't bring myself to ride it. Not now after everything that had happened, and not knowing what I still had to do. I threw on my helmet, hopped on the bike, and headed for ANC headquarters where I knew I'd find Knight.

It took me maybe fifteen minutes to get there—I hadn't allowed for traffic. Once I pulled up to the white, nondescript building, I felt my heart start thudding in my chest as I realized the weight of what I was about to attempt—I was going to beg for my job back. Having been retired as an ANC regulator for a few months, I'd been helping Knight out with cases whenever he needed an extra hand. Now I needed to be much more than that. I needed to be reinstated as a Regulator, in the employ of Splendor ANC, per my father's orders. And even though I'd always loved my job, now I was coming back to it for all the wrong reasons.

I parked the bike and took off my helmet, tucking it under my arm as I started for the double doors. Opening them, I waved to Elsie, the receptionist, who looked surprised to see me.

"Hi, Dulce!" she called out pleasantly, standing up, as if to get a better look at me.

I smiled and placed my helmet on the counter. "Hi, Elsie, I'm here to see Knight. Can you ask him if he can spare a few minutes?"

"Sure thing," she said with a smile and speed-dialed him, announcing my arrival. I could hear him on the line telling her to send me in immediately. He sounded as surprised as Elsie had been when I walked through the doors. She hung up and motioned down the hallway. "He's all yours." She swallowed and then another sweet smile claimed her lips again. "It's really good to see you again, Dulcie."

"Thanks, Elsie, and good to see you too," I said as I hauled my helmet back under my arm and started the trek down the hallway. I waved to my old coworkers as I passed their offices. Reaching my old desk, I noticed it was empty but Trey was still sitting at his desk, which was just across from mine. Some things hadn't changed.

"Yo, Dulce," he said in a nasally sort of voice. Then he held up one finger as if to say "give me a minute". He scrunched his eyes together and lifted his head, inhaling three short breaths as if he were wrestling with a sneeze. Eventually the sneeze won and exploded out of his mouth in a brash display of spit. Trey DNA bathed everything within a two-foot radius around him. Thank Hades I was standing a good four feet away. Afterward, he reached for a wadded-up and wet looking napkin from his pocket and blew his nose, something which sounded like a duck with whooping cough.

"Whatcha doin' here?" he asked finally, once he'd regained his respiration.

"I came to see Knight," I said simply. "Sorry I didn't come by last night to get Blue." Blue was my dog—a yellow Labrador and as I mentioned earlier, Trey had been dog sitting for me during my sojourn to the Netherworld.

He shook his head, the vibration of which ricocheted all the way to his enormous belly which wrapped around him like an overstretched water balloon. "Nah, it's cool. He's been real good." Then he paused for a second or two before glancing up at me with cow eyes. His four chins made him look like a male orangutan. "Hey, do you mind if I keep him another night? We're really just gettin' ta know each other, and on my lunch break, I went to the store and got him some steak bones. We're gonna have us a party tonight!" Then he smiled broadly and I could see the eagerness in his eyes.

Poor Trey needed to get a dog because a girlfriend was pretty much out of the question. But, girlfriend or dog, either way, it was obvious he was lonely. I just smiled and nodded, trying not to remind myself that I was now just as lonely. Nope, I would not, under any circumstances, feel sorry for myself.

"Thanks, Dulce, thanks a whole lot," Trey said, beaming at me. I was spared from further small talk when Knight popped his head out from behind his office door and cleared his throat.

"Dulce," he said, with warm surprise, even as he raked me from head to toe, smiling appreciatively. Knight loved nothing more than seeing me in my bike leathers.

"Hi," I said with a smile as I tried to ignore how freaking beautiful he was. How I'd managed to hold out so long where Knight and sex were concerned, I had no clue. Maybe it was my incredible sense of fortitude, or more so, my incredible sense of idiocy.

"What brings you here?" the sex god asked.

I didn't answer but, instead, quickly darted into his office, establishing the fact that I didn't want an audience. As soon as I walked into his office, I noticed the panoramic picture window that captured the beauty of Splendor Park with its poppies in full, spectacular orange and yellow blooms. Somehow the vista evoked a sense of wistfulness that suddenly started washing over me. This same office had once been Quillan's. That was before I'd caught him double dealing. His actions had gotten him kicked out of the ANC, only to return to my father in the Netherworld. I imagined that must've been a tough conversation between Quillan and my father since Melchior was pretty serious about having a touch point in the ANC.

Knight closed the door behind him as I seated myself in one of the two visitor's chairs across from his large oak desk. He took his chair and reclined backwards in it, studying me curiously.

"I hope I'm not interrupting," I started as I gulped down the sudden sense of foreboding that flooded me. I'd rehearsed this scene over and over in my head until it was as regular as clockwork. But now that I was actually here, I wasn't sure I could go through with it. 'Course there was no abandoning ship now.

"You aren't interrupting," he answered quickly, furtively. "What can I do for you?"

"I, uh, I'm here to ask for my job back," I said shamefully, suddenly wanting to cut right to the chase. But I was nervous, which was evidenced by the bouncing of my leg.

Knight studied me for a few seconds, rocking back and forth in his recliner chair, and then stopped rocking. He leaned forward with his elbows on his desk and I wondered if maybe it was going to be harder to get my job back than I'd expected.

"It's yours. It's never been anyone else's."

I heaved a sigh of relief and only then realized I'd been holding my breath. "Thank you," I began but he interrupted me as he resumed his idle rocking.

"What brings you back? I thought you liked your retirement?" He propped his large feet up on his desk, crossing them at the ankles as he smiled at me and my stomach flip-flopped.

"Um, I need the money." I said the first thing that came to mind and was thrilled with my answer. Knight was well aware that I was typically barely scraping by in the finance department, so this response had the ring of truth. Yes, my career as a lying sack of shit was off to a good start. Yay me.

He nodded and removed his feet from the table, facing me squarely. "I'm glad to have you back, Dulce, very glad."

"I'm glad to be back."

He nodded again, but his mind seemed to be elsewhere, his attention riveted on his fingers as he pressed them against one another. It seemed we were both fidgeting. "I've been thinking more about my release," he started and his words turned my stomach over, the acid rising up my esophagus. "I still don't know what to make of it." I just nodded and tried to appear ill-informed. "I actually talked to Caressa about it this morning," he continued.

I gulped down the frog that was climbing up my throat as well as the suffocating urge to scream out "FUCK!" at the top of my lungs. "Oh," I said feebly, going from sounding merely ill-informed to just plain stupid.

"I asked her about your release and how it came about." He shrugged as if whatever he was discussing was

commonplace and uninteresting; but I knew there was
method to his madness. He was testing me.

The frog came back up my throat and I nearly choked
on it. I thought I was going to vomit. "Oh," I said again, that
apparently being the only word that existed in my
vocabulary at the moment.

Knight glanced at his steepled fingers again. "And,
funny thing, but she said she never actually escorted you to
the portal at all." I gulped so hard I was afraid I'd swallowed
my tongue. "She said she had nothing to do with your
release whatsoever."

I felt the breath catch in my throat and worried I might
wet myself as I watched him raise his eyebrows, awaiting
my response. I should have known better. While I was in the
Netherworld, Caressa arrived to escort me from High Prison
to the portal which would take me back to Splendor. I,
however, talked her into letting me escape, promising to do
my best to obtain Knight's release. Caressa latched onto the
idea immediately, not wanting to see her friend suffer for
something he hadn't done. But when it came down to it,
Caressa said it would've looked too suspicious if she
released me. Instead, she thought of the alibi that I
overpowered her and got away. We even added some actual
facial blows to solidify the story.

Apparently Caressa had realized it wouldn't behoove
either of us if she told Knight the truth so obviously she
hadn't. Add to that the faux pas I'd just made when I told
Knight that Caressa had taken me to the portal and I was
well on my way to weaving a web of deceit and apparently
not doing a very good job of it. But damn me for not
touching base with Caressa before Knight got the chance.

"Hmm," I started (thank Hades I didn't say "oh").
Racking my brain for something non-incriminating to say, I
came up with a big, blank slate. Double damn me!

"Strange?" Knight queried, arching a brow in my direction. "I could have sworn you said she escorted you to the portal ... personally?"

I felt my heart drop to the floor and shatter into a million pieces before forcing myself to pick up the pieces and face the music. I had to come up with a plausible excuse and, harder still, I had to *own* it—for Knight's sake. "Um, yeah, well I sort of forgot to mention that I got away first," I said, sounding ashamed and embarrassed.

"And what happened then?"

Yeah, what happened then, Dulcie? I asked myself, wishing the floor would open up and swallow me whole. I pushed my thoughts aside, and focused on a believable explanation. I took a deep breath. "I went after the judge who presided over your case," I began. My voice pleasantly surprised me by sounding even and calm, although I had no idea where this story was going.

"Judge Thorne," Knight corrected and raised his brows as if he hadn't expected me to go after the judge; it seemed to amuse him at the same time.

I nodded as I took another deep breath and continued lying through my teeth. "Yeah, and I pleaded with him to reconsider your conviction and punishment. I told him it was all my fault."

"But he wouldn't listen," Knight finished for me.

"No, he wouldn't," I said, feeling slightly relieved when it appeared that maybe, just maybe Knight was buying this. "So after arguing with him for a few hours, he ordered an ANC escort to accompany me to the portal. End of story." Phew, that actually wasn't half bad. 'Course it also hadn't been half good.

"So why did you say Caressa took you to the portal?" Knight asked, his tone hinting that he was annoyed I'd lied to him. Well, if that little white lie annoyed him, I hoped to Hades he never found out about the whopper I was fabricating now.

"I just knew you'd be upset," I said quickly and shrugged. For a second, I wished I'd paid more attention in my high school drama class. Triple damn me! "I couldn't give up on you, Knight," I added with a flutter of my lashes, hoping that might convince him. When all else failed, it was best to rely on feminine ingenuity. The only problem with that was that my feminine ingenuity usually eluded me.

He shrugged. "I see." But somehow I thought I'd persuaded him.

There was a moment of distinctly uncomfortable silence and I realized I needed to change the subject—I felt like I might throw up in front of Knight or pee on myself if I didn't. "Yeah, so anyway, I, uh, wanted to ask you about something else."

Knight nodded, signifying that this conversation was over ... for now at least. Thank freaking Hades for that. "What?"

"Bram," I said, starting a conversation that actually interested me. It wasn't just a ploy to throw Knight off the scent of my lies.

"Bram?" Knight repeated and I spotted an expression of aggravation in his eyes. Knight was less than fond of Bram and Bram certainly wasn't fond of Knight. But c'est la vie.

"Bram seemed to know his way around the Netherworld pretty well. He even had his own portal," I started as I eyed Knight to see his reaction.

Knight nodded but didn't seem especially interested. "Interesting."

"Did you ... know him in the past, before you came here?" I asked as I wondered what Bram's involvement with the Netherworld was, especially how high up the chain he was. Based on my observations in the Netherworld, it seemed Bram had some pull of his own.

Knight shook his head. "I never set eyes on him before moving to Splendor." Then he pushed his chair back, stood up and approached me. I stood up as well, not appreciating the stare down he directed toward me. I glanced up at him in question.

"I missed you last night," he said, moving to kiss me. I stepped back, my unease arising not only because we were in his office, although the door was closed, but also owing to my new line of work. Whatever we shared before couldn't continue.

"Knight," I started with a hesitant smile. "You can't just kiss me here."

He narrowed his eyes on me. "Why not? No one has a clue what's going on in here. The door is closed."

I rubbed my hand down the nape of my neck and sighed. "It's just ... I just don't like it. It's not professional. You know how I am."

He chuckled and nodded. "Yes, I know how you are." He took a few steps back and made a big show of it, laughing all the while. "Dinner tonight? My place?"

I swallowed the bile in my throat and shook my head. "Um, I was hoping to write tonight." Knight knew I was in the process of writing a book—a book I'd started a few months ago.

"Oh," he said and my heart felt like a noose was squeezing the life out of it. I dropped my eyes to my fidgeting fingers, but was unable to resist watching his response and looked up at him again.

"I, um, I ... I still need a little time," I said, hedging because I really needed to say it was over between us. But somehow I just couldn't bring myself to do it.

He nodded and smiled at me consolingly. "I understand, Dulce, take as much time as you need. I'll be here."

I was reticent, but nodded and returned his smile with a sheepish one. Then I started for the door before the tears that were flooding my eyes began to stream out uncontrollably.

###

Later that evening, I actually did attempt to write. I'd always wanted to start a career as a novelist and I'd even managed to attract a very well-known agent to represent me along the way. Said agent was currently soliciting my first book, a story about Bram titled *A Vampire and a Gentleman.*

I sat down at my computer and opened the word document I'd started two months ago, but I couldn't will my fingers to start typing. It seemed like whatever inspiration I once possessed which allowed me to begin the follow-up to my first novel had abandoned me, high and dry.

I sighed deeply and clenched my eyes together, hoping to focus on something other than the look in Knight's eyes upon seeing me retreat when he'd tried to kiss me. I just felt so empty, so guilty about knowing what I had to do and not being able to do it. But the longer I waited, the longer I put off the inevitable, the worse the ultimate blow. I had to break up with Knight and it had to be the next time I saw him. I absolutely refused to do it over the phone, but I couldn't prolong it any longer than I already had.

Guilt suddenly overwhelmed me, guilt over the fact that we'd had sex. It was the worst thing I could have done, knowing I had to end things with him. It hadn't been fair to either of us, and yet I hadn't been able to control myself. I was so overcome with love for him, so happy to see him, so relieved that he was safe, and that he'd made it back to Splendor. But those were all excuses and from now on, excuses weren't going to be worth a damn to me. I was going to live by the rules of black and white, yes and no.

I eyed the blinking cursor again and just sighed, my inspiration drained and parched. Before I had the chance to turn off the computer, the cell phone from Quillan began ringing. I felt my stomach drop and it was almost like an out of body experience as I watched myself reach for it.

"Hello?" I asked, my voice deep and nervous.

"Meet me at Crespy and Palm in thirty minutes at the tattoo parlor," Quillan ordered, and before I could respond, he hung up.

FOUR

Crespy and Palm weren't exactly in a nice part of Splendor. Maybe not quite as bad as the loading docks where the portal from the Netherworld spat Quillan and me out, but close enough. And the tattoo parlor, aptly titled "Ink," was a place I'd kept strict surveillance on during my entire time as a Regulator. It was owned by a Titan named Baron Escobar. Baron was one of three Titans I had the misfortune of meeting, and like most Titans, Baron was enormous. If I remembered correctly from his ANC bio, (the guy had a long rap sheet in Splendor—mainly for illegal potions activity), he was over seven feet tall. And he was broad as well—like an ox. So to me, coming in at just five foot one, this guy was like talking to the Empire State Building.

Baron was bad news, period. He was renowned for his nasty disposition and a flagrant temper that was attached to a very short leash. Yep, Baron wasn't exactly the patient sort. I'd already had numerous run-ins with him; and if asked to rank Splendor's "bad guys" according to their severity, I would've put Baron close to the top. So you can imagine my excitement in meeting Quill at Baron's tattoo parlor ...

Yes, I had prepared myself, knowing full well that Baron and his entourage of mutual fuck ups were going to have a field day with the news that I was now one of their much esteemed company. I mean, I was sure the news was going to come out tonight if it hadn't already. I was actually hoping Quill had already informed them—it would save a big song and dance that I wasn't in the mood to get into.

I pulled into the parking lot of Ink and sighed as I wondered what I was about to walk into. The street was completely dark, the light bulbs from the streetlights having been broken purposely and never replaced. The tattoo parlor was the only active business on Crespy Street. It sat surrounded by empty buildings and warehouses that had been vacated years earlier. And, yes, I did have a feeling Baron had something to do with the dereliction.

The parking lot of Ink was overgrown with weeds, the asphalt crumbling into multiple potholes. I eased the Suzuki into a spot next to a white Camaro. Somehow the Camaro seemed familiar to me—I thought it might have been Quillan's. Glancing into the car, I noticed no one was in it which meant I'd probably have to meet Quill inside, something I wasn't thrilled about. Aside from my bike and the white sports car, there were five Harleys lined up in front of the door and a large black Hummer H2 parked just beside them. The H2 was Baron's.

I turned the bike off and stood up, removing my helmet and placing it on the seat. It wasn't a good idea to carry it under my arm because I wouldn't be able to adequately protect myself, if the need arose. And I had a funny feeling that the need was probably going to arise. As far as I was concerned, I was about to walk into a den of lions—lions who would very much enjoy mauling me into oblivion.

I took a deep breath and started forward, remembering the twin blades I'd strapped to both sides of my outer thighs. The Op 6 in my shoulder holster was most definitely going to be confiscated, but maybe my leathers would conceal the blades. I could only hope. 'Course if the blades were seized as well as my gun, I could always rely on my fairy powers which weren't anything to scoff at. With just the shake of my hand, I could materialize a mound of fairy dust in my palm, the limits of which were pretty endless. I could light the entire place on fire, freeze one of Baron's asshole thugs or at the very least, create a chasm in the ground and swallow everyone. I had to wonder if I could do all three at the same time. Hopefully I wouldn't find out because I needed to meld in—I needed to become one of them so I could get my job done and get the hell out of there. But what was more, I needed to figure out how I was going to get myself out of this whole mess. Either way, opening a can of whoop-ass wouldn't make me any new friends.

When I reached the front door and knocked, it opened immediately. A cloud of cigarette smoke wafted directly into my face. I gagged and tried to breathe through my mouth just to avoid smelling it. Facing the bouncer again, I recognized him, although his name escaped me. He was a hulking were who looked down at me and flashed a partially toothless grin. His canines were missing, which I found strange and a little off-putting, considering he was a were.

"The former ANC Regulator, huh?" he asked me with an ugly smile. So the cat was already out of the bag ... Good. That just saved me a lot of explaining.

"I have business with Quillan and Baron," I said acidly, glaring up at him and throwing my hands on my hips as I gave him all the sass I could muster. Hey, just because I was forced to work with Daron didn't mean I had to like it and, more so, didn't mean I had to be peaches and cream. Nope, I was going for sauerkraut and vinegar.

The were said nothing more, but harrumphed as it the joke was still on me and opened the door wide. I entered, feeling his gaze on my ass as I passed him. I turned around, my hands still on my hips, and narrowed my eyes at him. "Where the hell are they?"

"Down the hall," he answered, nodding his head toward the dark hallway. Before I could start walking, he grabbed my arm, pulling me toward him. Then he grinned lasciviously as he patted me down, ensuring that he copped a good feel of my breasts in the process. Just as I predicted, he felt my Op 6. I frowned as I took off my jacket to remove it, and handed it to him. My expression must have convinced him that it was the only weapon on me because

41

he didn't feel for the daggers strapped to my thighs. Things were looking up. I pulled away from him, and threw my jacket over my shoulders as I faced the interior of Ink.

The main room had two reclining chairs and a small stool that swiveled between them. The inside of the place was just as dingy as the outside: old linoleum floors, browned with age and filth, reflected the same decay and neglect as the surrounding buildings. The walls, once white, were yellowed from decades of cigarette smoke—the smell was pervasive. I'd felt a headache growing between my temples as soon as I'd entered the confined space.

Black and white samples, detailing the various kinds of tattoos available, hung around the room haphazardly. My eyes fastened on a skull with a snake going through both eye sockets; then shifted to the image of a naked woman spread-eagled. At that tasteful image, I decided to stop looking. Steeling myself, I started down the hallway. The combined smell of smoke, alcohol and vomit was nearly enough to make me hurl, but I strode on, trying to avoid breathing.

So this is what I was destined for? This was the type of place I was going to have to hang out in, the types of people I'd now be dealing with? I didn't even have the wherewithal to feel sorry for myself. Instead, I reached the end of the hallway, which terminated into a closed door and I rapped on it with my knuckles.

The door opened, the sound of "Black and Yellow" by Wiz Khalifa pouring out of the small room in a flourish of bass. A woman stood before me; she was wearing nothing more than a tiny black g string and heels that were so high, she towered over me. Glancing down at them, I had to guess they were at least six inches. The woman had a rocking body—huge fake boobs with a tiny waist that flared into curvy hips and long legs. Her face, though, was another story. Her nose was, in a word, generous, and her skin was wrinkled and sallow, hanging off her cheekbones as if all its elasticity was long gone. She looked like she'd been the inspiration for the phrase "rode hard and put away wet."

"Hi," I started as she eyed me from head to toe, smiling as she took in my leathers and matching jacket. I tried to see past her to count how many people were in the room in case I needed to protect myself, but she basically blocked my view.

"Hi yourself," she answered back in a high-pitched, seductive tone. She probably assumed I was another of Baron's playthings—my leathers being part of a costume. But the idea of sex with Baron left me completely grossed out. I'd rather cut off my own arm ... with a butter knife.

"I'm here to see Quillan and Baron," I said quickly, cutting right to the chase. I wasn't in the mood to make small talk with a floozy.

She frowned at my less than friendly greeting, but was spared any further correspondence when Baron's loud voice bellowed out over the other voices and music, "Who is it, Dolly?"

She backed away as if to say "see for yourself," and I glanced around the dimly lit room. There were two old couches in the middle and a dartboard along the back wall. Baron emerged from behind a corner, probably the bathroom, if I had to guess. I saw a huge smirk on his ugly face and I scanned the room quickly, looking for Quillan. He wasn't anywhere to be seen.

"Ah, Dulcie fuckin' O'Neil," Baron said, with a sigh, like I was exactly where he wanted me. "The bitch responsible for making the last five years of my life ... difficult." He was putting it mildly. I'd single-handedly busted his ass for multiple offenses and put him behind bars at least twice.

"Baron fucking Escobar," I answered, with one eyebrow arched, hinting at my pseudo-ennui. "Pleasure to see you too."

He laughed with a bellow that seemed to ricochet throughout the room. "It's always a pleasure seeing you," he began as he eyed me up and down. "It's the dealin' with you part that's a pain in my ass." He had the overall look of a boxer—a wide, flat nose, a nose which had been broken numerous times in fist fights. His eyes were set so far apart, he looked sort of like a dolphin; and he had an enormous lantern jaw—like he was half dolphin, half pit-bull.

"Well we can't all be," I started and then glanced at Dolly who was hobbling back toward us, looking like she was about to trip over her stilts, "gracious."

Baron folded his beefy arms across his barrel chest and regarded me with a grin, making me dread whatever was going through his head. "Seems like your new name should be 'Shitty Luck'."

I shifted my gaze from Baron to the three men who were standing around the dartboard, watching us curiously. As far as I could tell, there were four people in the room who might cause trouble. No, Dolly didn't count. And dammit all but where the hell was Quillan? I should have just waited on the bike until he pulled up instead of presuming the white Camaro was his. Stupid me.

"Call my luck what you will, but my name is still Dulcie," I said icily.

Baron shook his head and the fake smile on his face melted away into an expression of anger. The look in his eyes was lethal. "You think you can just show up here like we're old friends or some shit?"

Yep, things were starting to go downhill. And if Quill was planning on showing up, now would be a good time. I tried my best not to look ruffled in the slightest. "Look, Baron, I'm not here to cause trouble. Quillan told me to meet him here." I even backed away a few steps until I nearly bumped into the slut on stilts.

Baron peered behind him to what I assumed was the bathroom and nodded. As soon as he did, two men walked

44

out with Quillan between them. So it wasn't a bathroom after all. 'Course, right now, I was more concerned with why Quillan was being restrained than the architecture of Ink. From the look of it, he hadn't been roughed up or anything, so at least that was a blessing.

"Dulcie," Quill said in a low, worried voice.

"What the hell is going on?" I asked, looking at Quill and then Baron.

Baron took a few steps toward me and smiled as if he knew something I didn't. "The elf told me you were working with him now, for the Head of the Netherworld. That right?"

I nodded, but said nothing. Out of the corner of my eye, I could see Quillan trying to disengage himself from the two weres holding him. He was unsuccessful.

"Baron, I told you the truth—Dulcie *is* working for us now," Quillan interjected, obviously nervous about where this situation was headed.

Baron didn't spare him a glance, but faced me, nodding as his eyes narrowed into another angry expression. "Well, we gonna have us a little hazing then. A welcome to our newest recruit."

I swallowed hard, not liking the sound of that at all. "What does that mean, Baron?" I demanded.

"Melchior won't approve," Quillan said from the corner of the room. It made me wonder if Baron was also aware that Melchior was my father.

"What he don't know won't hurt 'em," Baron answered, facing Quill with an expression that said Quillan better not say a word about it—to Melchior, or anyone else.

"No one touches her," Quill said, his voice razor sharp as he again attempted to unwind himself from the weres. But they had him and weren't letting go.

Baron faced me again, apparently uninterested in Quill's protests. "So you got two choices."

I nodded, but I didn't believe for a second that I was going to walk out of here untouched. Given the fact that I'd been Baron's enemy, I definitely had something coming to me. This wasn't a surprise. "And what are my options?" I asked, sounding unfazed.

Baron took the steps separating us and towered over me, grinning. I didn't step back, but held my ground, determined not to let him intimidate me. He leaned forward and gripped a handful of my hair, yanking my head back so I was forced to look up at him.

"I either beat the shit outta you or screw the shit outta you. Your choice." Then he sneered a wide and terrifying grin. "Screwin' you won't hurt so bad. You'll get to likin' it."

"Dammit, Baron!" Quillan yelled from the opposite side of the room, but I knew Quill had no authority here. No, if I wanted to be accepted into this band of thieves, I had to undergo punishment. I had to let them haze me in return for my arresting and convicting them. It was now a matter of quid pro quo, this for that. I had to overcome my past as an ANC Regulator who busted their asses mercilessly. I had to become one of them. I had to earn their trust.

But that said, there was no way in hell this pig was getting inside of me. I held my jaw tight and glared at him. "I guess it's going to be a beating."

He pushed me away from him, obviously pissed off by my decision. I could see Quillan straining with his opponents again but I knew my bed was made. I just hoped there wouldn't be too much damage to show for it. Yes, as a fairy I could heal myself with my magic but that didn't take away from the fact that this was going to hurt like a bitch. But I was ready.

Without any warning, Baron pulled his arm back and cold-cocked me right across the face. My head flew back as I lost my footing and smashed against the floor, feeling the blow all the way to my toes. I took a deep breath and shook my head, trying to clear the stars before my eyes. I pushed up on my hands and leaned over, attempting to regain

control of my body again. I could feel blood running from
my nose and mouth. The viscous drops bled down my jacket
front, pooling into a puddle of what looked like molten gold
on the floor in front of me. I felt Baron's hands on both of
my upper arms as he pulled me upright. I wavered a bit, but
then held my ground, not at all looking forward to what else
he had up his sleeve.

"Dulce! Are you okay?" Quill called, out, but I
couldn't spare him a glance. Instead, I watched as Baron
swung his arm from behind his head into my other cheek.
The blow seemed to have a domino effect through my body
and I felt my head spin, the upper half of me falling forward
as the lower half gave out. I lost my balance and crumpled
into a heap on the ground. A dull ache started behind my
eyes and I closed them to ward away the pain, forbidding
myself from blacking out.

"Enough!" Quillan yelled, but his voice was drowned
out by the pounding of my heartbeat thumping between my
ears.

Don't black out, Dulcie O'Neil, I told myself. *Keep it
together!*

"Baron, that's fair!" I heard Quillan yell again.
"You've hased her enough!"

I forced myself into a sitting position and opened the
eye that wasn't swollen shut, only to find Baron kneeling
down next to me. He smiled an ugly and wide grin.
Apparently he wasn't finished with me.

"You picked the wrong choice," he said gruffly, his
eyes settling on my bust. Wasting no more time, he gripped
my shirt and yanked me toward him. Then he pushed me
down, none too gently. I closed my eyes again, feeling like I
was fighting a concussion or something. But the feel of
Baron on top of me snapped my eyes wide open, well, at
least one of them.

"Nah, I picked the right choice," I managed to spit
out, the salty taste of my own blood souring my mouth.

"To hell with you," he exhaled into my face, his breath stale from cigarettes and alcohol. As I tried to clear the stars from my vision, I could feel his hands on the button of my pants. Then I felt him unzipping them and attempting to pull them off my hips. *My daggers!* He gave me the perfect opportunity to go for them when he started unzipping his fly.

"Get off her!" Quillan yelled as he overpowered one of his captives. He punched the other one and dove for me. But the weres were on him in a split second, dragging him back to the far side of the room. Yep, this was my fight.

I reached my hands beneath my leathers and started shimmying them lower as Baron laughed enthusiastically, probably thinking I wanted the disgusting Titan between my legs. When I had each dagger in hand, I waited for him to lower himself on me again. Then I acted, pulling the daggers up and out of my pants, until each was poised to impale both of Baron's balls.

"Unless you want to become a eunuch, I suggest you get the fuck off me," I whispered with a groan, as if to say I wasn't kidding. There was shock on Baron's face, then anger in his eyes, but he saved his acorns and pulled away from me, retreating from whence he'd come.

I pushed away from him and stood up with some difficulty, sliding the daggers back into their straps as I pulled my pants up, pleased with the fact that only the very top of my black lace panties had been visible. I cleared my throat. "Do we or do we not have work that needs to get done?" I demanded, first facing Baron and then Quillan, as I wished the headache pounding between my temples would fade away.

Quillan smiled at me with an expression of relief. "We have much to discuss," he concurred.

I faced Baron and shrugged, still trying to catch my breath. "Well, what the hell are we waiting for?"

He took a deep breath and motioned to the doorway, which I'd originally thought led to the restroom. "Ladies first," he grumbled.

I said nothing as I walked past him, shaking my palm until a mound of fairy dust emerged. Then I threw it over my head, the particles falling around me like a shower of glitter. I imagined my pain as well as the wounds themselves vanishing into nothing. After another second or so, during which time the dust settled onto my skin, I felt completely healed and back to being Dulcie.

"Dulce?" Quillan said from behind me. He placed a concerned hand on my shoulder as I turned to face him and smiled encouragingly. We walked over the threshold of the next room and I noticed it was much smaller than the first one. It had nothing but a table and four club chairs that looked older than I did, complete with cigarette burns in the brown Naugahyde. I took a seat and swiveled to face Quillan. "I'm okay, Quill."

He shook his head and seemed to be studying my face, as if making sure my magic had healed the swelling and bruises. Eventually he smiled at me, taking the seat beside mine. When he did so, he put his hand on mine and squeezed it

FIVE

Even though I was in the lion's den, I had to admit I was more than grateful to have Quillan right there with me. Despite whatever had happened in our past, he was now the only person I could trust—well, with regards to this mess, anyway. As far as working for my father went, Quillan was my only friend and I needed him now more than ever before.

I glanced around the table with a big gulp. Baron was sitting across from me, two of his men on either side of him and a burly-looking goblin who, I imagined, was probably his bodyguard, standing behind him.

"The shipment of *Yalkemouth* is comin' through tonight," Baron said with no emotion in his voice as he faced Quillan. He narrowed his eyes once he glanced at me, probably reminded of how close he'd come to losing his gibblies. I glared right back at him.

Yalkemouth was an illegal narcotic which had started picking up speed in the streets of Splendor earlier this year. It was concocted from the tiniest drop of dragon's blood mixed with sugar water to help the taste. In larger quantities, dragon's blood was liquid death to any Netherworld creature unfortunate enough to come across it. All the bullets provided to the ANC were made of dragon's blood. Not surprisingly, there had already been fifteen deaths reported from *Yalkemouth* overdoses.

Apparently the high from *Yalkemouth* was exactly that—high. The most common side effects were hallucinations of out-of-body experiences, whereby the victims would see themselves separated from their corporeal bodies and their "essences" (as they termed it) would simply float away. The victims, in an act of desperation, since their souls were about to have lots in common with errant kites, would try their best to hang onto their essence. However, once they realized they couldn't reach their souls on flat land, they would climb whatever they could find. This wasn't such a big deal if said victims were inside a house, for example, where most just toppled off their couches or kitchen tables. But if the victims happened to be outside ... Well, there had already been reports of deaths from creatures falling off bridges, buildings and rolling down the sides of mountains.

"Where is the shipment arriving?" Quill asked as he exhaled a pent-up breath that spoke of his anxiety. I looked at him and was suddenly struck by how much older Quillan looked than he should have. As an elf who could live well beyond two hundred years, at thirty-two, Quill shouldn't have had a single line on his face. But I could already see the frown lines in his forehead and the beginnings of crows' feet in the corners of each of his eyes. His previously shiny gold hair seemed lackluster now, with threads of grey weaving around his ears.

This obviously wasn't an easy life, which was all the more incentive to get out of it. And although I didn't have an escape route planned yet, I wasn't giving up. There was something inside me that refused to yield, something that was rallying, something increasingly pissed off as the days went by. I just refused to do this forever—and to carry on with the likes of Baron and his entourage. But mostly I refused to give my father the satisfaction of knowing that I would bend to his will. As to figuring a way out, I just needed a little more time—I needed to clear my head and come up with a plan. But for now, that plan would have to wait.

"Loading docks," Baron answered as he started tapping his thick fingers against the surface of the table, which was worn in some places, stained in others.

"What time's it comin' through, boss?" the were at the right of Baron asked, chewing on one of his long, dirty fingernails. He had the general look of a were—big and burly with shaggy, disheveled hair that looked as if it hadn't seen a shampoo bottle in decades. He had a longish beard and his teeth were yellowed from too much smoking, I guessed. All in all, he was totally gross.

"Tonight," Baron answered as his eyes fell on me, a trace of mirth visible in their dark black depths. It was almost like an untold challenge—he was testing me to see what my reaction would be—to see if I was nervous or anxious about my newfound role. Well, even though I was more than anxious, I wasn't about to let him know that.

"What time?" I asked, my face and voice revealing nothing. I'd not only taken his bet, but I'd doubled it.

He smiled slightly and dropped his gaze to my bust casually, but I knew better than to think he was being casual. No, he was reminding me how close he'd come to forcing himself on me. He was trying to goad me. I felt my blood begin to heat up and forced myself to calm down, and not to react because that's what he wanted from me.

"O dark thirty," he said, his eyes still fastened on my breasts.

I held his gaze. "You might want to be more specific." He glanced up at me and I dropped my attention to the table, as if I were looking at his nuts which had nearly been sliced from his body only a few minutes earlier. Two could play this game. "I mean, after midnight, but before sunrise isn't exactly buttoned down." I looked up at his face again. "Is it?"

He eyed me and his smile widened, as if he were turned on by my pretending to focus on his man appendage. "One a.m."

"Hey, Baron, how about you drop this game you're playing with Dulcie and give us the information about the shipment?" Quill demanded, his voice irritated and his eyes burning.

Baron said nothing, but cleared his throat, facing Quill. Apparently the charade was now over. I patted Quill's hand beneath the table to say thanks. He didn't face me, but squeezed my hand all the same. Yep, it was nice to know someone had my back.

"Melchior said there'd be fifty cases comin' through the loadin' docks," Baron said finally, his manner now strictly business. And when he said "the loading docks," I figured he meant the *Yalkemouth* would be traveling by way of portal from the Netherworld to Splendor, arriving the same way Quill and I had.

"And the dupe?" Quillan asked.

"There'll be five cases comin' through on a ship to the far west of the loadin' docks," Baron answered.

And now everything made sense. Melchior was sending out a decoy, which was meant for the ANC to find and bust. The five cases of *Yalkemouth* would be the ANC's bust, meanwhile the fifty from the Netherworld would slip in unnoticed.

"And I'm going to bust the dupe?" I finished hoarsely, figuring out where this was going.

Baron glanced over at me and nodded, his eyes still on mine rather than my chest. Thank Hades. "You an' your ANC buddies can fuck around with bustin' Horatio and the five cases. You just keep them outta my bidness, got it?"

Horatio apparently was the hairy were sitting beside Baron because, at the mention of his name, he started grumbling something about getting beaten up again. Baron gave him a discouraging look and he shut up. And, really, he had nothing to worry about. Once we busted and imprisoned him, he'd merely be deported to the Netherworld where he'd probably just have to lay low for a few weeks. After that, Melchior would see to it that he was released to return to the crime ring. Basically it was like a revolving door, really just a hop, skip and a jump away from a walk in the park.

"What's the name of the ship?" I asked, realizing that was a necessary detail.

"It's a tanker called Alice," Baron finished. "It'll be pullin' in at one a.m. an' there ain't gonna be no more ships tonight, so you can't fuck it up."

As if I was going to fuck it up in the first place. I exhaled a frustrated sigh when something suddenly occurred to me. "How are you going to keep Trey from picking up on what's really going on?"

Trey could see glimpses of the future, his super power in the eyes of the ANC. Although half the time his gift couldn't delineate times or dates, or even locations, Trey's abilities were still an unknown that could seriously threaten the well-being of this plan. I mean, the last thing we needed was for Trey to get an inkling about the fifty cases of *Yalkemouth* on the opposite end of the loading docks. That would blow the plan all to hell.

Baron waved me away with an unimpressed hand. "Melchior already took care of it."

I glanced at Quill with a question in my eyes. "What does that mean?"

Quill smiled down at me. "Melchior knows about Trey's gift. He has a witch in the Netherworld who magicks all the narcotic shipments to ensure there isn't any residue on them that Trey could pick up on."

I just nodded and thought this whole thing had been so well choreographed, so staged. What really struck me was that it had been this way for years. The entire time Quillan had been the head of the ANC in Splendor, this had been going on underneath my nose and I'd had no clue.

"You have access to the vault?" Horatio asked me.

Baron turned his full attention on me, and realizing what this meant, I immediately shook my head. "The only person who has access to the vault is Knight," I said staunchly. The only tip off I'd ever received that something unsavory was happening in the ANC was when I'd finagled my way into the vault. It was being used to warehouse the illegal potions we Regulators confiscated. Every week, cauldrons from the Netherworld would arrive, the sole purpose to destroy all the confiscated potions. When I broke into the vault (well, broke into it is a bit harsh, seeing as how Knight granted me permission), I immediately noticed that none of the potions had been destroyed at all. Later, I learned that Quill was redistributing them on the black market, something Baron was obviously interested in resuscitating—at least judging by the expression of curiosity in his eyes.

"Absolutely not," I reiterated, shaking my head. "I'd be found out in a second."

"She's right," Quill said as he viewed the room, as if to ensure that everyone assembled understood that this wasn't a good idea. "Vander's the only one with access. It would be too suspicious."

I stood up, after deciding I'd had enough. "So one a.m. tonight, Alice the tanker ship on the west end loading docks. Anything else?"

Baron glared at me as if he were annoyed that I was done with our little rendezvous since he hadn't announced "meeting adjourned." When he didn't say anything else, I pushed my chair out from underneath the table and started for the door, Quillan right behind me. "See you in three hours," I said.

"This is your night ta prove yourself, O'Neil," Baron called out to my exiting figure. I paused with my hand on the doorknob.

I turned around to face him and smiled assuredly. "It's in my back pocket, asshole," I said with as much disdain as I could muster before showing myself out.

"Watch it, Dulce," Quill said and sighed heavily.

I glanced up at him, unfazed. "What? He *is* an asshole."

"You know his temper."

"Yeah and now he can get well acquainted with mine."

Once freed from the confines of Ink, I approached my Suzuki quickly, and noticed an electric blue sports car, complete with black stripes on either side, parked beside it. Quillan beeped it unlocked and I glanced over at him as I wrestled with my helmet.

"Are you okay?" Quill asked as he faced me with concern in his eyes. I wasn't sure if he was referring to my emotional sanity or my close encounter with Baron. Maybe both.

"I'm fine," I answered tersely, "I just want to go home." I turned the key in the ignition only to hear it click a few times. I turned the key again and nothing. The engine was dead. "Son of a fucking bitch!" I yelled and slammed my palm against the tank. Quillan walked over and took the key from me and motioning me aside, straddled the bike as he inspected it and attempted to start it himself.

"It's dead," he announced, standing up and eyeing me sadly. "I think it's the starter."

"You've gotta be kidding," I grumbled and shook my head like I couldn't believe it. Talk about shitty timing!

"I'll take you home," Quillan said as I tore off my helmet and felt like I wanted to cry.

"What am I going to do with this?" I asked, meaning that I didn't want to be tied to Ink in any way, shape or form; and everyone at the ANC knew what I drove. It wasn't any stretch of the imagination at all to think that Knight, Trey or anyone else from the ANC might happen to do a drive-by to make sure Baron was on the up and up. Seeing my motorcycle in the parking lot was not a good thing.

"The bike is done, Dulce," Quillan said in a grounded tone, as if he were afraid I was super attached to it or something. "Baron has guys who can strip it and sell the parts. I'll let him know on the way to your house."

I nodded and approached Quillan's car, scanning it quizzically. "Is this a Mustang?" I asked, finding some of the lines fairly reminiscent of the iconic Ford.

"2013 Shelby GT 500," he answered with obvious pride.

I gave him a raised brow as I opened the door and seated myself. "Mustang?" I asked again once he was within earshot.

He chuckled and helped himself into the driver's seat. "Mustang," he answered.

I secured my seatbelt and then sighed. "I guess it beats a 1961 Galaxy Town Victoria."

###

I walked in my front door at a little past ten p.m. Locking it behind me, I immediately noticed my answering machine blinking red. From the looks of it, I had two messages. I checked my cell phone lying beside it and lifting it up, saw that it also had messages. Probably Sam and Dia wondering what in the hell had happened to me while I'd been in the Netherworld. Even though I knew I needed to face them at some point, I just couldn't bring myself to do it now. Not after the crappy evening I'd just endured. But what was even scarier was that there was something inside me that wanted to sever all ties to my old life, something that wanted to invalidate any and all associations with my friends because I realized I was now a different person. Even worse, knowing me could be detrimental to their wellbeing. I mean, who knew what sorts of power trips Melchior could hold over my head now? He already had Knight for insurance, so it wasn't too much of a stretch to imagine Sam or Dia could be next. Yep, my father had me exactly where he wanted me, and that was a desperate place to be.

Trying to avoid the naked truth in my thoughts, I searched the fridge for something to eat, but it was just as bare as it had been the last time I'd opened it when Knight had visited after his release from the Netherworld.

Knight ... just the image of him filled my gut with a deep-rooted sorrow, and a tremor that rattled me. I felt like I'd soon cave into a puddle of jelly.

At the sound of my doorbell, I pulled myself together, forced myself to put on my poker face and see why the hell someone was visiting so late. The fact that my alone time was now nonexistent was really getting old. I huffed over to the front door, expecting to find Quill or Baron and checked the peephole, instantly recognizing Bram. A sense of guilt washed over me as I remembered I'd never paid Bram a visit to tell him I was okay. And that was bad—especially after he'd acted as my guide and protector in the Netherworld.

With a sheepish smile, I pulled the door open and found the dashing vampire glaring at me. "Then it is true?" he asked, pushing past me and showing himself into my living room.

"What's true?" I asked as I closed the door behind us. I was actually happy to see Bram. Somehow, along the course of our Netherworld adventure, I'd actually grown fond of the vampire. If nothing else, he was definitely amusing.

"That you have escaped the Netherworld and returned to Splendor." With his raised brows and frown, he looked pissed off. There was something livid in his eyes, which surprised me. I mean, even though it wasn't exactly polite that I'd failed to inform him that I was back, I didn't imagine he'd be this bent out of shape.

"Oh, yeah, it's true." I took a deep breath and caught his eye. "About that, I, uh, had been meaning to come by and tell you."

"And yet it appears you did not find the time?" he chided, crossing his arms against his chest.

That was basically the short of it, but it wasn't like I could tell Bram exactly what I'd been up to. Yes, I'd never painted Bram as a "good guy," but I also was fairly convinced he was nowhere near the likes of a Baron or even my father. Nope, Bram basically ran in his own circle.

"I'm sorry, Bram," I started, shaking my head, not really knowing what I could say to lessen the blow of my obvious bad manners.

"Perhaps I was not important enough?" he pouted. Jeez, he was really wringing everything he could out of this. But, I guess I deserved it.

"I really was meaning to come tell you," I said in as sincere a voice as I could. "I feel really terrible about it, I mean it."

"I see," he grumbled but I could tell his mood was lightening. *Note to self: apparently Bram likes panderers.*

"How did you find out that I was back, anyway?" I asked, trying to change the subject because there was only so much ass-kissing I was prepared to do. And where Bram was concerned, I'd already reached my limit.

"I make the goings on in Splendor my business, sweet," he answered and when he called me by my pet name, I guessed he was well on his way to forgiving me. Forgiving me was important because I wanted to keep Bram on my good side. He wasn't the type of person to have as an enemy. Nope, he was powerful. Just how powerful, though, I wasn't sure, but that's exactly what I intended to find out.

"And I was quite concerned with your whereabouts," he continued, inspecting his fingernails as he spoke. "It has been the only subject to occupy my mind."

"I'm sorry," I said again, trying to belabor the point. "I really am, Bram."

He said nothing for a few seconds, just watched me as if to gauge how sincere I was. And the truth of the matter was that I was sincere—I did feel bad about it.

Finally, he dropped his stern expression and smiled handsomely. "Apology accepted."

And now it was time to move on to more important topics. It was time to learn just how involved Bram was with the Netherworld. I cleared my throat and thought about the best way to approach him, as well as what my chances were of getting some straight answers out of him. Figuring there really was no "right" approach, I just opted for friendly. "Have a seat," I said, motioning to my couch.

Bram looked surprised at first, but quickly acquiesced and seated himself on the far end of the sofa. He eyed me curiously, as if wondering why I'd invited him to stay. Well, he was about to find out.

"Bram, I have questions for you," I started and sat down in a chair beside him. I pulled it out so we were facing one another.

"As I have questions for you, sweet."

It didn't surprise me to know he'd have questions for me. Bram was always nosy. "I know you're curious as to how I got home," I began, searching for a plausible excuse. Remembering that I'd nearly blown my cover with Knight regarding my story about Caressa and the portal, I decided to learn from past mistakes.

"Quite so," the vampire replied; and when I didn't respond immediately, he prodded. "Go on."

"I escaped," I said simply.

"Escaped?" he repeated dubiously.

"I overpowered Caressa and tried to talk Judge Thorne into taking me back into custody in exchange for Knight's life," I spewed out, nearly tripping over the lie.

Bram said nothing, but eyed me suspiciously as if he found it hard to believe. "And yet the Loki has returned, as have you."

I nodded, reminding myself to stick to my story. "Judge Thorne wouldn't listen to me and decreed that I be escorted to the portal by one of his guards." I took a deep breath. "As to why Knight was released, I don't know."

"I see."

I shrugged, thinking I needed to play up my surprise a bit more. "I mean, I thought for sure he was never going to get out."

"It is quite the riddle, is it not?" Bram asked and then smiled in an off-putting sort of way.

"It is," I agreed and even nodded to reaffirm my words.

"And you have been reinstated in your position at the ANC?" he continued. Bram was definitely at the top of the gossip totem pole. He always had been, though, which was why I found him so useful in my position as Regulator. He got the inside scoops before anyone else did.

"You're impressive, I'll give you that," I said softly and then smiled at him.

"Why did you insist on becoming a Regulator again?" he asked, his tone slightly more casual, but I knew his indifference was merely an act—Bram wanted to know what was going on. He made it his business to know the ins and outs of ANC business.

"I missed it," I answered nonchalantly before turning to the subject of my own questions. "How high do you rank in the Netherworld pecking order?"

Bram smiled, revealing his fangs, clearly appreciative of the question and even more clearly impressed with himself. "High." He narrowed his eyes on me. "Why was the Loki truly released?"

I swallowed hard. "I don't know," I bluffed. "Are you familiar with the head of the Netherworld?"

Bram's smile dropped. "Yes."

I felt my heartbeat quicken. "How familiar?"

"Familiar enough." He paused a moment or two before that debonair smile was back in full effect. "Are you familiar with the head of the Netherworld?"

"No." I paused to catch my breath, completely aware that he was testing me, that he knew more than he was letting on. "Are you involved with his affairs?"

"No," he answered quickly. Maybe too quickly. "Are *you* involved with his affairs?"

My heart thundered through my ears, sounding like waves crashing against rocks. I almost felt like I was going to pass out. "No."

"Are you aware that he shares the same last name with you?" Bram asked in a casual, bored tone.

I swallowed hard. "There are many people with the last name O'Neil," I said simply, even adding a shrug, trying to portray the image of someone bored, apathetic and uninterested.

"Very true," he answered noncommittally.

"Why were the prison guards so frightened of you, Bram, and why do you have your own portal entrance to the Netherworld?"

He smiled, long and languidly. "Why do you share the same last name as the Head of the Netherworld? And why was the Loki returned when Melchior had him exactly where he wanted him?"

I didn't say anything for four seconds and I'm sure I was wearing my anxiety. Bram smiled even more broadly.

"It seems we are at a standstill, Dulcie, sweet."

SIX

Somehow Bram knew Melchior was related to me and I was pretty sure it wasn't just a guess based on the similarity of our last names. Since Bram hadn't said anything for the last few seconds, he was right—we were at a standstill.

"How did you know?" I asked finally. My voice sounded hoarse as I realized I'd been first to show my hand.

Bram smiled slightly, like he was pleased I'd finally acknowledged my familial relationship to Melchior. I watched as he relaxed against my couch and sighed dramatically. "I assumed from the moment I met you, sweet."

The word "assumed" held a lot of weight because it implied that Bram didn't *know* I was related to Melchior. And I must say I was relieved he hadn't been in the know—I mean, it's not exactly a good feeling when you realize everyone around you knows more about your life than you do.

"Well, he's my father," I finished, my jaw tight and my tone betraying the fact that I wasn't happy about it.

"Ah, I see," Bram said, nodding thoughtfully. "And it seems you just learned this?"

It was my turn to nod. "Yep."

"And your story regarding the escape from Caressa?" he pried, eyeing me with a drawn brow as if he knew I hadn't exactly been telling the whole truth and nothing but the truth.

I inhaled deeply and exhaled just as deeply. "It wasn't true."

Bram's left brow continued to reach for the ceiling but, otherwise, his countenance remained unchanged—the same expectant, yet unconcerned look he tried so hard to achieve. "And what is the truth?"

"Before we get into this dog and pony show," I started, my voice suddenly sounding bossy and harsh, "this has to be a quid pro quo, Bram. If I'm going to spill the contents of my diary to you, I expect the same in return."

Bram threw his head back, laughing heartily before his merriment died on his lips and he faced me with a wide smile and shook his head in wonder—like he seemed to approve of my sense of humor. "Of course, sweet, of course."

I nodded and continued. "The truth is that I broke into the Head of the Netherworld's office with the express purpose of holding a gun to his head and forcing him to release Knight." Bram's eyes went wide, but he said nothing while I merely shook my head, admitting that my plan *had* gone off with a major hitch. "The joke ended up being on me when I found out Melchior was my father."

"Quite the sobering joke," Bram said in an aristocratic tone, his English accent dripping. Sometimes I wondered about how, after living in California for a hundred years, his accent still sounded like he'd just jumped off a plane from Heathrow airport. Yep, Bram was one of those people who impressed himself often and it wouldn't have surprised me in the least to learn that Bram talked to himself just to hear the sound of his own voice.

"Yeah, I wasn't exactly laughing," I admitted.

"Then you negotiated the Loki's release with the Head of the Netherworld?"

"Yes," I replied, feeling suddenly uncomfortable with the direction the conversation was taking. The matter of what those negotiations with my father entailed was now just a matter of connecting A with B to arrive at C.

"And what did your father gain in return for releasing the Loki?"

"A daughter," I said simply, not wanting to delve much deeper than that. I already felt as if my business was now standing in front of us, completely naked and embarrassed.

"You have sold your soul to the devil, it appears?" Bram deduced aptly and I felt my stomach drop. Sometimes he just had this uncanny ability to see right through me. It was almost as if I were a book and he'd merely opened me to the chapter where my innermost thoughts and feelings lay.

"Then you're aware of my father's ... business dealings?" I asked, eyeing him pointedly.

Bram was quiet for a few seconds and then simply nodded, saying nothing. But I wasn't about to put up with his silence. Not after I'd just spilled my proverbial blood. Now it was his turn to do a little bleeding. "How long have you been aware of it?" I asked, finding it somewhat ironic that I couldn't put a word to my father's underhanded ways, that I couldn't refer to them as what they were—illegal.

"The entire time I have lived in Splendor," he said softly, pursing his lips together in something that most resembled a frown.

That was when I remembered Bram telling me, upon our entrance to the Netherworld, that he hadn't stepped foot on Netherworld soil in one hundred years. Jeez, that had to mean good ol' Pop was older than I'd imagined. I mean, I knew elves could live a very long time—the oldest on record having lived to see her four hundred and twelfth birthday—but this was still a surprise. "How old is my father?"

Bram cocked his head to the side as if my question had given him cause for pause. "Perhaps one hundred fifty," he finished.

I couldn't help the astonishment that overtook me. I just hadn't figured Melchior was so old—he didn't look a day over fifty. "And how long has he been the Head of the Netherworld?"

Bram didn't hesitate. "A century."

"Then you came here to Splendor to get away from him?"

Bram cocked his head again, this time to the other side. I was convinced he encouraged these long pauses just because he liked to build up anticipation. If nothing else, Bram was a drama queen.

"I would not use those exact words," he finished.

I shook my head, feeling exasperation starting to fill my entire being, my ears even heating up with it. "Bram, can't you, for once, just cut this melodramatic crap and give it to me straight?"

He huffed like he was offended, but then dropped the charade a few seconds later, thank Hades. "Ask me what you care to know."

I leaned forward, realizing what this meant—that the ordinarily reclusive Bram was going to let me in. Questions swarmed through my mind. "What was your connection with Melchior and why did you leave the Netherworld to come here?"

"I was your father's partner," he finished succinctly as my eyes widened.

"What do you mean?"

"Before O'Neil ever became the Head of the Netherworld, he was first and foremost a business man."

I frowned, surprised. I wasn't sure why, but it was like I hadn't ever conceived of the idea that Melchior had ever been anything but a lying, double-dealing, piece of shit. "What sort of business?"

"Importing products from Earth to the Netherworld," Bram said softly and his eyes took on a faraway sort of glaze—like he was reliving a time long gone.

"What sort of products?"

Bram shrugged. "Automobiles, horses, food, clothing, building supplies ... anything that existed on Earth that could be considered useful in the Netherworld." He sighed deeply which was all for show because he had no respiratory system. "O'Neil and I were quite close friends," he continued. "Little by little, your father's ...

"Please don't call him that," I said, suddenly deciding that just because I was related to Melchior didn't allow him to bear the title of my father. A father was someone who, in my mind, had been involved in his child's life, or at the very least, cared about his child. And there was no evidence that Melchior had ever given a crap about me. As far as I was concerned, Melchior was basically a sperm donor.

"How would you prefer I label him?" Bram asked, his eyes softer as if he understood my need to distance myself from good ol' Dad. Well, knowing him first hand, Bram had to be aware of what a rotten person he was.

"Melchior is fine," I answered. "'Course, the devil works too."

Bram nodded with a sad smile. "Very well." Then he started with his story again. "Melchior's interests turned away from imports and he became increasingly enthralled with the politics of the Netherworld. Eventually, he ran for the office of Head of the Netherworld and was elected."

"So the Netherworld is a democracy?" I asked, completely confused because it had seemed anything but.

Bram shook his head. "Many moons ago it was, sweet, but not so any longer. Melchior has taken it from a republic to ... how shall I say this ..."

"Don't sugarcoat anything," I interrupted, my expression and tone staunch. "As far as I'm concerned, my father is my father in name only."

Bram nodded. "Melchior is a tyrant," he finished.

"Why hasn't anyone tried to get rid of him?" I demanded, finally broaching a question that had been plaguing me all along. "I'm sure the creatures of the Netherworld don't want to live under a tyranny."

"Quite so," Bram agreed. He steepled his fingers together only to begin drumming them against his thighs. He was obviously a fidgeter. "The last attempt on Melchior's life was a century ago."

"And what happened?" I asked, now on the edge of my seat.

Bram shrugged. "The interloper was captured, tortured and his corpse paraded through the streets to discourage future attempts on Melchior's life; apparently the warning achieved its purpose as there have not been any other assassination attempts since."

I swallowed hard, thinking it sounded like a punishment from the middle ages or something more befitting the court of Henry VIII as opposed to the Netherworld a mere century ago. "And is that why you came here to Splendor?"

Bram simply nodded. "I chose not to subject myself to the oppression of Melchior any longer and, instead, opted for a quieter life."

"I'd hardly call owning No Regrets a quiet life," I said, but my thoughts weren't really on Bram's nightclub. Instead, they were centered on the feeling of a knot twisting my stomach. My father was much worse than I'd given him credit for. I glanced at Bram again, needing one more question answered. "Are you aware of his ... extracurricular activities?" I asked.

"If by 'extracurricular activities,' you mean his illegal potions importing, yes, I am."

"Are you working for him?" I continued, hoping and praying the answer was no. Why? Because I liked Bram and didn't want to think that my father had not only royally fucked up Quillan's and my lives but Bram's too. But somehow, in my heart of hearts, I didn't think Bram was in the employ of Melchior.

"No," he said resolutely and then faced me, concern in his eyes. "How deeply are you involved, Dulcie?"

I held my breath for a few seconds as I debated over whether or not to admit anything more. But, really, what more was there to admit to? "Deep," I finished in a small voice.

Bram nodded and his expression was suddenly drawn, his eyes narrowed. "Was it worth it?" he asked, flicking his eyes back to mine.

It was the same question Quill had asked me. I just simply nodded, knowing if I had to make the choice all over again, I wouldn't change a thing.

I got the call from Knight around one fifteen a.m., and of course, I'd been waiting for it. He called to say that Trey had just gotten a vision of a potions delivery in the loading docks and that I needed to hurry. Of course, I was already dressed in my leathers, my helmet waiting beside the front door. Once I hung up the phone, I locked the door behind me and started for my ANC provided (read: Knightley Vander provided) red Ducati Diavel motorcycle. Throwing one leg over the seat, I strapped on my helmet and turned on the engine until it was purring excitedly, and I was off.

It took me exactly ten minutes to reach the west end of the loading docks where I could already see the tanker ship, Alice, present and accounted for. Just as Baron had claimed, she was the only ship in sight. I pulled off the road, maybe one hundred feet from the docks, and hid my bike beneath a massive oak tree. A salty breeze traveled up from the docks, wrapping around me in a chilly embrace. I shivered in spite of myself and hopped off the Ducati, toying with my helmet as I pulled it off and placed it on the seat. Unzipping my leather jacket, I slid the Op 6 from my shoulder holster, palming it in a low ready stance, the muzzle pointing down. I stayed mostly to the shadows offered by the oversized oak trees along the stretch of road leading down to the docks. I had to look every inch the alert and prepared Regulator. Even though Baron and his men were more than aware that I was coming, I had to maintain the charade for Knight.

I continued down the dark road, the sound of insects chirping from the tall grass beside me in chorus with the lonely calls of a few seagulls who flew overhead. I glanced around myself, looking for any sign of Knight or Trey, but nothing. At a bend in the road, I took cover behind a knotty-trunked pepper tree and looked down at the loading docks, which were now maybe fifty feet from me. I could see the men of the ship unloading large crates of Hades only knew what direct from the Netherworld. Whatever portal this ship had come through had to have been pretty large because the tanker was, in a word ... enormous.

I didn't recognize the men who were unloading the crates and figured they had nothing to do with Melchior. As far as Horatio was concerned, there was no sign of him. I pushed out from the darkness of the pepper tree and continued down the road, the moonlight now spotlighting me as I hurried for cover under a large pine tree maybe ten feet away. Once I reached it, I looked around myself and wondered where the hell Knight was.

Well, wonder and you shall receive, because only seconds later, I heard Knight calling me from off to my right, where he was kneeling behind a crumbling brick wall, Trey just beside him. I hurried over to them, kneeling down in front of Knight who gave me a friendly smile.

"Good to see you, Dulce," he said, his smile widening.

I returned the smile hesitantly before facing Trey. "What's going on?" I asked and then eyed the loading docks again, searching for any sign of Horatio or, failing him, Baron. But all I could see were the sailors unloading numerous crates. I could only hope we hadn't come too late.

'Course, I had to imagine Horatio would take his sweet time, knowing his sole purpose was to be caught.

"I don't get it," Trey said and shook his head as if he were frustrated, alternating his stare between Knight and me. "I know I saw something in the vision," he finished, his upper lip wet with perspiration. "It just doesn't make any sense that nothing's happening now."

"And you're sure it was supposed to happen tonight?" Knight asked him, his tone conveying the fact that he, himself, was dubious.

"Yeah," Trey said, emphatically nodding. "I had the distinct feeling that it was happening right as I was seeing it. When have my visions ever been wrong in the past?"

They hadn't been.

"What exactly did you see?" I asked.

"I saw crates of something that looked like *Yalkemouth* or maybe *Arson Flower* or *Monravia*. I couldn't really make it out in the vision, but it was a general feeling I got that hinted at one of those three," Trey finished and then glanced at me apologetically.

"But so far, we haven't seen anything out of the ordinary," Knight finished and shrugged as he glanced at the tanker again.

"Interesting," I said, looking at Knight only to find his attention riveted on me. When I faced him, he simply smiled and I felt myself gulp down the need to throw my arms around him and kiss him.

Knight said nothing but handed me a pair of binoculars. I took them and focused on the loading docks and the men unloading the crates. On the opposite side of the ship, I watched as Horatio seemed to suddenly appear from the shadows, like they simply spat him out. Well, it was about damn time! I felt my heart speed up as I watched him motion to someone onboard. The sailor appeared with a large white crate between his hands, complete with rows of bottled *Yalkemouth*, the fluorescent blue liquid peeking out through the slats of the crate. He handed it to Horatio.

"Looks like it was *Yalkemouth*, Trey," I said and handed the binoculars to Knight who took them immediately. He glanced through the lenses for a few seconds before returning them to his jacket pocket.

"Let's move," he said simply and stood up, Trey and I following. "I don't want to lose him," he added, pulling his Op 7 from his waist, holding it in low ready as he started down the road, being careful to stick to the shadows the entire time.

I followed Knight down the road which terminated in a cement walkway, the five ramps leading down to the docks looking like outstretched arms sprouting from the concrete. Our tanker ship was at the bottom of the second ramp.

Turning to face Knight, I watched him pause and figured he was deciding the best way forward. He checked behind him, then, holding up the binoculars in the direction of Horatio, who was still busily unloading his illegal imports, Knight shook his head, the look of impatience plastering itself across his face.

"He's already unloaded three cases of *Yalkemouth*," he said in a steely voice.

"Who is it?" I asked.

"Looks like one of Baron's guys," he answered. "A were." It wasn't like Knight was on a first name basis with Horatio or the likes of Horatio, so I wasn't surprised that he didn't know Horatio's name.

"So what do you want to do?" I asked, knowing whatever we were going to do, we needed to act fast because Horatio only had two more crates left to unload. And if he unloaded them too slowly, that in itself would seem suspect.

Knight shrugged. "We need to act."

I glanced down at the ship and noticed the sailor handing Horatio the final crate of *Yalkemouth*. Horatio plopped the crate on top of the others and made a big show of being out of breath. Then he hoisted the top crate and started for a Ford Explorer, the only car in the parking lot, which was parked as close to the docks as possible. Once the first was loaded, he returned for crate two and seemed to be taking his sweet ass time. He was obviously waiting for us to make our move and probably wondering where the hell we were.

I glanced at Knight and watched him looking at the scene before him as if he were taking stock of every detail, deciding the best approach to take. We obviously couldn't just walk down the ramp to the ship single file like we were on a field trip. I guessed we'd probably get back on the road. It disappeared around a hillside just above the cement walkway, leading to the loading docks. There were some old, craggy oak trees along the hillside which would offer us ample cover.

"Let's stick behind those trees," Knight said, motioning to the small hillside. Yep, I'd been right. Point for me.

Neither Trey nor I said anything, but simply followed Knight back up to the road, being careful to stay in the shadows and remain undetected. Once we'd reached the hillside, we continued along the tree line, skulking in the shadows. I glanced down at the goings on in the ship below us. The sailor who had been helping Horatio returned to the other side of the ship where he started helping his fellow sailors unload. Yep, he hadn't been involved in Horatio's business any more than just in helping him unload the crates. I wasn't sure why but somehow that fact was a relief to me.

My gaze fell to Horatio again as I watched him pick up the third crate and start for the Explorer. When we were maybe ten feet away from Horatio, Knight turned toward me and motioned that he was going to take Horatio down. I nodded and clutched my Op 6 even more tightly.

"I'll be right behind you," I whispered.

Then I watched Knight sprint down the hill, landing on the concrete just behind Horatio with a soft thud. Before the shorter, stouter man could respond, Knight knocked him down. Horatio released the crate and it crashed down next to him, the bottles of *Yalkemouth* breaking as the fluorescent liquid began leaking from the broken bottles.

The sailors all turned at the sound of the confrontation and when a few began to walk towards Knight, I stood out before him, pulling open my jacket to reveal my badge.

"This is ANC business," I said sternly.

The sailors nodded and the one who had been helping Horatio glanced at him nervously before facing me again. "I had nothing to do with it," he said, swallowing hard. "I was just helping him unload whatever that stuff was."

I nodded. "It's okay. Just keep going about your business."

The man didn't say anything else but returned to the far side of the ship as I brought my attention back to Knight. Horatio was still on the ground, Knight's knee in his back. Trey was standing at Horatio's head, his Op 6 aimed at the were. I watched as Knight pinned Horatio's arms behind his back and read him his Miranda rights.

Horatio didn't attempt to put up much of a fight for obvious reasons and a few seconds later, Knight hoisted him to his feet and started toward us.

I didn't even glance at Horatio and I noticed he did his damndest not to look at me.

"Where are you parked?" I asked Knight.

"Up the street," Trey answered. "I'll go get the car and meet you at the top of the docks." We both nodded and Trey re-holstered his gun before running up the ramp to the cement walkway and back to the road from which we'd come.

I glanced at Knight and smiled, keeping my Op 6 trained on Horatio. "Not bad."

Knight chuckled. "It's good to have you back."

SEVEN

When I walked through my door, I was exhausted. After the whole Horatio ordeal and everything that led up to it, I felt like I needed a hot shower and a long nap—as in, sleeping-for-the-next-two-days long. I tore off my jacket, throwing it on the chair beside the door and bemoaned the fact that Blue wasn't around to greet me. I'd have to make a trip to the pound and get Trey a new friend, so he'd relinquish mine.

As I walked into my living room, I thought about getting something to eat, then about taking off my clothes and getting into the shower; but instead, I did nothing. I just stood there like I'd misplaced my brain, like an idiotic zombie. And before I could second guess myself, I suddenly burst into tears.

And it's not like I'm often given to fits of crying. In fact, I could count on one hand the occasions in my life when things have been so bad that I've cried. But even though part of me was shocked by my emotional side, it was in complete control of me. In fact, I wasn't really crying—it was more like sobbing, my entire body was consumed by a convulsion of tears.

It was as if everything that had happened over the last two weeks was suddenly raining down on me, straining my ability to cope. I guess it's true what they say—that everyone has her breaking point. And I was definitely at mine. My entire life had turned upside down and, really, I was living my own worst nightmare. I'd become something I couldn't respect, something that was so unlike me. I was being controlled by someone else, my father, and worse, allowing it. And the mere thought of that sickened me because I'd never subjugated myself before, and always

76

looked down on those who did. Yes, I had to remind myself that my reasons were sound and good—that saving Knight's life meant everything to me, but that didn't mean I wasn't searching for a way out of it. I just needed some time to think, to plan, and in planning, figure out a way to extricate myself and all of my affiliations with Melchior. I just needed time, but so far, time alone was fleeting, if not impossible to find.

Pretty soon, I started hyperventilating and couldn't catch my breath so I told myself to cool it. What good were my tears going to do me anyway? It wasn't like they'd magically flick Melchior O'Neil off the face of the Earth, er, the Netherworld. It wasn't like they'd ensure Knight would be forever safe. No, all in all, they were completely useless and as such, I was done with them.

I shook my head, wiping the water from my eyes and threw myself into my couch, waiting for my breathing to return to normal again. I could feel my tears drying and hoped it would only be a matter of seconds before I could respirate like a completely collected, rational and normal person. Before I had the chance to fully regain control of myself, my cell phone buzzed in my jacket pocket; that is, my *personal* cell phone, not the one Quillan gave me. Standing up, I grabbed it and I held it up to my face, trying to make out the name through my glassy vision.

It was Knight.

I took a deep breath to feel more calm and a little more in control of myself before I answered. "Hi."

"Dulce," Knight started and his rich baritone warmed my entire being like hot fudge. "Just wanted to check in and see how you were feeling about things."

"Things?" I asked, testing my voice more than his comment. I sounded okay. Maybe a little tired but not like I'd just had a crying fit alone in my living room.

"Yeah, you know—your first bust now that you're back as a Regulator for the ANC ..." I could hear the smile in his voice. Then his tone became a bit quieter. "And everything that's happened between us." I was about to respond when he interrupted me. "Are you going to be up for a while?"

"I guess," I answered, thinking that even though I was more than exhausted, I probably wouldn't be able to sleep. I'd been suffering from sleep deprivation ever since I'd found out Melchior was my father and more, that I was working for him.

"Do you want company?" Knight asked, his voice sounding hesitant. That stuck in my gut because "hesitant" was not a word to describe Knightley Vander. He was outgoing, confident, strong. Sometimes annoyingly so.

"Sure," I said as warmly as I could, but inside me something was about to wither and die as I realized it wasn't right to continue pretending things were fine between us. I knew what I had to do and pretty soon, things wouldn't be fine between us.

"I'll be there soon. Want me to pick anything up?" His tone was warm, happy.

"At two a.m.?" I asked, surprised. "Nothing will be open."

"Shit," he laughed. "Sometimes this job makes me forget what time of day or night it is." He sighed. "I'll see you soon."

Then he hung up the phone and I collapsed onto my couch again, trying to quell the tears that were threatening to re-emerge, but now for a different reason. Now, something within me was snapping at the realization of what I was about to tell Knight—that we were through, that we couldn't date anymore. Of course, I couldn't tell him the real reason—that reason being that my father coerced me into his control by holding Knight's life on the line. Instead, I planned to tell him that things had gotten too complicated for me and that I wasn't comfortable throwing myself into a relationship. I'd buffer that excuse with another one—that since I was now working as a Regulator for the ANC again, I wasn't comfortable carrying on a relationship with my boss. Besides, a relationship between Knight and me *was* against ANC policy, seeing how he was my manager. I had to admit that I was surprised Knight had never mentioned as much. Sometimes, he definitely bent the rules to suit himself. At any rate, given my past, my reasons for breaking up with him wouldn't seem so farfetched. He always knew I had commitment issues. I'd been so badly hurt by my last relationship, I'd basically given up on men.

I was spared further soliloquies when Knight knocked on the door, a purposeful sound. I stood up and quickly glanced at the mirror on the wall above my couch. I checked my reflection to ensure I didn't look blotchy and red-eyed, or that I'd completely hit rock bottom and been crying my eyes out. I looked okay actually. Maybe a little red, but I could explain that away with allergies. 'Course, as a fairy, I didn't get allergies—being a creature of nature and all—but whatever.

I pulled the door open and greeted Knight with a small smile. He was wearing dark blue jeans and an untucked, long-sleeved, black T-shirt that matched the blackness of his hair. His hair was a little longish, curling around his ears and it gave him a certain unkempt ruggedness that was sexy as all get out. He smiled at me, his full lips spreading into one of the most breathtaking grins I'd ever seen and I felt my entire body deflate on itself. Not only was he beautiful, but he was all around a wonderful person. I felt the exact opposite of a wonderful person—like I was a huge, steaming, stinking dog turd on the bottom of his shoe.

"Come in," I said in a near whisper, opening the door wide. He walked past me and threw himself into the chair beside the couch, propping his large feet on my coffee table. He looked so comfortable, as if he'd just come home from a long day of busting criminal ass, and planned to forget the day's events in my armchair. Although he dwarfed my chair, he looked as though he was exactly where he belonged.

"Long night," he offered and I closed the door, locking it, before taking a seat on the couch.

"Did you take care of locking him up?" I asked, referring to Horatio.

"Trey did while I wrote up the paperwork. He was one of Baron's guys. Horatio something or other." After Knight had taken Horatio into custody, he'd let me go home, explaining that he and Trey could take care of things and I looked like I needed to get some z's. Knight knew me well because he obviously assumed I wasn't going to sleep, which was why he was sitting in my living room now.

"When are the cauldrons coming?" I asked, referring to the shipment in which we disposed of our illegal narcotics busts. Until then, they were kept locked up in the vault. I'd already promised myself to personally see to it that the *Yalkemouth* was destroyed.

"This week," he answered, eyeing me curiously. "So, Dulce, are you going to tell me what's wrong?"

"Wrong?" I asked, feeling taken aback and sounding just as surprised. Was I wearing my emotions on my sleeve again?

He nodded with a stern expression—like I wasn't going to schmooze myself out of this one. "You look like you've lost ten pounds over the last week and you have bags under your eyes."

"Well, you're beautiful yourself. Thanks for noticing."

He shook his head and leaned forward, squeezing my right thigh just above my knee with his large hand. "I'm serious, Dulcie, what's up?"

I shook my head, refusing to look at him. Then remembering myself, I forced my eyes to meet his and held his gaze. "Nothing's up."

He shrugged and relaxed back into the chair. "Sam said you've been ignoring her—not returning her phone calls. And Dia called yesterday, wondering where the hell you were? Apparently, you aren't returning anyone's calls? I had to convince Sam that you were fine and talk her out of an intervention."

"Intervention?" I repeated with a frown, feeling irritation creeping up within me. "That's taking things a little too far." I shook my head as I considered it. "Holy Hades, I've just been ... busy."

"Doing what?" he demanded and his eyes narrowed on me as he crossed his long legs at the ankles. Relaxing against the chair back, he folded his arms behind his head and looked as if he had all the time in the world to listen to me lie my ass off.

"A little of everything." I shrugged. "I've got a lot on my mind."

"That's fair," he said, standing up and approaching me. He dropped down to his knees in front of me and took my hands in his, forcing me to look into his stunningly beautiful blue eyes. "Dulcie, I know you've been through a lot. We've been through a lot. I just want you to know that I'm here for you. If you ever need to talk, if you need a friend, you have me."

I had to choke down the guilt that suddenly welled up within me. More unshed tears were now ready to betray my words again. "Thank you," I managed and then took a deep breath, looking away from him because I knew if I gave him any more eye contact, I'd lose it.

"I know how independent you are and I know how strong you are, Dulcie, but sometimes you need to break your barriers down and let people in. Sometimes you need to talk about things to get through them."

I faced him again and smiled, dropping my eyes to the ground as I realized he was completely right, but I couldn't open up to him. I couldn't talk to him about everything that was going on because it would put his life in jeopardy. "I'll see Sam tomorrow at work and we'll go to lunch," I said hollowly.

"No," Knight said, with an emphatic shake of his head, leaning forward as he did so. "You and Sam take the day off and spend some quality time together. I'll call her in the morning and tell her to expect you at nine a.m., bright and early."

"Knight, you don't have to do that," I started, but his lips were tight, his jaw clenched, which meant he would not be dissuaded. "Thank you," I said finally, allowing him to take each of my hands in his.

"I care about you, Dulcie," he said frankly. "And everything I said to you when we were in High Prison was true."

I felt my stomach turn. We both admitted our love for each other while rotting away in the main prison of the Netherworld. I was awaiting my sentence and Knight was basically sitting on death row. But as far as whatever we said or didn't say, I couldn't think about those things now. If I did, I knew it would break down my resignation as well as my dedication to doing what I had to do.

"Knight, I realize we were both under a lot of pressure when we were in the Netherworld," I started, hating the way it sounded, and, more so, having to pretend that Knight didn't mean as much to me as he did.

"Dulcie, I meant everything I said," he reiterated, his gaze just as penetrating as his tone. His hold on my hands tightened.

I nodded and said nothing, at a complete loss for words. Well, I knew what I had to say, but that didn't make it any easier. And so far, I was sucking at it.

"Did you mean everything you said?" he asked, after I was silent for a few more seconds.

And this was the moment when I knew I had to force the words out—I had to tell him that we couldn't be together any longer but the words seemed stuck in my throat, as if they were clinging to my tongue with all the strength left in them.

You have to do this! I screamed at myself. *Knight's life depends on it!* But I was still silent. *For fuck's sake, Dulcie!*

"Knight, I ..." I started.

Immediately, I could see the pain in his eyes. He knew what I was about to say—probably from my expression or maybe the tone of my voice or the words I'd just uttered. The expression of hope he'd shown earlier was suddenly gone, replaced with dejection. His eyes looked hollow.

"I don't want you to think I didn't mean what I said," I corrected myself quickly, hating myself for inflicting the pain in his eyes. "But things between us can't continue."

His glance was filled with angst but mostly anger. "Why?"

I swallowed hard, feeling as if my tongue was swelling and gagging me. It suddenly occurred to me that I couldn't blame all of this on my break-up baggage with my last boyfriend, Jack. Now it just seemed as if that excuse wouldn't hold weight. Why? Because the problems with Jack couldn't hold a candle to everything that had happened between Knight and me. I mean, we'd openly admitted our undying love for each other! Those words were so strongly heartfelt and deep, I couldn't imagine anything I said now would hold weight. It was like I was just speaking in hypotheticals—in one-sided masks of reality that would easily fall over as soon as a gusty wind approached.

"I can't work with you and date you at the same time," I admitted at last. The words sounded cheap and flimsy as soon as I uttered them. "It's against ANC policy."

Knight narrowed his eyes and stood up, retreating to the far side of the living room. His back was to me and his shoulders seemed tight, making his posture straight and rigid. When he turned to face me, there was anger in his eyes and grimness to the lines of his mouth. "That's bullshit, Dulcie, and you know it."

I stood up and took a deep breath, trying to convince myself not to lose it. One tear and he'd know I was bluffing, that I wasn't being honest with him or myself. "Whatever my reasons, Knight, I can't do this anymore. Things between us from now on have to be strictly platonic."

He glared at me. "So this whole thing was set up."

"Set up?" I repeated, shaking my head, although dawning realization hit me like a bomb. That was exactly what this looked like—a set-up. He thought I'd only asked for my job back so I could break up with him, blaming it on not being able to work together and date. Although it was the farthest from the truth, the truth was nearly as bad.

He nodded and took a step closer to me. I felt like I was shriveling beneath his stringent gaze. "You wanted your job back because you knew it would be an out where you and I are concerned."

"No, that isn't why," I started, shaking my head again, only this time more adamantly. Before I could defend myself, he interrupted me.

"Then why, Dulcie? Seems pretty damn convenient if you ask me."

My heart started beating frantically. I didn't want to get into an argument with him. I'm not sure what I expected—or what I'd thought his reaction was going to be, but I wasn't at all prepared for this. "I just, um … I just felt like I belonged in law enforcement," I said sheepishly. As soon as I said it, I realized my reason needed to sound more legitimate than that. A lot more legitimate if Knight was going to buy it. "Going to the Netherworld reinforced my reasons for getting into law enforcement in the first place. I needed to come back where I belong," I said as a wave of nausea washed over me. I hated the fact that I was a complete and total hypocrite.

"The ANC is where you belong. It's in your blood," he agreed, but crossed his arms against his chest to reveal that he was still angry all the same.

"Please believe me when I say that getting my job back has nothing to do with ... this."

"Then what does this have to do with?"

"I just don't think it's right to work with you and date you, Knight. It's a conflict of interests, especially because you're my boss."

"Then I'll change the arrangement so you can report directly to Caressa."

I swallowed hard. "Knight, Caressa doesn't work in our office and no one else reports to her. It would be too weird and I don't want special favors merely because you and I are in a relationship."

"So you'd prefer to be completely out of the relationship?"

And that was exactly what I was trying to say, but apparently, not doing a good job of saying it. "Knight, I care about you," I started, but he sighed and shook his head.

"But not enough, it seems." He glared at me for a few more seconds and the pain in his eyes nearly undid me. "Damn me for falling for you, Dulcie." He shook his head and stared at something in the distance. "The warning signs had always been there, but I ignored them. I thought you would let me in, that I could help you break down your walls and forget about your past, forget about Jack." He faced me again. "But I was completely wrong." He chuckled acidly. "And fuck me for being completely wrong."

I felt my heart breaking because everything I'd just told him was a complete lie. I was as much in love with him now as I'd ever been. And he *had* been successful in breaking down my walls! It was solely because of Knight that I was able to put Jack behind me and move on. Knight really had saved me, but of course, I couldn't tell him that. Instead, I had to watch silently after I painted the worst possible picture of myself. I had to simply sit back and allow him to believe that I didn't love him.

"I'm sorry," I said dumbly, knowing there really wasn't anything more I could say. Anything more would be considered blabbing the entire truth, thereby sealing his fate to an early death.

Knight didn't say anything for a while, just stood there looking at me with an overall pissed off expression. Then he shook his head and exhaled as he started for the door. "Dulcie, you have issues and the sooner you can attack those issues, head on, the happier you're going to be."

"I realize," I started, but he held up his hand, intimating that I should talk to it because the face wasn't listening.

"I actually pity you," he continued and with his other hand on the doorknob, he turned back around to face me. "I just hope for your sake, one day you don't wake up and realize you wasted your entire life by dwelling on the past."

Then he turned around and walked out of my house, closing the door behind him.

EIGHT

At nine a.m. the next morning, I showed up on Sam's doorstep and rang the doorbell. She answered immediately, a huge smile spreading across her pretty face. Her light brown hair was pulled back into a low ponytail, highlighting her large brown eyes and rosy cheeks. She sort of reminded me of a young Sally Field. She was wearing her "Kiss Me, I'm Wiccan" apron which had to mean one thing—she'd either been cooking or baking. Lucky me.

"Who the hell are you?" she asked, throwing her hands on her hips as she pretended to be irritated, but the smile curling her lips gave her away.

"I know, I know," I said, guilt rampaging through me as I shook my head as if to say I had no words for being such a bad friend. If she only knew the half of it ...

"Well, come on." Sam held the door open wider and grabbed my hand, pulling me inside. "I thought I'd make us breakfast." Then she eyed me suspiciously, tapping her index finger against her mouth. "Knight is right—you *have* lost weight and you look anorexically thin, like LeAnn Rimes in a bikini thin." She brought her eyes back up to mine. "*Not* a good look."

"Thanks ... to you and Knight," I grumbled.

"Don't worry; I'll fatten you up," she said and pinched my left butt cheek ... a little too hard.

"Ouch, Sam!" I yelled, swatting her hand away.

As soon as I walked into her house, the aroma of eggs and bacon welcomed my nostrils. I knew I was in for a treat because Sam was an amazing cook. "Mmm, what smells so completely awesome?" I asked, my stomach growling in agreement, as I dropped my backpack on her sofa, followed by my leather bike jacket. Motorcycle riding was getting old fast just based on the need for constant wardrobe changes. Sidling up to her counter, I took a seat on one of her barstools, swiveling around to face her.

She smiled proudly. "Well, eggs and bacon with fresh-squeezed orange juice, made from the oranges from my tree, I might add. And then we have blueberry breakfast casserole, zucchini and sweet potato frittata, and snicker-doodle bread."

"Um," I started, a look of mild concern on my face. "Aside from me, what army do you plan to feed this morning?"

Sam waved me away with her hand as if she were brushing away crumbs. "I have all these recipes my friends keep pinning on Pinterest, so you're just a good excuse to try them out."

I said nothing but shook my head and smiled at my best friend, suddenly incredibly grateful to Knight that he'd orchestrated this whole thing. Of course, thoughts of Knight led to memories of last night and I had to firmly push them from my mind, reminding myself for the nth time that what I'd done had to be done—that in the long run, I was doing Knight a huge favor.

"Okay, Dulce, go sit at the table because breakfast is ready," Sam said, untying her apron and reaching for what I imagined was the blueberry casserole—the verdant blue splotches in the otherwise white dough being my first clue. I followed her to her dining table, pulling out my chair as I watched her gingerly place the casserole on a trivet. Then she returned to the kitchen for dish number two. The fresh squeezed orange juice was already sitting in a clear jug on the table and the eggs and bacon on a large plate just beside the orange juice.

"If I didn't know better, I'd say you were trying to get into my pants," I said with a laugh, filling my glass with OJ.

Sam glanced at me and smiled widely. "As if! And, besides, I'm well aware that somebody else already filled that position, no pun intended."

I smiled at her very-much-intended pun before my smile turned into a frown and a resigned, despondent sigh. I watched her deliver the frittata and the snicker-doodle bread, placing both directly in front of me. She handed me a serving knife, motioning that I should cut myself a slice of the bread. Then she busied herself with piling a heaping spoonful of scrambled eggs on my plate, three pieces of bacon and an even larger serving of frittata. When she started in on the blueberry breakfast casserole, I had to say something.

"Go easy, there," I begged. She offered me a raised brow but gave me a reasonable serving. Then after fussing around me like she had the Queen of England at her breakfast table, she sat in her seat and started serving herself.

"So why the sigh?" she demanded. I should have known better than to think my best friend would ever let anything slip by. So, figuring the news would soon be known anyway, I decided it was best for Sam to hear it directly from the horse's mouth.

"Knight and I broke up," I said, in a dejected tone.

She didn't respond for a few seconds, taking a bite of her blueberry casserole as she stared at me. Swallowing it, she took a swig of orange juice, surprising me by asking, "What do you think of the blueberry casserole? Good?"

I hadn't even tried the casserole, or anything else for that matter, but I couldn't say my mind was on food. "Um, did you hear what I just said?" I was completely thrown when she hadn't jumped on the topic, not that I wanted her to, but, still, it surprised me.

She simply nodded although I noticed her jaw was clenched and she looked annoyed. "Of course I heard you, but I chose to ignore it."

I frowned at her. "That doesn't sound like the Sam I know and love so well."

She was about to take another sip of her juice, but seemed to change her mind and plunked the glass down so hard, some of the juice splashed out. "I just don't get you, Dulcie," she said, shaking her head as she glared at me. "Knight is a great guy. And what's more, he's perfect for you." She was silent for a few more seconds. "I just don't understand why you destroy every chance you have for happiness, not to mention that I think it's totally shitty to hurt Knight like that."

"I said 'we broke up' not 'I broke up with him'," I corrected her, even though the truth of the matter was that I had been the architect. It annoyed me, however, that Sam automatically assumed all the blame rested on my shoulders.

"You didn't have to say who did it, because I just made an educated guess based on how well I know you," she retorted. "So was I right? Were you the one who ended things with him?"

I nodded and then immediately held up my hands in a rendition of *it wasn't my fault*! "I didn't mean to," I started, wondering what exactly I was going to tell her. Earlier, I decided to just blame the whole thing on my hang-ups from my relationship with Jack, but I knew I couldn't lie to her, my best friend. But I also couldn't tell her the truth. Aye, there *was* the rub. "I didn't have a choice, Sam."

She frowned again. "Didn't have a choice? Everyone has a choice." Then she eyed me speculatively.

I shook my head. "I ..." I stared down at my fork on which I'd speared some eggs, but the thought of getting them past my lips was completely out of the question. I'd just lost any appetite I might have had. That burning feeling of acidic bile in my stomach, which had become a permanent tenant ever since my return from the Netherworld, was back in full force.

"Dulcie, what's going on with you?" Sam asked, putting her fork down as she stared at me. "You're not acting like yourself."

"I'm fine," I started and tried to act unconcerned, but Sam saw right through me. I should have known she would.

"Whatever it is, we can get through it together."

I swallowed hard. "It's not so simple," I started, finding myself at a loss for words.

"Well, for God's sake, tell me what it is!" I just took a deep breath and so she continued. "You've been so weird lately, I wasn't even sure if you were going to show up this morning."

"Of course I was going to ..." I started, but she interrupted me.

"Ever since you got back from the Netherworld, you've been different, Dulcie. You've been avoiding everyone, not answering your phone, not returning phone calls. What happened to you while you were there?" I tried to answer, but she shook her head, signifying that her tirade wasn't over. "Do you realize you never even told me what happened while you were in the Netherworld or why you went, for that matter? You've kept me completely in the dark."

I took a deep breath. "I left you a message to let you know I was back and that I was okay," I said. My words rang hollow and weak. She was right, I hadn't treated her like the friend she was—really, Sam was the closest person to me. She was more like family than a friend.

"Dulcie, I was worried sick about you, wondering what the hell you were doing there. Not to mention, what was going to happen to you and Knight? And talking to Dia didn't make matters any better. The two of us were nervous wrecks. I couldn't sleep that whole week! And then all you can say is that you're back and you don't want to talk about it?" Her tone was becoming frantic and it was pretty obvious she'd been keeping all of this bottled inside her, finally reaching her boiling point.

"I'm sorry, Sam," I said in a mousey voice as I exhaled deeply, searching for some excuse as to why I'd failed her as a friend. "I've just been through so much lately, I barely know what to think of any of it myself."

"That's what your best friend is for," she responded, her tone softer. "Whatever you're going through, I'm here to help you. You don't have to go through it alone." She took a deep breath. "But in order for me to help you, you're going to have to tell me what the problem is."

But I shook my head, knowing she was wrong, that I couldn't tell her anything or I'd be endangering her. "Sam, I can't tell you the specifics, and please don't push me because I can't and I won't."

She eyed me with concern. "What happened to you in the Netherworld, Dulcie?"

I swallowed hard and shook my head again. "I can't talk about it."

She reached across the table and took my hand, her eyes piercing through me. "Are you in trouble?"

I took another deep breath. "Not at the moment and that's why I can't talk about anything. Just trust me when I say I'm handling it, okay?"

"What does that even mean?"

I stood up, feeling claustrophobic, like the feelings of turmoil were suddenly caving in on me, suffocating me with angst. I started for the door. "Sam, I can't do this," I said, my voice wavering between anger and sadness. "I have to keep you safe and as part of that, I can't tell you what's going on." I reached for my backpack and jacket. "You have to just trust me on this, okay?"

"Okay," she said and stood up, pulling at my backpack as she motioned for me to sit down again. "Please don't go. I won't press you anymore, I promise."

I just nodded and offered her an apologetic smile as I returned to her dining table again. "I'm sorry, Sam, but things are just going to have to be this way for a while, until I can figure a way out."

She started worrying her lower lip, something she did whenever she was frustrated or upset. "Does Knight know about any of this?"

"No!" I responded automatically. The thought that she might tell him started wreaking havoc with my stomach. "And he can't know anything! Not even that we had this conversation, okay? Promise me you will keep this to yourself."

She nodded. "I promise."

"Charm promise it," I said, knowing that if she charmed herself into promising, she literally wouldn't be able to break the power of the spell, no matter how hard she tried.

She frowned at me, probably because she was annoyed I hadn't trusted her enough not to say anything without the protection of a charm. Eventually, though, she stood up and walked over to her potions cabinet. Her potions cabinet was a two-foot-by-two-foot white box with matching doors that she'd mounted on the wall beside the front door, for easy access. She bottled a multitude of charms in vials in case she needed them right away and didn't have the time or energy to go through the rigmarole of performing each one.

The charm I sought, one which discouraged blabbermouths, was pretty commonplace so I wasn't surprised when she located it right away, taking out a vial filled with amber liquid. It was about the size of my thumb. She closed the cabinet doors behind her and then removed the cork from the top of the vial. Once it was free, she eyed me askance (another reminder that she was miffed I'd made her do this) and downed the liquid, saying aloud: "Whatever Dulcie O'Neil tells me, I will keep in strict confidence."

She carried the vial to the dishwasher and put it in for the next load. Then she faced me with anxiety in her eyes. "Does all this have something to do with why you broke things off with Knight?"

I nodded, my eyes suddenly feeling heavy with exhaustion. "It has everything to do with why I broke up with Knight."

She nodded and dropped her gaze to the floor before glancing up at me again. "Then you do still love him?"

Even though I was surprised to hear her using the "L word," mainly because I hadn't realized I'd been so obvious in my affection for the Loki, I just sighed and nodded. I figured on this one count, I might as well be honest.

"Is there anyone you can talk to about this, Dulcie?" Sam asked, her expression filled with concern. "Is there anyone you trust whom you can talk to?"

There was one person—Quill, but he was as deep in all this shit as I was. Plus, I didn't think he'd appreciate me lamenting my shattered relationship with Knight. I shook my head. "I have to figure a way out of it, Sam, but I'll find a way." I offered her a tentative smile. "You know me."

She returned the smile, but hers was wistful. "If anyone can, it's you. I just hope you know what you're doing and I also hope you aren't in serious trouble." She sighed heavily. "I really wish you'd tell me what's going on, Dulce. I'm sure I could help you."

I shook my head. "I can't tell you anything, Sam."

She nodded and dropped her eyes to her lap where she'd folded her hands neatly, like she was posing to have her portrait painted. "I have something for you," she said as if just now remembering and stood up, walking to the far end of the living room. She opened the top left drawer of her entertainment center and produced a white box. Walking back, she handed it to me without a word.

I opened the box and found a bracelet inside it. It was made of silver wire and appeared to be knitted. The wire knit framed a greenish-blue stone in the middle of the bracelet. The stone was maybe the size of my thumbnail. I glanced up at Sam and smiled. "It's beautiful, Sam, thank you."

"It's called a Viking Knit," she said. "It's hand woven wire, and back in the days of the Vikings, they used the same weaving for their chainmail armor."

"Wow," I said, rubbing the stone between my fingers.

"It's one continuous strand of wire."

"It's really beautiful."

"Thanks," she said and looked as if she was very proud of it. "I made it myself."

I glanced up at her, surprised. "Oh my gosh, Sam! Wow, I'm really impressed! I love it." I rubbed my fingers across the slick surface of the stone, watching it sparkle in the light. "What sort of stone is it?" I asked.

"A protection stone," she said softly. "Also something the Vikings carried with them. They believed it warded away evil spirits. I charmed it to protect you against anyone who would do you harm."

"Thank you," I said again, throwing my arms around her.

"I'm really worried about you, Dulcie," she said as she rested her head against my hair.

"I'm going to be fine, Sam, I promise." Even as I uttered the words, I couldn't say I believed them.

She shook her head and sighed as she pulled away from me, smiling as she took each of my hands in hers. Her eyes were shining with unshed tears. "Whatever it is you've gotten yourself into, the bracelet should help keep you safe."

I watched as she took the bracelet from my hand and placed it on my wrist, securing it as she did so. I shook my hand, the bracelet sliding down my wrist and resting at the top of my hand. The silver knitted metal gleamed in the sunlight streaming through Sam's windows. It was beautiful.

I glanced up at my best friend. "Thank you for being you, Sam."

###

I spent the majority of the day with Sam, and I had to admit, I needed every minute of it. Being able to forget the stress of my overwhelming life for a few hours did wonders for me. When I got home, I actually felt rejuvenated, recharged. 'Course, the added energy could also have been from all the food Sam had forced down my throat. I'd eaten more today than I had all week.

As soon as I walked in my door, I noticed Blue outside in my yard, pawing on the sliding door to be let in. Taped to the glass was a note. I walked over to the door and opened it wide, nearly falling over as Blue jumped up on me. He showered me with doggy kisses, his tail wagging as he peed all over the floor and then looked up at me in an embarrassed sort of way.

"You silly boy," I said, laughing as I walked to my kitchen, grabbed a handful of paper towels and cleaned up his mess.

Then with Blue on my heels, I approached the sliding door and pulled the note off the glass, unfolding it to read:

Dear Dulce,

I didn't want to keep Blue too long cause I'm sure you miss him. He's a really great dog and if you ever need someone to dog sit again, call me first, k?
Really glad you're back. We all missed you tons.

Love, Trey.

PS: There's this convention coming up for Star Wars and I got this Chewbacca   costume that's super cool and I was wondering if you would go with me to the convention? It wouldn't be like a boyfriend-girlfriend thing (Knight would kill me) but like a friend thing. I just don't want to look like a loser going by myself, you know? Oh, and don't worry about a costume—we can find Princess Leah or Padmé or I also have a pretty cool ewok costume I wore last year. That might be a little big on you though ... Don't worry about a costume, we'll figure it out, k? Cool beans?

> *P.P.S: Thanks again for letting me keep Blue so long. I really like him.*
>> *Later gator!*
>> *Love, Trey.*

I put the note down on my kitchen counter and couldn't help the sadness welling up inside me. I just felt as if I'd not only been a bad friend to Sam, but to Trey and Dia as well. And I couldn't even think about Knight. But the frustrating truth was that this whole situation was a catch twenty-two because I had to keep my distance from everyone in order to keep them safe. I didn't want Melchior knowing who my friends were because I didn't want him to use that knowledge against me ... or them.

I didn't have the chance to continue feeling guilty because the cell phone from Quillan suddenly started ringing. Feeling my throat constricting as I wondered what in the hell Melchior or Baron wanted from me now, I reached for it and flipped it open.

"What's up?" I asked, my voice tremulous.

"Meet me at the portal by the loading docks in ten minutes. Melchior has requested to see us both."

NINE

"Hi," I said, once I recognized Quill. He was standing next to his blue Mustang, which he'd just parked in the lot of the loading docks. I'd pulled in beside him a minute or so earlier. He closed his door, beeping the car locked as he faced me with a wide smile. His glance moved from me to my bike as his eyes narrowed.

"Is that your bike or a loaner from the ANC?" he asked and motioned to the Ducati, inspecting it as though he were displeased.

"Mine, but provided by the ANC." I removed my helmet, wedging it under my right arm as I stepped off the bike. The light of the full moon was so bright, it was like standing under a spotlight. The cold, salty ocean air whipped around me, chilling me through my leathers, while the smell of dead fish made me want to retch.

"Where's the Wrangler?" he asked.

I sighed, remembering my Wrangler and missing the yellow Jeep. "Gone. Totaled in an accident."

He didn't say anything but noticed my helmet underneath my arm and unlocked the mustang again, holding his hand out for it. I gave it to him and he plopped it on the passenger's seat. He was as aware as I that if I left the helmet unattended on my bike, it probably wouldn't be there when we returned from our errand to the Netherworld. Like I mentioned earlier, the loading docks weren't exactly the best neighborhood.

"And that?" he asked, referring to the leather jacket, which I was still wearing. "Remember, you'll get wings in the Netherworld."

That was one of the curiosities of the Netherworld which I liked least. As a fairy, wings would instantly sprout

98

from my back as soon as I crossed over to Netherworld territory. The worst part was that my wings seemed to completely have a mind of their own. They'd start flapping unexpectedly and for no reason at all—annoying, to say the least. And they were also the reason I had to wear an oversized, baggy T-shirt which I'd slit in half down the back in order to make room for them. So, yes, it would be wise to leave my jacket behind. I took it off and handed it to Quill, waiting while he locked the door again.

"You totaled the Wrangler?"

The pervasive silence between us was telling. Quill had to be thinking the same thing I was—that once upon a time, when we were much closer, he would have already been aware of details like this. Now, however, there were parts of my life to which he wasn't privy. We definitely weren't the friends we used to be.

"Yep," I said and shrugged like the accident hadn't been a big deal although it had been a *very* big deal.

"Were you hurt?" he asked in a soft voice, his tone troubled and contemplative.

"As you can see, I'm fine," I said simply, not wanting to focus on the past any more than I wanted to focus on the shreds of Quill's and my former friendship. It was enough that we were maintaining some sort of pseudo friendship now, something born from necessity, considering the fact that neither of us belonged to the social circles in which we were now included.

He glanced at me curiously, but refrained from commenting, instead facing the Ducati again. "You'll need another mode of transportation."

"Why?"

"Don't want you to give off ANC everywhere you go."

I shook my head. "I thought my added value to this cluster fuck was all because I'm active ANC?"

Quill's eyes traversed me from head to toe as he took a deep breath and shook his head, apparently appreciative.

"You look good in leather," he said with a soft smile. But at my less-than-impressed, raised-brow expression, he got back to the point. "Being active ANC isn't the only reason you're valuable to your father or me, Dulcie. You know that."

"Actually, I don't, but let's skip that conversation," I retaliated, wanting to think about my father as little as possible. "You think I need to drive something different to avoid suspicion?" I figured Quill was worried that leaving my ANC bike unattended in questionable places such as the loading docks, might draw speculation should anyone in the know (namely, Knight, Trey, Sam, etcetera) happen upon it. He actually had a good point.

"Yep," he said and nodded. "Apparently, we think alike."

"Well, an untraceable vehicle can be part of the agenda we discuss with Daddy Dearest," I muttered and started forward.

"Portal is this way," Quillan corrected me. He motioned for me to go in the exact opposite direction I was headed. I glanced at him dubiously, trying to remember the previous location where the portal spat us out the last time we returned from the Netherworld.

"That way?" I asked, my hands on my hips and eyebrows scrunched in an expression of "Um, you're wrong, Quill."

"Yep, the portal always changes location. It's a safety measure," he explained.

"Interesting," I said, shrugging as I started toward him again. "How do you know where it's going to pop up?"

He rolled up his left sleeve and pointed to his watch. "Portal compass. Remember?"

I nodded, as I recalled him using the same device to locate the Netherworld portal that brought us here. But on to more important topics ... "So what does Melchior want with us?"

Quill glanced down at me and smiled before shrugging. "That's the twenty million dollar question. Who the hell knows?" He took a deep breath and shook his head, leaving me with the feeling that he wasn't exactly fond of my father, even if he were Melchior's right-hand man. "He's summoned me to discuss incredibly unimportant shit in the past."

"Such as?"

He sighed as he thought about it, his frown slowly giving way to a smile as he apparently remembered a case in point. "To tell me a joke," he said and shook his head, the humor leaking out of his expression while something close to irritation crept in. "He summoned me once to tell me a stupid ass joke that I already knew." Then he laughed again, but the sound was forced, like he was pretending to find it funny, while there wasn't a shred of true amusement in him.

Somehow, I couldn't share in Quillan's feigned humor. I didn't regard my father's actions and his personality flaw of ordering people around very funny. Disrespectful, unnecessary and self-centered, yes, but funny, no. I stopped walking and took a deep breath. Quill paused in front of me and turned around to face me with a curious expression in his eyes.

"I'm not going to do this forever, Quill," I said, my lips tight. "I'm not going to let him dictate my comings and goings for the rest of my life."

Quill was quiet for a few seconds as he apparently searched for something to say. "Once you're in, there's no getting out, Dulcie." He said the words as if he were already resigned to them, and almost as though he believed them wholeheartedly. The truth of the matter was that he probably did because he'd been involved in this lifestyle for so long, any embers of fight left within him had died a long time ago.

I will never allow that to happen to me, I insisted to myself. *As long as there is breath is my body, I will fight or die trying!*

"There's a way out of everything," I said resolutely. "And I'm going to find it."

"Dulcie, I hate to break your bubble, but you're already in the thick of it. There's no getting out."

I shook my head and clenched my teeth as I faced him with steel resolve. "I'm in it for the moment, but this arrangement isn't permanent. I'll find a way out."

He approached me then, placing a hand on either of my shoulders, the look in his eyes patronizing. "Your father is more powerful than you can imagine. You can't just go after him with your guns blazing. All you'll end up doing is sacrificing yourself and Melchior would just replace you."

I didn't say anything but nodded, knowing Quill had been brainwashed by my father for too long, his backbone having been compromised. But as for me, I wasn't used to taking no for answer and as long as there was breath in my body, I'd get myself out of this shit if it was the last thing I did.

And from the sound of it, it very well could be.

Once we located the portal, Quill stepped through and within a few seconds, I was quick to follow. That bizarre feeling of balmy gel enveloped me but before I could respond to my growing feelings of claustrophobia, I felt a swish of air across my face and then felt like I was falling. I opened my eyes, realizing in a split second that the portal had kicked me out and into my father's office ... at ceiling height.

I shrieked and in apparent reflex, my wings suddenly started beating insanely, just saving me from hitting the floor. But now that I was airborne, I had a new problem—

landing. I still couldn't exactly control my wings. Once they started beating, it was nearly impossible to get them to stop.

Quillan, apparently observing my quandary, reached out and grabbed hold of my leg, pulling me down beside him. Once my feet touched the ground, my wings continued to frantically thrash back and forth. I had to hold onto Quill's arm so I wouldn't float away again. Suddenly realizing we weren't alone, I looked up into Melchior's amused eyes. Taking a deep breath, I forced my poker face.

"The portals do have a way of depositing unsuspecting travelers in quite random places, such as the ceiling." My father's voice infiltrated the room and I felt myself recoiling.

I cleared my throat as my heart pounded in my chest. He looked the same as I remembered. His grey hair framed a very handsome face for a man of his age—appearing to be in his fifties although he was over one hundred, a fact which still amazed me. His emerald green eyes were the exact shade of my own, so similar, in fact, that I had to ask myself how I'd never made the familial connection between the two of us when I'd first met him.

"Quillan Beaurigard and my very own flesh and blood," my father greeted us as he took a few steps forward. His eyes fastened on me as his smile grew. "How are you both?"

"I've been better," I said with a frown, anchoring myself more firmly to the chair behind Quillan, my wings still beating incessantly.

My father had nothing to say, but never lost his irritating smile. Instead, he faced Quillan with an expectant expression. "And you, Quillan?"

"I'm good, thanks," Quill said, taking a deep breath, and eyeing me before looking at Melchior again. He seemed nervous. "To what do we owe this honor?"

Melchior nodded and walked around his executive desk, an ornate and overwhelming piece of cherry furniture, embellished with gold accents that matched the hutch directly behind it. In a word, it looked ... expensive. It also looked incredibly ostentatious and overdone. Melchior opened the top drawer of his desk and took out a black box. Then he walked back to us and handed the box to me.

"A present for my daughter," he said simply.

But there was no way in hell I could or would accept anything from him. "Gifts weren't part of this bargain," I said without humor.

"Then don't think of it as a gift," my father answered, his lips drawn tight as he pushed the box further into my face.

I withdrew from him, clinging to the chair which was anchoring me in place. "How about I don't think of it at all?"

My father sighed and gave Quillan an expression that said, if nothing else, he found me exasperating. Then he faced me again and this time, there wasn't any trace of levity in his eyes or the hard line of his lips. "You will need it," he said simply. "It's a portal compass."

Realizing he was right, I took a big bite of humble pie and reached for the box. I mean, he had a good point—I couldn't always rely on Quillan when it came to catching a ride to the Netherworld. As my wings began to calm down, I released my hold of the chair back and stood still for a few seconds, testing myself to see if I might become airborne again. Once my wings appeared to be sitting peacefully, I opened the box. Inside, I found a silver watch, a Rolex, complete with diamonds to represent each hour. Smaller diamonds trimmed the periphery, highlighting the pink watch face. Obviously, my father knew nothing about me— I hate pink.

"Quillan will teach you how it works," Melchior said as Quillan obediently nodded.

Sighing heavily, I pulled up my sleeve and immediately saw Sam's Viking bracelet. A sense of warmth filled me as I thought about my best friend. Not wanting to taint the beauty of her bracelet with the gaudiness of Melchior's watch, I pulled my sleeve down and offered my other wrist, allowing Quillan to fasten the watch on me.

I glanced at Melchior, my lips tight, my hands crossed against my chest. "Now that we've taken care of that, Quill mentioned that I shouldn't be driving my ANC provided bike—that it would be too obvious should it be spotted while I'm in your employ."

Melchior nodded thoughtfully and then smiled. "I have a fleet of vehicles at my disposal on the basement level of this building. My secretary will call the guard to inform him that you are in need of one." He paused as if considering the logistics before adding, "It will be shipped to you."

I turned to Quill, expecting him to get this show on the road. As far as I was concerned, I'd just ticked off everything on my list.

"How did the *Yalkemouth* import go with Baron?" my father asked, spearing us both with his trenchant gaze.

I didn't respond, so Quill nodded. "Good, just as planned."

"Very good, very good," my father said, but suddenly seemed uninterested, like there were bigger things on his mind. I figured he had to have known the import went off without a hitch, probably getting the report from Baron, himself. "Horatio arrived in High Prison just yesterday," he continued.

"And?" Quill asked.

"He is living the high life in one of my apartments for the next three weeks at least. Then I will release him back to Splendor."

"Beats High Prison," I said angrily, remembering what a shithole it was and how I'd worried Knight and I would never get out.

"That it does," my father agreed, seemingly not sensing the acidity in my words or, more fittingly, not caring.

"Okay, so let's cut through the crap here," I said, my temper finally getting the best of me. "Why did you call us here?"

My father faced me and frowned. "You will not speak to me in such a way ... I am the Head of the Netherworld and you will treat me with deference and respect."

"I don't care who you are," I began as my fingers dug into my palms and my hands balled into fists. "I agreed to do your bidding, but that's it. As far as I'm concerned, you are a piece of ..."

"Dulcie!" Quillan silenced me, grimacing with a knitted brow meant to discourage me from further speaking my mind.

"Do not forget, girl," my father interrupted him, turning his fuming eyes on me, as well as his long and bony index finger, "that I can end the life of your friend with merely a phone call," he finished, referring to Knight. "If you care for him as much as you appear to, you would do well to keep that in the forefront of your mind."

I gulped and tried to take a cleansing breath, realizing my father had bested me ... again. Yep, he had me exactly where he wanted me; and it was the second to worst feeling I'd ever had. The worst feeling was hearing that Knight was sentenced to death.

"Now that we've addressed your quarrelsome nature," my father continued and with a discouraging glance at me, returned his attention to Quillan, adding, "I would like to discuss my reasons for requesting your presence." I said nothing while Quill merely nodded and smiled at my father, so he continued. "First, I would like you both to meet someone."

Melchior walked back to his desk and turned the dial of the rotary phone. Immediately, the sound of ringing blared out over the speaker phone (the logistics of which I still hadn't figured out).

"Yessir?" A woman's voice picked up. Probably Melchior's assistant, if I had to guess.

"Please send Christina in," my father responded, lifting the handset, only to replace it again at the sound of a dial tone. None of us said anything for the next five seconds as we awaited Melchior's guest.

There was a knock on the door. "Enter," Melchior called out.

The door opened and a woman walked in. She passed by both Quillan and me as she approached Melchior. She offered him a smile and extended her hand which he instantly clasped in his own, kissing the top of hers. I could only wonder at the nature of their relationship. Melchior admired this woman—I could see as much in his eyes, but as to what his admiration meant, who knew? Either way, I'd find out—the information seemed like a necessary arrow to have in my quiver.

"Melchior, it is good to see you again," she said with a slight New York accent. She was small in height (even shorter than my five foot one) and her frame, though also petite, was very toned. She was dressed well, wearing tailored, black dress pants with a matching black, unbuttoned blazer. Beneath the blazer peeked a purple tank top. But what really captured my attention were her shoes … They were white snakeskin, peep-toed heels with metal spikes on the heels, which had to be at least four inches high. I suddenly viewed my own ensemble of leather pants, black sneakers and faded, ripped, long-sleeved T-shirt with disinterest.

I watched her make small talk with my father as I admired her incredibly long, straight dark brown hair that ended at her butt. And speaking of butts, hers was pretty nice. Um, not that I was into checking out women's butts, but sometimes you can't help but appreciate a good one. And she had a good one.

"Christina, I would like you to meet two of my colleagues," my father said. He faced us both as I felt like choking on his description of us as "colleagues." "Minion" would've been more fitting, or in Quillan's case, "groveling, ass-kissing puppet."

The woman spun around and smiled at us both, her front side just as attractive as the back. Quillan had apparently come to the same realization as his eyes raked her up and down wolfishly. She offered him her hand and smiled politely as he shook it. Then she approached me and offered her hand again with another practiced and radiant smile. As soon as I shook her hand, I felt a sense of familiarity welling up within me. She had a certain power within her that spoke to the same power within me.

"You're a fairy," I said in surprise, having only ever met one other fairy in my lifetime—the fairy hooker, Zara. Even as the words left my mouth, I had to question them, because as far as I could tell, Christina didn't have wings. And in the Netherworld, all fairies had wings.

Her eyebrows raised in surprise as her smile widened. Her large eyes were nearly as dark as her hair and framed with perfectly shaped, dark brown brows. She was probably around the same age as me, maybe twenty-six, twenty-eight, with a young face. Her sensuality radiated out of her and I could only imagine how popular she was with the boys. But strangely enough, even dressed to the nines as she was now, something about her didn't seem totally girlie. Something about her hinted to the possibility that she could get muddy and do so happily.

"That's a true gift you have," she said, her dark eyes dancing. "And, yes, you're right; I am a fairy."

I frowned. "Where are your wings?" At the mention of "wings," mine suddenly unfurled. And like a Jack Russell on Red Bull, they began beating in full-steam-ahead-mode until I had to grab the chair back to keep myself grounded. Mortified, I could only assume I looked completely ridiculous.

"I have a special device in my jacket, which keeps them under control," Christina started as she dropped her gaze and tried to hide a smile. "It's one of the less-than-thrilling side effects we fairies have to suffer in the Netherworld." She waited for my wings to calm down and added, "I'm Christina Sabbiondo, pleased to meet you."

I smiled in return, finding her easy affability refreshing. I had to remind myself that she had some kind of relationship with my father and, as such, I shouldn't like her. "Dulcie O'Neil," I said abruptly.

Christina's eyebrows stretched for the ceiling as she turned back to face my father and said: "O'Neil? As in a relative of yours, Melchior?"

He nodded with the expression of a proud father. It was something which didn't suit him and it made me want to throw up all over Christina's expensive shoes.

"Yes, Dulcie is my daughter," he said, glancing at me as if I were a prize winning sow. I glared at him as I muttered something unintelligible, while my wings continued to imitate a hummingbird on fast forward.

Christina faced me again and seemed to be studying me. "Ahhh, I can absolutely see the resemblance. You both have stunning green eyes."

I failed to reply because I was all out of pleasantries. Besides, where my father was concerned, it was better to hold my tongue than piss him off again. Especially since he didn't hesitate in reminding me that Knight's safety was always on the line.

"I wanted to introduce the three of you," Melchior started, "because I am tasking all of you with a team project."

A fucking team project? I said to myself, suddenly feeling like I was an unenthusiastic candidate on "The Apprentice."

No one replied, we just glanced back and forth at one another, waiting for Melchior to continue. He walked across his office to a coat closet in the corner of the room. Upon opening it, he reached for something and returned with a white Styrofoam box which looked like an organ transporting device. He opened the box and I almost expected him to pull out a lung. Instead, he placed a vial on his desk. It was about the width and height of my index finger, and filled with white pills that looked like Tic-Tacs. Melchior popped the cap and offered each of us a pill.

"What is it?" I demanded, feeling my heart drop. As a veteran ANC Regulator, I'd busted plenty of potions traffickers on the black market, and I was very familiar with illegal narcotics. But I'd never laid eyes on this small white pill before.

"It's an antidote, or should I say, an anti-buzz," Melchior said softly.

"An antidote to what?" I inquired, my tone of voice sounding less than thrilled as I continued to study the white pill.

"To *Draoidheil*," my father answered, as if the very word would ring a bell or two in my head. But, at the moment, the only thing ringing inside me was my temper.

"What is that?" Christina asked, sounding like an eager student. Apparently, I wasn't the only one who hadn't seen nor heard of *Draoidheil* before, much less the white pill.

Melchior reached inside the box again and produced another vial. This one was filled with what looked like iridescent glitter, although the particles were far smaller, almost like very fine sand. He handed the vial to Quill, who inspected it before handing it to Christina. She started to uncork the vial, but stopped when Melchior "tsked" her.

110

"I would not do that," he said simply.

Christina's eyebrows raised as she gulped and handed the vial to me; but I wanted none of it and simply shook my head. She gave me a strange expression before handing it back to Melchior.

"What does it do?" she asked.

"In Gaelic, *Draoidheil* means magic," Melchior said simply. "And that is precisely what it is and what it does."

"Magic?" I asked in a droll tone, feeling like I'd just found a Golden Ticket to Willy Wonka's Chocolate Factory. 'Course, I would've exchanged Melchior for Willy in a split second. And I didn't even like sweets.

My father faced me and frowned. "If I were to open this vial and hold it beneath your nose, with one whiff, you would be under the influence of *Draoidheil*. As simple as smelling a flower, whatever you most wanted in life would be yours."

"What?" I asked, frowning helplessly as fear began uncoiling within me. I'd never heard of a narcotic being activated by merely smelling it. Inhaling, yes, smelling, no. "What does that even mean, whatever I most wanted in life would be mine?"

"Not in actuality, of course," Melchior backpedaled. "But its influence would convince you that whatever you most desired; love, money, companionship, fame, intelligence ... was yours."

"And that's the narcotic's high?" Quillan asked, although it was really more of a statement. He glanced at the vial again with shock in his eyes. I'd never heard of anything like this before and apparently neither had he.

Thoughts started swarming through my head, causing alarm bells to peal through my entire body. "If I were to throw that vial into the air, with all of us in here," I started.

"We would all be under its influence," Melchior finished for me.

"For how long?"

"Perhaps five hours," Melchior responded, his countenance eerily casual and calm.

"How long does one vial of *Draoidheil* last?" I persisted.

Melchior held the vial up to his eyes, as if he were inspecting it. "The narcotic was designed to have an expiration date of two days after the uncorking of the vial."

"And let me guess, it's incredibly addictive?" I continued, the frown on my lips drooping all the way to my feet.

My father glanced from the vial to me and smiled pleasantly. "Precisely so."

A short shelf-life with an addictive chemical would predicate incredible demand. From a capitalistic standpoint, it seemed a winner. But from a humanistic standpoint, it was anything but.

"And how addictive is addictive?" Quillan asked cautiously.

"Currently, the most addictive potion on the market," Melchior answered. "One whiff and you would be at the mercy of the *Draoidheil*." I felt my mouth drop open in shock as Melchior held up the vial with the white pills in it. "That's why these little specimens are so important."

"Those pills invalidate the power of the potion?" Christina asked, her tone revealing she was as shaken as the rest of us.

"Yes, if taken right before or after exposing oneself to the *Draoidheil*," Melchior continued, "they nullify its effects." He glanced at Christina, then at me, adding: "I call it *Snake Oil*."

"Fitting," I said snidely, my heart racing as I began to put the pieces together. "This isn't on the streets," I said softly. "I've never seen it before."

My father's eyes narrowed on me. "Precisely so." He smiled then. "I am tasking the three of you with the mission of introducing and distributing it."

TEN

No one said anything for at least five seconds—and the cloying silence in the room became uncomfortable. I was still in shock, allowing my father's words to sink in. I just couldn't come to grips with the idea that A, there was a potion available as dangerous and potentially devastating as *Draoidheil;* and B, that I was now in charge of distributing it. I could already imagine what that would entail—widespread addiction. It was the recipe for a large-scale disaster, the outcome of which would be absolute dictatorship for my father. Why? Because it would mean an immense amount of unlimited money—unlimited because the stuff was so addictive. And of course, Melchior had designed it that way for exactly that reason—to ensure his own tyranny.

The more I considered it, the more it concerned me. It wasn't farfetched to imagine half the population, on Earth and in the Netherworld, addicted to this stuff. One sniff and boom, you were hopelessly addicted! Actually, half the population was probably being conservative. It wouldn't be much of a stretch to imagine that eventually, everyone could become addicted since the stuff was basically airborne. Yep, this really was the perfect seedbed to Netherworld dominion, as far as Melchior was concerned.

"And does it work on humans?" Christina asked, her tone curious but wary.

I hadn't even considered that side of things and gulped hard. Most Netherworld potions didn't have any effect on humans (with the exception of one or two). Likewise, things like heroin, marijuana, cocaine and meth, for instance, did nothing to my kind.

Melchior shook his head and relief washed over me. "Not so far."

That meant he was working on it. My sense of relief was short-lived and soon disappeared. The human market was probably where Melchior ultimately wanted to lay claim. There were far more humans in existence than Netherworld creatures, so he had to look at them like unmilked cash cows.

It seemed every time I turned around, I sunk deeper and deeper into the quagmire known as the illegal potions trade. If I thought I was up to my neck before, now I was up to my eyes and it was becoming increasingly difficult to invent a way out. But I still hadn't given up. I wouldn't give up now, knowing *Draoidheil* was on its way. I had to prevent this; somehow, I had to stop Melchior. But the question was *how*?

"Perhaps you would care to see a demonstration of the potency of *Draoidheil*?" my father asked. He said it with such ease and nonchalance, like we were on a field trip and he was going to show us how to pan for gold.

"Okay," Christina said nervously, her eyes suddenly going wide as she probably wondered if she'd just offered herself as a guinea pig.

My father smiled at her warmly and shook his head, as if to say, "Calm down and relax." Then he picked up the headset to his phone and dialed. His secretary answered almost immediately.

"Barbara? Will you come in for a moment?" he asked, sounding casual, but matter-of-fact.

"Of course," she answered in a chirpy voice as Melchior hung up.

Then he picked up the vial of white pills and emptied them into his palm, taking out one before replacing the others. He brought the pill to his tongue and swallowed it in an instant, turning to face the three of us. "Now would be a good time to take yours."

I'd nearly forgotten the white pill I clutched in my hand. For a split second, I thought the pill might be something entirely different than an antidote; and maybe this was some sort of setup. But after witnessing my father swallowing his and confident that I wanted nothing to do with the *Draoidheil*, I swallowed mine, hoping for the best. With last minute panic, I glanced at Quill and Christina, and relaxed a little after noticing they had both taken theirs.

At the sound of a hesitant knock on the door, I saw Barbara poke her head in. She was a redhead with a plain, non-descript prettiness about her face—like with the right makeup she might even be considered beautiful.

"Come in," my father greeted her warmly. I watched as she closed the door behind her and approached us, smiling curiously before settling her gaze on my father. She was probably in her mid thirties and maybe five foot six, if I had to guess. She was dressed conservatively in a slim fitting, two-piece grey skirt suit, but it was still obvious that she had a good figure.

She approached my father and then paused, as if awaiting his instruction. He simply pulled out the vial of *Draoidheil* and handed it to her as my stomach dropped. It just seemed so wrong that he'd lured his trusting secretary to be his test subject. Why that should have surprised me was curious since there was really nothing redeeming about my father at all … A sobering thought.

"We are researching new scents," he started, sounding like he was the chairman for a perfumery. "Our panel seems to agree upon this one." He paused. "We thought we'd ask your opinion."

I desperately wanted to stop her from reaching for the vial, but I knew I couldn't. Instead, I stood there with my heart lodged in my throat and watched her bring the vial to her nose and sniff it. At first nothing happened. Her face appeared to go blank, and I thought maybe she hadn't gotten the scent of anything. She started to move the vial toward her nose again, as if she needed another sniff, when the *Draoidheil* appeared to have hit her.

She sort of hobbled back a few steps, at which time Melchior grabbed the vial from her, to stop her from spilling it. Then a momentary look of bewilderment pasted itself across her pale face. She closed her eyes as a huge smile widened her mouth. When she opened her eyes again, she focused on Melchior and her pupils were dilated.

She definitely looked like she was on something.

"Melchior," she said in soft voice, closing the gap between them. She took one of his hands in hers while running the fingers of her other hand through his hair. At that moment, it was pretty obvious what she most desired — my father.

Yuck in a basket.

My father seemed slightly uncomfortable, although not surprised by her display of affection. He eyed the three of us almost apologetically before taking control of the situation and turning it into a show-and-tell again. He smiled at Barbara, something she must have taken as an invitation because she suddenly tried to kiss him. He pulled away.

"What do you most desire, Barbara?" he goaded her, obviously still trying to prove a point.

"You," she responded automatically. "You've always known that. I just never imagined you'd ever give in to your feelings for me."

He looked at us again, holding Barbara's wrists to keep her at arm's length. "The *Draoidheil* makes you believe that whatever you most desire is yours," he said to the three of us. He focused on Barbara again. "Case in point."

"Point taken," I grumbled, hating that Barbara's secret was being so blatantly flaunted in front of people she didn't even know. I couldn't imagine how mortified she'd be if she had any idea what she was saying and doing at the moment. Hopefully, the *Draoidheil* would mess with her memory. When my father made no move to end his little show, I attempted to. "I think we've seen enough," I said, trying to sound calm and even-keeled. "Give her the antidote ... please."

Melchior said nothing. He merely nodded and shook the vial of pills over his palm, before selecting one pill and handing it to Barbara. She stopped attempting to sexually harass him and eyed the pill curiously, making no motion to put it in her mouth.

"Swallow it," my father said abruptly.

Barbara dutifully placed the pill on her tongue, and a second or so later, swallowed. I assumed it would take the antidote at least a few minutes to work, depending on how long it took to reach her bloodstream, but I was wrong. Almost instantly, her demeanor changed, the lovelorn look in her eyes was replaced with perplexity as she glanced around the room in utter confusion.

"Do you feel well?" Melchior asked, studying her in a detached, clinical sort of way. I felt extremely sorry for her, knowing that she was in love with my father who was incapable of loving another person. Of that, I was convinced; he was entirely too much in love with himself.

She faced him and shook her head, bringing her hand to her cheeks then her forehead. "It's strange but I feel a bit flushed, I'm not sure why."

"Perhaps you should leave early today, Barbara," Melchior said, patting her back as he escorted her to the door. "Sit down at your desk for a while before you drive, though, will you?"

She nodded obediently as he closed the door behind her. He faced us again and slapped his hands together like he'd just proven his thesis. "Any questions?" he asked.

I didn't say anything. I was afraid that if I started, I wouldn't be able to stop. I saw Quillan simply shake his head, with the look of defeat on his face. Christina was the only one of us who seemed at all interested, and although she didn't have any questions, this new project seemed to excite her, all the same.

"If you don't mind showing yourselves out, I still have important business that demands my attention," my father said. He returned to his gargantuan desk, took a seat and faced his computer as we started for the door. None of us said a word as we traipsed down the hallway to the bank of elevators. Even our ride down was silent. Once we reached the lobby, I cleared my throat and Quillan sighed.

"Guess we're going to have our work cut out for us with this *Snake Oil* stuff," Christina said. She offered me a tentative smile as we walked out of my father's building and headed for the portal to return to Splendor.

"I'd say so," Quill said, his tone of voice sounding somewhat reserved as he glanced at me for the third time since leaving Melchior's office. Knowing Quill as well as I did, I would have bet money that he was fretting over how I was taking everything that had just happened. He had to know I was reeling at the moment, anger and shock churning in my stomach.

Somehow, I imagined my father had to have been getting perverse pleasure out of being able to bend me to his will just like that. Well, he could think whatever the hell he wanted to think, but we were definitely not "like father, like daughter." No, I was now even more determined than before to find a way out of this and what was more, I was arriving at the realization that the only way out of this mess was in going after the mastermind, himself.

"Are you headed to Splendor?" Christina asked Quill, interrupting my train of thought. We'd arrived in the parking lot of the ANC Headquarters. Apparently, this time the portal was at the far end of the parking lot, just beside the dumpsters.

I couldn't help but notice Christina was avoiding me, probably sensing my temper was about to blow. I tried to at least partially mask my foul mood, not wanting Christina to suspect I was less than thrilled to be a player in this team. Why? Well, first and foremost—I had to think of Knight. And I also didn't think it would be a good thing for Christina to know I was only working for my father because I *had* to. Yep, better to keep that under wraps. The less my father's people knew about me, the better.

"Yes, both Dulcie and I are headed to Splendor. You?" Quill responded.

Christina nodded and the sound of her heels tapping against the concrete grabbed my attention. I glanced down and noticed she had tattoos of purple and green hummingbirds on the tops of both of her feet. It made sense—fairies were supposed to be the "children of nature," and most of us were naturally attracted to flora and fauna, hummingbirds always a fairy favorite. I guess I'd just missed the boat where all things nature were concerned.

"I live in Sanctity, but given recent events, I think I might stay in Splendor for a while so we can discuss a plan moving forward," she answered as she pulled her incredibly long hair into a ponytail, offering me a glimpse of her ears. As fairies, Christina's and my ears came to points at the top. Hers, by the look of them, however, weren't as pointy as mine. Something which made my mood even better.

Scolding myself for comparing ears (and even more irritated that mine came up short), I forced my thoughts back to her last comment, something suddenly occurring to me. "You live in Sanctity?" I asked, turning to face her. Sanctity was the next town over from Splendor, maybe twenty or thirty minutes away.

Christina smiled sweetly, merely nodding. Quill stopped walking and checked his portal compass watch, I assume, to ensure that we were still going the right way. Apparently, we were because he proceeded forward again, Christina and I in tow.

"I've never seen you before," I said finally, pulling my attention from Quill and narrowing my eyes at her. "And I'm pretty sure the ANC records only itemize Zara, the hooker, and I as the sum total of the local fairy population." All Netherworld creatures that lived on Earth had dossiers in the ANC which specified the type of creature they were, how they earned a living and where they lived. It was the easiest way to keep track of them. And I wasn't bluffing— Christina didn't exist in the ANC database, as far as I knew. I definitely would have remembered another fairy living nearby.

She eyed me with surprise. "Ah, that's right! Your father mentioned that a member of his entourage worked in the Splendor ANC. That must be you." Her smile broadened. "Very smart of him, placing his own people in the enemy's lair." Then she laughed. All I managed was a half-assed laugh-giggle that came out more like a grunt, but sounded worse still, like a burp.

"Yeah, smart," I managed, wanting to direct her to the question at hand. I raised my brows at her in impatience when it didn't seem she had anything more to offer. "So you managed to avoid ANC profiling?"

She simply smiled again. "I, um, stay beneath the ANC radar," she said simply.

"Interesting," I admitted, studying her pointedly. "And why is that?"

The look she gave me combined with the smile that was still on her lips told me she was hiding something. Something big. And that's when I zeroed in on her little game. She was tough, strong and smart. But she didn't want anyone to know that. She exploited her beauty and femininity in a way that got men to doubt her, finding her nothing more than a pretty face. Well, unluckily for her, I didn't possess a penis. And since my father had deliberately placed her on this task force, I assumed he saw through her game as well. That or maybe he was enamored of her, which, come to think of it, could very well have been the case. Either way, she was someone I had to watch.

"One of the benefits of knowing your father," she finished simply.

I said nothing more but just nodded.

"Should we regroup in a few hours?" Quill asked, eyeing us both, although his eyes rested on me.

I looked down at my newly acquired compass watch and noticed it was nearly five a.m. Yep, another night without any sleep. Great, just great. "I can't," I said, rubbing my eyes, wondering when I was going to get a decent night of sleep. "I'm due at the ANC in three hours."

"Ah, I forgot," Quill admitted before smiling apologetically. "Let's resume discussions later. I'll call you both tonight."

I just nodded as Christina whipped her cell phone out to exchange numbers with Quill. All I could think about was getting home and crawling into bed so I could at least get two hours of shuteye before I was due in the office.

I was thirty minutes late when I arrived at the ANC. After parking as quickly as I could, I pulled my helmet off, and cradling it beneath my arm, hurried up the ramp to the double doors. I'd overslept ... as in right through my bedside alarm, one which rang shrilly. Yep, I was that tired.

Stepping through the double doors, I waved to Elsie before hightailing it down the hallway, pausing to say hello to Sam on the way. When I reached my desk, I noticed Trey was already at his. 'Course that really wasn't much of a surprise because Trey was always at least a half an hour early every day. He considered work a social outlet.

"Hey, Dulce," he said, looking up at me from where he'd been picking at his cuticles

"Morning, Trey," I replied, remembering I hadn't gotten back to him about the Star Wars Convention. "Oh, about that convention ..." I started.

He glanced up at me, his eyes wide. "Yeah?"

I cleared my throat, feeling like the queen of all assholes. "I don't think I'll be able to make it."

"Oh," he said, dropping his gaze to his ample lap.

"I just have so much going on right now, Trey," I continued, feeling like I needed to make him understand. "I really wanted to go though."

"Nah, it's cool," he said with a disenchanted smile. "There's always others."

"Okay," I said, hoping I sounded sincere although the truth of the matter was that spending a day with Storm Troopers, R2D2 and Ewoks wasn't my idea of fun. "Thanks for the invite though."

He nodded and seemed a little dejected as he focused on the cuticle of his left thumb. Apparently recalling something, he glanced up at me again. "Big guy was looking for you earlier," he said with a whisper of a smile. "And just a warning, don't piss him off 'cause he's not in a good mood."

"Great," I said, not ready to deal with Knight and his foul mood. I dropped my helmet on the table and left my backpack on my chair as I started toward Knight's office.

"Hey, Dulce," Trey called out behind me.

I turned around to face him. "Yeah?"

"Everything good with you?" he asked, studying me carefully, as if looking for a clue in my posture.

I felt my stomach drop as I realized I had to do a better job of appearing normal, as in not stressed out. The last thing I needed was everyone getting concerned about me. At the thought, I was suddenly consumed with exhaustion. This double life was getting to be too much, taking too large a toll on me. I needed to tell Quill that I had to have a night off so I could catch up on my sleep. "Yeah, I'm fine, Trey," I said softly. "Just been really busy."

"Okay," Trey said and smiled at me encouragingly. "Just wanted to check on you."

I didn't say anything more, but turned around again and started for Knight's office. When I reached it, I noticed the door was closed. I could see him reclining in his chair with his long legs up on his desk as he chastised someone over the phone. He spied me through the slats of his blinds and motioned for me to enter. I opened the door and walked in, sitting down in the chair directly in front of him.

At the sight of him, I felt my stomach tighten into a knot, which worked its way up my esophagus and into my throat until I almost couldn't breathe. Hot Hades, he was just so gorgeous. I wasn't sure where my libido had been the last few days, probably hibernating given recent events, but facing Knight now, it was back in full force. I couldn't seem to take my eyes off his incredibly broad shoulders, or the shapely swells of his muscular thighs.

"I don't give a shit, just make it happen," he said into the phone, his tone heightened. I tried not to gulp too loudly as my gaze worked its way up his remarkable body to his even more incredible face. His eyes were on me, sharp and hungry. Or maybe I was just imagining that last bit.

"I don't care what it takes," he said in a steely firm voice, letting his legs slide off the top of his desk. They were loud when they hit the floor. He leaned forward, resting on his elbows, never taking his eyes from mine. "I want those sons of bitches tried in our system, not theirs." Then he shook his head and scrunched his brows together, in obvious irritation. "Just do it and don't call me back until you have good news. I have to go, I have someone in my office." He was quiet for a few more seconds. "Call me tomorrow," he said before hanging up.

"You wanted to see me?" I piped up, my voice sounding antsy and rushed.

"You're late," he said with an undisguised frown.

I dropped my eyes to the carpet and started fidgeting with the zipper on my jacket, only then realizing it was damn hot in Knight's office. I took off the jacket, fully aware that Knight's eyes were glued on me the entire time. If anything, it just made my body temperature increase. I had to remind myself that I was Dulcie O'Neil and therefore, shouldn't be nervous and definitely shouldn't be fidgeting. I faced Knight with a renewed sense of self and held my jaw tight. "I overslept."

"I see," he said, narrowing his eyes, apparently dissatisfied with my attitude. "Don't be late again. Consider this warning number one."

I gave him a replica of the pissed off expression he was giving me. "Noted."

He glared at me for another few seconds before exhaling and quickly dropping it. "I want you to compile all the bios of every known potions trafficker through Splendor, Haven, Sanctity, Estuary and Moon," he ordered as I felt anxiety working up my spine.

What in the hell would have prompted him to request this information? "Why? I mean, what do you need it for?"

He sighed and sounded exasperated, like he didn't want any questions. Well, too bad for him because I was anything but a yes-man, er yes-woman. "We received a tip this morning that a new street potion will be hitting the black market soon and I want to cover all my bases."

I think my heart actually stopped for at least two seconds. Maybe more. "A ... a what?" I asked, in a whisper soft voice.

"A tip," he said, shaking his head like he couldn't understand why was I asking so many questions.

"From whom?" I persisted, hoping the rapid pulse in my neck wouldn't give away my worry that I was about to piss myself.

"Anonymous," he answered, eyeing me inquisitively, and picking up a pencil that had been lying on his desk. He started drumming the eraser end against his desk, making a sound almost as maddening as nails on a chalkboard. "Where were you last night?"

I felt my cheeks color and dropped my gaze to the floor before forcing my eyes back to his. I just sucked at lying. "Why?"

He shrugged like it wasn't a big deal. "Got the tip last night. I called you and came by, but you weren't around."

I gulped air, hoping he couldn't read me as I wished I could lie more convincingly. "I, uh, had plans."

His eyes narrowed and his jaw tightened. "I see." Then he stood up and started for his door, opening it extra wide as if to let me know he was finished interrogating me. "I need those bios by lunch," he said sternly as I stood up and started for the door.

"I understand," I answered simply.

"Trey and I are going to run some reconnaissance later today. That's why I need the bios before lunch."

And the only reason he'd mentioned that was because he wanted to make sure I knew he'd asked Trey along for this mission, instead of me. I said nothing although I was burning inside. Knight was more than aware that paperwork wasn't my forte and, more so, that I hated it. It was something Elsie usually did or if she weren't around, Trey. But I held my head high, refusing to give in to him. Instead, I faced him squarely. "I'll have them to you by lunchtime."

Knight said nothing, but stared at me as if trying to read me. Uncomfortable with his scrutiny, I returned to my desk.

ELEVEN

As I sat at my desk, pouring through the profile pages of miscreants in Splendor and neighboring cities, I couldn't stifle the trepidation winding its way up my gut. Ever since Knight had admitted to receiving an anonymous tip about what could only have been the *Draoidheil,* I felt like I was going to throw up or, failing that, have a young-life crisis. I couldn't understand who could've leaked the information so quickly. I thought maybe Melchior had already informed his traffickers that the *Draoidheil* was on its way, and in their excitement, word got out. But it was how word got out that had me the most concerned. Obviously, I hadn't mentioned it to anyone and I assumed Quillan hadn't either. Christina seemed like she was currently Melchior's favorite pet, so I was fairly certain she was innocent of blabbing. But if it weren't any of us, then who had it been?

Knight and the ANC were now aware the *Draoidheil* was on its way, which only created an added complication It was also something I hadn't expected that would only make it harder for Quill, Christina and I to distribute it. I'd have to remember to inform them about this new obstacle as soon as we saw each other again. The more I thought about it, the more irritated I became. It just would have been so much easier if the ANC hadn't found out, because now the three of us would have to plan a way around this and be extra careful. But first things first, I needed to find out how much Knight knew ...

'Course, currently I was stuck doing the mindless gofer job that Knight assigned me, so that's what I'd focus on. I glanced at the clock on the wall next to me, noting I had one hour left before lunchtime. I'd already located and printed the bios of traffickers from Splendor, Moon, and

Sanctity. All I had left were Estuary and Haven and I could have those done in twenty minutes, tops.

"How's it goin' over there, Dulce?" Trey asked as he looked over the top of his monitor at me, his wide face reminding me of the moon rising into the sky.

"Good, I'm nearly done," I answered, offering him a quick smile before returning my attention to the twelve or so bios left to do.

"Quick work," he said as he hovered over his monitor, obviously not realizing I was on a deadline. I looked up at him and nodded, noticing he still made no move to sit down again. Instead, he continued standing there, wearing the expression of a kid too ashamed to admit he'd just wet himself.

"Yep," I said, clicking "print" on the next bio. Then imagining I might be able to get some info out of Trey, I asked, "So what was this anonymous tip Knight was talking about?"

Trey shrugged and dropped his eyes back to his computer, sitting down immediately. Obviously, he knew something but even more obvious was the fact that he wasn't about to spill the beans. "Not really sure. He said he'd fill me in while we were patrolling." Clearly, he'd been ordered to keep his trap shut. Well, lucky for me, I was really good at prying traps open.

"Oh, I thought you might know, since you're always on top of the best gossip." Usually, he'd leap at the opportunity to fill me in on any news around the office—it seemed like he was proud that everyone came to him first for the juicy details.

"Oh, yeah, not this time. It's pretty hush-hush I guess." Then he was quiet for a few seconds. Hmm, this might be harder than I thought.

"Wow, so *you* don't even know about it? That is hush-hush."

"Yep," he answered succinctly and I gave up.

"I'm sure you and Knight will figure things out." I didn't meant to sound so pissed off—like I was upset Knight had left me out of the loop. Well, truth be told, I *was* pissed off because I guessed the only reason Knight had failed to inform me was because he was angry I'd broken up with him. Another reason why it was never good to mix business with pleasure.

Trey stood up then, and propping his pudgy arms on the top of his monitor, he offered me a consoling smile as he studied me. "Things will get better between the two of you, Dulce,"

I felt my eyebrows arch in surprise as I realized Trey was more in the know than I could have imagined. I mean, I didn't tell him Knight and I had broken up. "So word's already gotten out about us?"

Trey nodded with the expression of someone disappointed. "Yeah, I found out from Sam."

"From Sam?" I repeated, suddenly worried that Sam had somehow broken the silence charm I'd insisted she put on herself. "What did she tell you, exactly?" I asked, eyeing Trey like a hawk.

Trey shrugged again and then ran his arm across his nose, apparently in an effort to scratch an itch. "Nothing really, just that you and Knight weren't together anymore. She said she didn't know why."

Relief sounded through me at the same time as a rock of worry filled my gut. It was just a huge bummer to realize the finality of Knight's and my breakup was now public news. I noticed Trey watching me expectantly, like he was waiting for me to fill him in on the hows and whys of it, which of course, was never going to happen.

"Well, sometimes things just don't work out," I said dismissively and faced my computer screen again. I tried to remain uninterested and casual as I forwarded to the next bio and hit "print."

"I thought you guys were really into each other," Trey continued, his lower lip sticking out so far, someone could trip on it.

"Relationships aren't as easy as they appear to be," I said in a stilted tone, not wanting to discuss any of this at all. It was beginning to leave a bad taste in my mouth.

"Knight's been different ever since though," Trey continued, sighing heavily. He leaned his large head on his arm, looking like a country singer about to lament his unrequited love in a woe-be-gone song.

I knew I should've just avoided the subject altogether because it wasn't like I could do anything about it. I'd done what I had to and that was that. But somehow, I couldn't help my own curiosity. "What do you mean?"

"He's just in a crappy mood all the time now and doesn't seem like he wants to hang out with any of us, like he used to."

I exhaled my pent-up anxiety and shook my head. "He'll come around eventually. I think he just has a lot on his plate at the moment."

"Do you have those reports for me yet?" Knight's irritated voice sounded from behind me and I felt myself jump in reflex. I glanced at Trey and grimaced, realizing Knight had probably just overheard the remnants of our conversation. Trey just smiled innocently and sat back down, leaving me to suffer the wrath of the Loki. If I'd thought Knight was in a bad mood before, overhearing me discussing our failed relationship certainly wouldn't help things.

I pulled the final printouts off the printer and stacked them on top of the other ones piled on my desk. Knight said nothing, but turned around and started down the hallway for the break room, his coffee cup in hand. He called out over his shoulder, "Just leave them on my desk."

I had no intention of leaving them on his desk. Nope, I had my own reconnaissance to do and that involved finding out as much as I could about this "anonymous tip." I walked the printouts into Knight's office and sat on the visitor's chair, waiting for him to return.

With nothing else to do, I busied myself by scanning his office. His brown leather jacket was draped over his bookshelf, which was piled high with file folders. There really wasn't anything too personal in Knight's office, aside from a picture of him standing next to Gabriel, his best friend from the Netherworld. Knight and Gabe grew up together. Gabe was also a Loki and gorgeous —almost as gorgeous as Knight. I only met him once, when Knight and I were being held captive in the Netherworld. Moving on from the picture, there was a BMW magazine on the top of Knight's desk and a motorcycle magazine beneath it. I shook my head with an amused smirk as I thought about what a man's man Knight was with regard to his love of speed. The only signature in the office that was truly Knight's was the smell—his office smelled just like him: crisp, clean aftershave mixed with pure and raw masculinity.

"I thought I said just leave them on the desk?" Knight grumbled from behind me as he closed the door, being careful not to spill his coffee. He walked behind his desk and took a seat.

"Yeah, you did," I answered, my tone flat. I definitely didn't appreciate his sudden aggression. "So why the bad mood?"

He raised his eyebrows with surprise, before frowning. "What bad mood?"

"Um, the bad mood that's been hovering over you all day. If you're trying to beat the competition for 'World's Worst Boss,' you're well on your way."

"Funny, Dulcie," he said, although his expression said it wasn't funny by a long shot.

"Haven't you noticed everyone around you seems to be walking on eggshells?"

He glanced at me as he sipped his coffee, looking completely irritated. "Is that why you came in here—to ride me about my office manners? If so, I'm not in the mood to hear it."

"No that's not why I'm here," I snapped, frowning as I leaned forward and gave him a little sass. "I wanted to bring you the printouts and ask what's going on with this new street potion you mentioned."

He arched a brow at me and motioned for me to hand him the stack of papers. I did and watched as he shuffled through them and then tossed them on the desk, leaning back in his seat and taking a deep breath. He rested his legs on the desk, crossing them at the ankles and stretched his muscular arms above his head like a cat just waking from a nap.

"I don't know if there's any credence to the tip," he started as he faced me again. "But we received a typed note saying to keep an eye out for a brand new, incredibly addictive potion."

"Does it have a name? And if so, was it anything you'd heard of before?" I asked, sitting on the edge of my seat as I waited for his response with visible anticipation. "Did the note say when the potion was going to hit the streets?" Knight looked at me closely, as if wondering why I was so curious. "Um, I'm back on the force again; or did you forget?" I replied to the unasked question in his eyes.

He dropped the suspicious expression and simply nodded. "The note didn't say what the potion was or when it's due to hit, but from the sound of it, it's something completely new."

"Where's the note?" I asked, trying to sound more businesslike, while burning with the need to see it. I hoped the note might give me some hint as to where it had originated and, more specifically, a hint as to who knew too much.

Knight said nothing, but pulled open the top drawer of his desk and handed a folded piece of white paper to me. His fingers brushed against mine and I felt my eyes go wide as they met his, which were narrowed and angry. I quickly looked away.

"And you checked it for prints?" I asked, unfolding the note as feelings of gratitude descended on me over the fact that I had something with which to attract my attention away from the heat in his eyes.

"Of course," he answered tersely, wrapping his arms across his broad chest. I glanced up at him for a second and immediately regretted it. He just looked so ... mad.

Refocusing my attention from Knight to the letter, I read:

New potion hitting streets soon from Netherworld. Nothing like it out there.   Instantaneous dependency. Could cause widespread epidemic. Increase patrols.

I felt myself gulping as my heart started pounding in my chest. Someone knew! There had to be a snitch somewhere in Melchior's ranks and the thought made me sick to my stomach. The next logical step was to deduce that if there was a snitch, he or she could easily have ratted me out ... if he or she hadn't already.

I took a deep breath and told myself to calm down. I was getting way too carried away, and playing the "what if" game wasn't going to help things. I handed the note back to Knight and offered him a raised brow expression, not really knowing what else to say. There was nothing in the letter that I could comment on. And, since there were no fingerprints associated with it, it truly was anonymous. Whoever left it had been incredibly careful.

"What do you make of it?" I asked, suddenly uncomfortable with the silence between us.

He shrugged. "Who knows if it's legit, but I'd rather be safe than sorry; so I'm going to treat it as if it came directly from Caressa."

"Probably smart," I said, the words dying on my tongue as I noticed his intent gaze on me.

"What do *you* make of it?" he asked, studying me as if trying to memorize every line of my face.

"Not much there to make anything of," I answered, feeling like I was choking on the words. He didn't lose that suspicious expression and at the thought of further questions, I quickly added: "Where do you want me to patrol?"

"I don't," he said simply, his jaw tight.

I felt my stomach drop and was suddenly scared to death that he knew more than he was letting on. There was just something in his eyes. "What do you mean?"

"I don't think you're emotionally stable at the moment," he said simply.

I nearly swallowed my own tongue. "Excuse me?"

He shrugged as if what he'd just said wasn't a big deal by any stretch of the imagination. "You've been sleeping in and showing up late to work, things you've never done before."

"I did it once!" I interrupted him, spearing him with my eyes. "One time, for fuck sake!"

He didn't seem fazed. "You're too thin, you look sick and you've distanced yourself from all your friends. All warning signs, as far as I'm concerned."

"Warning signs of what?" I demanded, glaring at him. He was basically doubting my ability to do my job, and I had to admit, despite my fuming, I was hurt. "And I haven't distanced myself from any of my friends, I've just been busy!"

"Doing what?"

"None of your business," I said in as collected a tone as I could muster. "All that matters is that I'm good at my job, Knight, you know that."

"You *were* good at your job. These days, I don't know what to think about you."

I rolled my eyes and gritted my teeth. "This is fucking unbelievable," I said as I shook my head.

"I think you have some things to figure out for yourself, Dulcie," Knight continued calmly, like he thought he was a shrink or something. "And as head of this branch of the ANC, I can't, in good conscience, put you in a potentially dangerous situation."

Feeling like I would either cry or pull my hair out, I exhaled deeply, and ran my hand through my hair in frustration. Instantly Knight's eyes glommed onto my wrist.

"What's that?" he demanded, pointing at my portal compass watch.

If I'd had anything in my bladder, I absolutely would have wet myself. Instead, it felt like I was in slow motion as I brought my gaze to the diamond-faced watch, which caught the sunlight coming through the window. It reflected rainbow prisms all around the room as I panicked, my heart beating frantically. Then I realized there was no way in hell that Knight could identify this as a portal watch. There was nothing about it to give it away. Instead, it appeared to be an extravagantly ostentatious timepiece.

"It's a watch," I said simply, berating myself for not having left it at my apartment.

"I can see that," Knight barked back at me. "Where did you get it?"

"A store." I said the first thing that came to mind, and realized my mistake immediately.

"You bought it for yourself?" Knight asked incredulously.

Well, the lie had already escaped from my lips, so there was no use in backing down now. As transparent as my lie would be, it was still way better than admitting that the Head of the Netherworld, a.k.a., the head of the illegal potions market, gave the watch to me. "Yes."

Knight cocked his head to the side and studied me. "Interesting, considering you detest the color pink not to mention diamonds."

I swallowed and prayed for a miracle. Unfortunately, one didn't come. "I, uh, needed a watch and didn't feel like shopping ... for a long time, so I just bought the first one I saw."

Knight stared at the watch again, before bringing his fuming blue eyes back to mine. "A Rolex? You bought the first Rolex you happened to see?"

I suddenly wished one of the flying Netherworld monsters had followed me home and gobbled me up, just so I wouldn't have to face the ire in Knight's eyes. "Yeah, I wanted to get something nice for myself," I answered sheepishly.

"Good to know you have, oh, ten thousand dollars just laying around."

Ten thousand dollars! My eyes nearly popped out of my head. I had no idea the watch was that expensive! I said nothing, but watched Knight shake his head as he exhaled. "It's great you've moved on so quickly, Dulcie. Kudos to you."

"That's not ..." I started, but he shook his head again, silencing me with his raised hand.

"I don't give a shit about your personal life," he interrupted me. "All that matters to me now is that you do a good job here. And lately, your attitude sucks."

I shook my head and felt exhausted from my hair to my toes. "If anyone has had a personality change lately, it's you," I spat back at him. "So don't try and tell me that I can't do my job when it's pretty clear where all of this is coming from."

His jaw went tight. "And where would that be?"

136

I wasn't about to back down, not now. "Obviously from the recent events between you and me."

He snickered an ugly sound and then the smile left his lips entirely as he glanced at my watch again. "Don't flatter yourself."

"I'm not," I answered, narrowing my eyes as the pain of his words singed me. "I'm simply looking at the facts."

"Dulcie," he started, a slight smile playing with his lips again, which pissed me off even more than his harsh words had. "I've had plenty of time to ask myself what happened with you and me and I've reached the conclusion that what happened was destined to be."

"What the hell does that mean?"

"It means that your hang-ups are bound to fuck up any relationship you get into."

I shook my head, at a loss for words to adequately defend myself. And the kicker of the whole damn thing was that I'd broken up with him merely to protect him! "Maybe and maybe not," I said finally, feeling completely defeated because there was nothing I could say that would make things better.

"It is what it is," he finished dismissively. "But don't worry about me because I'll move on." He narrowed his eyes. "I am moving on."

I didn't want to admit to myself how much his words stung me to the core, and of course, I wasn't going to admit anything to him. I simply held my tongue and nodded, trying not to lose my poker face. "Then I'm happy for you."

He glared at me for a second or two before a mask of indifference pasted itself over his face. "And as far as this investigation goes, you're off it."

I stood up, feeling sick to my stomach and left his office.

###

The cell phone on loan from Melchior buzzed in my pocket at exactly seven p.m. I pulled it out and noticing "private caller" on the window, figured it had to be Quill. Really, he was the only one who ever called me on the damn thing anyway.

"Hello?" I answered, impatiently.

"Dulce." It was Quillan. "Christina is going to pick you up in thirty minutes."

Yes, I was dead tired and needed to sleep, but after my day with Knight, I knew I wouldn't be able to. "Sounds good," I said with a deep sigh.

"I'll see you both soon," Quill answered. Then he apparently remembered something. "Your father had one of his cars shipped to the empty warehouse at the loading docks. You can take it home tonight, but just be sure to park it somewhere where no one will notice it; and make sure no one's around whenever you're getting into and out of it."

"I'll park it in the Vons lot around the corner," I said. "And I'll go for incognito when I'm driving it."

"Yeah, that sounds good," he answered quickly and then paused for a few seconds. "Are you okay?"

I wanted to scream at the top of my lungs that no, I wasn't okay by any stretch of the imagination, but held myself in check. "I'm great."

TWELVE

After I got off the phone with Quill, it suddenly struck me as odd that Christina was coming to pick me up—mainly because it wasn't like we were friends or anything. I shrugged the concern away, though, figuring Quill was just nervous about me using my ANC bike on Melchior business. And when it came down to it, it would be an opportunity for me to grill Christina for information, and find out exactly how close she was to my father.

Christina rang my doorbell precisely thirty minutes after I hung up with Quill. This time, she was dressed in dark blue jeans with flared legs, white sneakers, and a white T-shirt, which made her natural olive complexion look even tanner. She didn't have a speck of makeup on, not even eyeliner or mascara, and even in this most natural state, she was still very pretty. Her hair was pulled back into a high ponytail, which I immediately noticed because I'd always had an aversion to wearing my hair up and revealing the points on my ears. Apparently Christina wasn't a self conscious fairy. Point for her, I guess.

"Hi," she said in a chipper voice as she poked her head in my entryway, scanning my house nosily. She pulled her head back out and offered me a heartfelt smile. "Cute place!"

"Thanks," I grumbled as I eyed her jeans and sneakers again. "You were lots taller last time we met."

She laughed and shook her head. "Those were my Sam Edelman's. Pretty hot shoes, don't you think?"

I couldn't argue because they were hot. "Yeah," I managed to squeak in reply.

"You saw me in my work attire; usually, I look like this," she said, glancing down at herself, and shrugging like "what you see is what you get."

"Much more practical," I commented, noting that I was wearing an outfit almost identical to hers. She seemed to notice it too and smiled at me in response.

"My dad always said not to get all dolled up every day because if you do, people will always expect you to look that way; but if you get dolled up every once in a while, people will really notice how beautiful you are."

"I like your dad's advice," I replied, locking the door and closing it behind us.

"It's good advice." She started down the walkway with me at her side.

"Thanks for picking me up," I chimed, feeling like I needed to do my part to seem sociable and friendly, especially since she was so gregarious. And you know what they say about catching flies with vinegar …

"Sure, Quill wanted you to be able to drive the car on loan from Melchior, so it made sense for me to pick you up."

I hadn't thought of that. Guess my brain wasn't working on all eight cylinders. 'Course, I'd had all of, what … four hours of sleep in the last few days? It was a wonder my brain was even working at all.

"Yeah, that does make sense," I said and watched as she whipped out her car keys and beeped her remote, unlocking the doors to a lifted, black Jeep Wrangler which was covered in mud. "You drive a Wrangler?" I asked in awe, suddenly finding respect for her. I mean, there are cars, trucks and SUVs, and then there are Jeeps.

She opened the driver's side door and sort of launched herself up and into the seat, something which probably sounds comical but somehow she managed it with the grace of a ballerina. I, on the other hand, wasn't quite as polished and bashed my knee into her glove box. She raised her eyebrows at me as if to ask if I were okay. I just nodded and buckled my seatbelt, watching as she pulled her door shut, turned the engine on, stepped on the clutch and put the Jeep in gear. It was even a stick-shift. Another point for her.

"Yep, I'm a Jeep girl. Sorry about the mud, but I took it off-roading the other day and still haven't found the time to wash it." She pulled into the street and looked over at me again. "I can be a huge procrastinator."

"Do you go off roading a lot?" I asked, finding myself naturally drawn to her. It was sort of hard not to because she just seemed so much ... like me.

"Yep, the bigger the rocks and steeper the hills, the better," she said, coming to a stop at the end of my street, and casting me an impish smile. "Live like there's no tomorrow, right?"

I just nodded ... I'd basically lived by that mantra the majority of my adult life. She took a right on Lucky Street and downshifted as my eyes roved over the inside of her Jeep—it was almost exactly the same as mine had been. "I used to drive a Wrangler, myself," I said, lamenting the loss of my most favorite vehicle. "It was canary yellow."

"You wanna know what's funny?" Christina laughed and shook her head, as her eyes narrowed on me. "I totally pegged you as a Jeep girl." She also apparently knew her way around my neighborhood because she took all the back streets, apparently good with this incognito stuff.

"Well, I *was* a Jeep girl," I said, pausing to allow myself to reminisce. "That was before I had an accident and totaled it."

She shook her head. "I'm sorry." Then she focused on driving, following the hairpin turn of the street. Once it was straight again, she turned to me. "Did you take yours off-roading a lot?"

"A few times," I said with a sigh, feeling my exhaustion gaining on me. I yawned, covering my mouth with my arm and then tried to shake the feelings of fatigue right out of my head. It didn't work.

"You gotta get some sleep, you know?" Christina said as she arched a brow at me. "You can't go all day and expect to go all night too."

"Tell that to Quill," I answered simply as I stretched my arms over my head and relaxed into the seat.

"I will." She came to another stop before turning left and jumping on Highway One, which led to the loading docks. As if suddenly unnerved by the silence in the car, she reached over and turned her CD player on. It was like the wrath of Hades was unleashed when the speakers blared a loud array of tantric beats. I nearly jumped out of my skin as the noise rattled the speakers.

"Shit!" I yelled, trying to calm my heart down as she reached over and lowered the volume. "I'm awake now, that's for sure!"

Christina giggled. "Sorry." She pushed the "forward" button on the face of the CD player, sparing me further torture.

"Do you like punk rock?" she asked with an amused smile.

"I don't know. Name some groups."

"Um, Pennywise?" she answered. Before I had the chance to respond, she added, "Here, this is *My Own Way* and it's one of my favorites."

Then, without waiting for my response, she turned up the volume as a barrage of drums and guitar assaulted me with a beat so fast, I felt like we should have been head-banging.

"I also love Bad Religion!" she yelled over the singer's voice and started nodding her head while slapping her hand against the steering wheel in time with the beat.

Even though our tastes in music were miles apart, the thought struck me that if this situation had been different, Christina and I might have been friends. Why? Because so far as I knew her, I liked her—an independent woman carving her niche in a male dominated industry, refusing to take no for an answer. And even though we were on separate sides of the moral spectrum, I couldn't stop myself from liking her. There was just something about her that made her easy to like. She was definitely the type of person I would enjoy spending time with—she wasn't afraid to get dirty and had an affability about her that was refreshing.

It was a damn shame she worked for my father.

Once the song was over, she turned the volume down and glanced over at me with a smirk. "So, what'd you think?"

I shook my head. "I consider myself lucky to have survived it."

She broke into a giggle, which was quickly reduced to a smile. "Oh well, I guess it's an acquired taste."

"You think?" As soon as I felt like I wanted to laugh, I changed the subject. I mean, there was no point in becoming friendly with her when things couldn't end well. I was now, more than ever before, convinced that I had only myself to rely on if I were to get out of this shitty situation. Who knew where that left Christina? Instead of making useless small talk, I should have been grilling her for information. "So how long have you been working with my father?"

The smile vanished from her lips, replaced by a pensive expression. She rolled her eyes, as if trying to remember. "Um, I think maybe six years now."

"Wow," I said, surprised it had been so long and disappointed all at the same time. I wasn't sure why, but I was hoping she was a new recruit, unaware of what she'd gotten herself into. Obviously such was not the case.

"Have you been working for your father your whole life?" she asked.

I shook my head, too tired to come up with yet another lie. "My father actually just came into my life a few weeks ago." I couldn't help my less-than-thrilled tone. I didn't think it was possible for me to actually sound happy about anything involving Melchior O'Neil.

"Really?" she asked, eyeing me curiously. "So what made you decide to work for him?"

"He asked me to," I answered, reminding myself it wasn't exactly a lie, maybe just a white one. I mean, he *had* asked me to work for him.

"Oh and how do you like it so far?"

At this point, I was tired of trying to be something I wasn't and no longer caring whether or not it would come back to bite me in the ass later, I opted for candid honesty. "I don't."

Her eyebrows arched in an expression of curiosity. "Why is that?"

I shrugged. "As you mentioned earlier, the hours suck."

She laughed at that, and then took the opportunity of a red light, to ask me, "So if you aren't enjoying what you're doing, why are you doing it?"

I sighed and shook my head. "Personal reasons."

She nodded as if she respected my answer and wouldn't try to pry. "At least the pay's good?"

"I wouldn't know," I grumbled, suddenly aware that I hadn't exactly made it onto my father's payroll. Apparently, Christina had. Well, good for her. "What about you?" I asked, turning the tables. "You don't seem like the type of person to be involved with something like this. It doesn't seem like you have anything in common with the Baron Escobars of the world."

"He's a real piece of work, isn't he?" she asked with a smirk as she shook her head, probably recalling her less than pleasant memories of the Titan.

"Piece of work doesn't even do him justice."

"With regard to the Baron Escobars of the world, I could say the same of you," she started. "Doesn't seem like you two have anything in common either."

"I don't, but I also don't have much of a choice since he works for my father."

"Yeah, I can see that. I guess your situation is a little more complicated. Mine is pretty straightforward."

"What is it?"

She shrugged and took a deep breath. "I started working for the ANC in the Netherworld and met your father during a convention. He was one of the presenters. I was really impressed with his business sense and asked him a ton of questions, probably too many. Anyway, he was really patient, and at the end of our conversation, he told me to drop my resume off with his secretary. So I did, never expecting to get a call back."

"But lo and behold you did," I finished for her.

She nodded with a smile. "Yep, and he asked if I was interested in working for him."

"Did you know what you'd be doing?"

"No, of course not," she sighed, as if remembering how she used to be, before her innocence was corrupted by street-potion-trafficking.

"Otherwise you probably wouldn't have agreed?" I asked, eyeing her surreptitiously.

She nodded and sighed. "I probably wouldn't have." Then she was quick to answer, "But I like the situation I'm in now, so I have no regrets."

And that, right there, was the difference between us.

Ten minutes later, Christina pulled into the parking lot of the abandoned warehouse beside the loading docks. I immediately noticed a bright red Mercedes sedan sitting in the parking lot and Quill standing beside it.

"Hmmm, looks like your dad sent the E550," Christina said with a smile. "Not too shabby."

"So much for being incognito," I said, shaking my head, thinking I was going to be about as inconspicuous driving the red, flashy thing as the flying monsters of the Netherworld.

"Invest in some good sunglasses and a big hat," she replied as she pulled alongside the Mercedes and killed the Jeep's engine.

I took off my seatbelt and opened my door. The smell of rotting fish was enveloping even this far north of the docks. Trying not to breathe through my nose, I jumped down from the Wrangler and faced Quill with a frown. "This better be quick because I haven't slept in four days."

"You beat me to it!" Christina called out. She was referring to our previous conversation when she said she'd talk to Quill about my sleep deprivation.

"I guess I did," I said over my shoulder before turning back to face Quill, my lips going tight.

"Nice to see you too," he said, smiling at both of us before his eyes settled on me and he dangled the keys to the Mercedes. "From your father," he said with a glance at the car. "He said to send his best one."

"I could care less. As long as it works, I'm happy," I grumbled.

"I know," Quill said, grinning at me as if he appreciated the fact that I was completely unimpressed by material things. "And I don't think this meeting should take that long."

I accepted the keys, and with Christina by my side, followed Quill toward the warehouse for our rendezvous. Overgrown bushes and piles of rubble from the neglected building created obstacles in our path and all three of us had to step over them. It was a feat for Christina and me since we had more in common with the Munchkins of Oz than I wanted to admit, at least where our height was concerned.

Looking up at the decrepit building, I noticed the paint was nearly completely chipped off what was left of the edifice. Graffiti covered the first six feet of the crumbling walls and the windows had been broken long ago, although glass still littered the ground. The inside was in as much disarray as the outside, with old, broken furniture scattered on the floor. What looked like the remains of an impromptu fire pit proudly occupied the center of the room, and next to it lay the bones of some unfortunate animal. I could only hope the transient who'd sought shelter here was now long gone.

"There will be six different shipments of *Draoidhell* coming in at the same time in six different locations," Quillan started, alternating his glance between the two of us. "Melchior wants these first shipments to hit the streets in exactly two weeks."

"Two weeks!" I repeated, suddenly feeling sick to my stomach. "That gives us no time to prepare at all!"

"Where will the drop-offs be?" Christina asked, apparently unconcerned about the timeline.

"He wants drop-offs to occur here, in Moon, Sanctuary, Estuary and Haven. There will be two drop-off locations in Splendor, on the loading docks and the East side."

"There is no way we can do this ourselves," I said, shaking my head, while the anxiety bubbled in my stomach.

"Melchior realizes that," Quill responded patiently.

"Then all the traffickers will have to be involved?" I said, recognizing that the three of us were just going to play the parts of orchestrators now, rather than potion pushers.

"Yes," Quill said, his lips tight as he faced me. "We'll have to contact everyone in the know and plan it out."

"In two weeks?" I continued with a frown, shaking my head incredulously. "And the dupe? Will there be six of those as well? Because that will require more ANC staff than we currently have."

Quill shook his head. "No dupes. Melchior's orders are that the ANC can't find out about the *Draoidheil* at all."

"No dupe?" Christina started, but I interrupted her.

"Too late. The ANC already knows."

Both Quill and Christina gaped at me. Christina's mouth hung wide open while Quill's brows knotted in the middle. Nope, there was no way either one of them had spilled the beans to the ANC, they both looked entirely too astounded.

"What the hell do you mean 'they already know'?" Quill asked in a harsh tone of voice.

I took a deep breath. "We got an anonymous letter the other day."

"What did it say?" Christina asked as she crossed her arms against her chest.

"It didn't name the *Draoidheil* specifically, but it did say an incredibly addictive potion was hitting the streets soon and to increase patrols. Knight is already on it." I didn't include the part about him keeping me off the case because of my alleged emotional imbalance.

"Who the hell could have?" Quill started and then shook his head, probably realizing anonymous meant anonymous.

"So we *are* going to need a dupe or six," I finished. "Unless Melchior wants Trey to sniff out the real stuff."

"Melchior doesn't want the *Draoidheil* in ANC hands," Quill said staunchly. "Period."

I threw my hands on my hips in exasperation and raised my voice. "Well, it doesn't sound like he has a choice." I took a deep breath, rubbing my temples because a headache was starting to form between them. "Besides, it's not like the ANC wouldn't bust it at some point anyway. Our track record is good."

Quill held his hands up. "I'm just the messenger."

"Well, we need to figure this out ASAP," I answered, still as pissed off as before. My father was delusional and I didn't feel like dealing with his maniacal fantasies in the exhausted state I was currently in. "Something's going to have to give because Trey is very good at what he does."

"I'll relay the information," Quill said, checking his watch. "I guess we're adjourned until then." Then he addressed both of us. "Tomorrow night?"

"If we need to figure this out in less than two weeks, yeah, tomorrow night," I answered begrudgingly as we started for the entrance of the building that led out to the parking lot.

The cold night air assaulted my cheek like a slap as I stepped into the moonlight, being careful not to trip over an old cement pylon.

"Have a good night," Christina said as she started for her Wrangler. "See you both tomorrow night."

"I'll call you tomorrow afternoon with a time," Quill answered, waving good-bye to her.

"Sounds good," she called back. "'Night, Dulcie."

"'Night," I said and reached into my pocket for the keys to the Mercedes as Quill and I watched her start the Wrangler and then drive away.

I glanced at Quill and sighed. "Let me guess, you need a ride home?"

He smiled apologetically. "Sorry to be an inconvenience, but someone had to get the Mercedes here."

"Yeah, yeah," I said as I unlocked the driver's door. Locating the button to unlock all the doors, I clicked it. Quill walked over to the passenger side and opened the door, seating himself as I did the same.

"Well, he definitely set you up," he said, sliding his hand across the tan leather interior. "This is one of the nicer rides I've been in and it drives like a dream."

I frowned at him, uninterested in the Mercedes for the moment. "I guess it beats the Ford Galaxy," I said absentmindedly.

"Uh, yeah," Quill answered as I turned the key in the ignition and felt the car hum beneath me. I buckled my seatbelt and put it in drive as I eyed my passenger.

"Where to?"

"South side of Splendor, Citrus Glen area."

I'd known that Quill had had to move after we discovered he was a potions importer, but I never knew where he moved to. Citrus Glen was one of the nicer areas in Splendor—a rural, but upscale area. "Nice," I said as I eyed the rearview mirror to make sure I wasn't going to hit anything while backing up.

"It's quiet," he answered indifferently and I could feel the penetration of his eyes on me. I glanced at him as he looked away, trying to pretend like he hadn't been staring at me.

I started back down the street that would take us away from the loading docks. Even though I was more than exhausted, the quiet in the car made me feel uncomfortable. "How come you never met Christina in any of your dealings with my father?" I asked as another thought occurred to me. "She said she's been working with Melchior for six years."

Quill shrugged. "Melchior has people all over the place who I don't know about."

I nodded, surprised by his answer, but accepting it at the same time. "Did you know she isn't in the ANC database at all?"

He nodded. "Lots of Melchior's people aren't."

"I guess that makes sense too," I said, stopping as the light turned red.

"Dulcie," Quillan started. He paused, as if there was something heavy on his mind and he was having difficulty finding exactly the right words. "I don't know if you and Vander were in a relationship, but I hope you realize it's going to have to end. Most of your connections will."

I was surprised by the subject change and felt a deep sadness inside at the thought of Knight and how our relationship had dissolved into something that barely even resembled a friendship. "Most of my connections will?" I repeated, swallowing hard as I thought about it. "Even my friendship with Trey, Dia and ... Sam?"

"Inevitably, they all do," he said, sounding resigned and tired.

I couldn't think about my relationship with Sam falling apart. It was just too painful to dwell on. "Things between Knight and me are already done," I said hollowly. "I guess you could say I had foresight."

Quillan nodded "I hope you understand it's for the best."

My lips were tight. "I do."

A few minutes later, we pulled onto Peach Tree Drive and Quillan pointed to a two-story, Spanish-styled home.

"This is me," he said simply.

I pulled over and parked in front of his house, impressed with the large olive trees that graced the walkway up to the dark oak front door.

"Looks like you're doing well," I said with a raised brow and a smirk.

He didn't say anything, but opened the car door and stepped out. Then he leaned over, presumably to say good night. "Do you want to come in and see the place?"

I really didn't want to, but his eyes were hopeful and I guess I didn't want to disappoint him. I nodded and turned off the engine, stepping out of the car and closing the door behind me. The moonlight reflected off his blond hair, making him look like some sort of angel. I met him on the sidewalk and then followed him up the brick pathway to his front door. He took a few seconds to unlock it and then stepped inside, turning on the lights.

I looked around, walking from the entryway into the living room, and was pretty impressed with the wide open space. The Spanish tiled floors and exposed beams in the ceiling definitely lent a California feel to the house. The coffee table and entertainment center were made of what looked like a richly stained pine and Quill's large sofas were slip-covered in white. His living room looked like something out of a magazine.

Taking a deep breath, I turned around, about to tell him how much I liked his house, but was completely stunned when I found him standing directly in front of me. Before I could react, his mouth was on mine, his hands in my hair. I was too shocked to respond for a second or two. But once I regained my wits, I pushed away from him, outrage billowing through me.

"What the fu ..." I started, but he interrupted me.

"I'm sorry," he said, frowning with shame. "I don't ... I don't know why I did that. It just ... it just felt like old times again, Dulce."

I shook my head and took a few steps away from him. "Well, it's not old times and it never will be old times again," I sighed, rubbing my eyes. I wanted nothing more than to be in my bed, asleep. "I have to go."

"Dulcie, I'm sorry. I didn't mean to upset you."

I refused to look at him and, instead, started for the door. "Let's just pretend like this didn't happen," I said over my shoulder.

Before he could reply, I opened his front door and closed it behind me.

THIRTEEN

For the first time in five days, I slept like the dead. After leaving Quill, whose kiss filled my mind with confusion mixed with irritation, I came home, crawled into bed and didn't wake up until the next morning at seven a.m. sharp. I got a good stretch of six hours of sleep, which was more than I could have hoped for.

The next day at the ANC went by incredibly slowly, mainly because my mind was on other things, like the *Draoidheil* delivery, for instance. Along with my mind, Knight was also elsewhere. For the entire day, I was the only one on duty, aside from Sam.

Of course, she was still incredibly nosy about what had happened to me in the Netherworld and I was just as emphatic about putting the kibosh on any conversations leading in that direction. And that was no small feat because the topic was still uppermost in both of our minds. When we went to lunch, I noticed numerous pregnant pauses and uncomfortable silences than we'd ever experienced before. I was haunted by the fear that what Quillan had mentioned the previous evening about all my connections coming to an end might actually happen.

And as to where the hell Knight had been all day, I had no clue. I mean, I knew he wouldn't call me to fill me in on his whereabouts, nor did I want him to. After our last interaction, it seemed no news was good news. At this point, it would be a wonder if he ever even spoke to me again. He'd been so pissed off about my watch, assuming it had been a gift from a would-be lover, that I didn't think we'd be real chummy again anytime soon. Although I was curious where he was and what he was doing, it was actually a relief that he wasn't in the office. Especially when

I considered how abrasive he'd been the last time I'd seen him. Yep, it seemed things were going to hell in a handbasket as far as my personal relationships were concerned. And worst of all, it didn't seem there was a damn thing I could do to prevent it.

Later that evening, Quillan called me just as he'd said he would. He told me to meet Christina and him at a deserted gas station down the street from Baron's tattoo parlor. Once I arrived, Quill outlined our plan so we could move forward where the *Draoidheil* was concerned. I now knew exactly where the shipments would be received, which smugglers would be handling each shipment and how many vials of *Draoidheil* filled each crate. I had a list of portal locations as well as ETAs when the *Draoidheil* was due to hit each site. Quill provided Christina and I with two vials each filled with white antidote pills.

As far as Melchior insisting on not getting the ANC involved, he'd taken extreme measures to ensure that no more information about the *Draoidheil* reached them. Once Melchior learned about the anonymous warning letter Knight had received, he instructed Quill to test both Christina's and my loyalty with a quick charm. It basically acted like a lie detector test to discern whether either one of us had written the letter. Of course, I passed with flying colors and Christina did too. Quill had taken the test earlier when Melchior first summoned him to the Netherworld to tell him the updated plan. Changes to the original arrangement included Melchior's slashing our timeline of two weeks down to a mere three days (something which caused my blood pressure to sky rocket). And, to stifle Trey's ability to glimpse the future, Melchior employed the entire race of Dryads.

Dryads were the most sentient of all creatures. They had the ability to perceive the past, present and future more easily than any other creature in the Netherworld. And their power was strong enough to deflect the psychic abilities of other sensitives (Trey, for example). Dryads had never been allowed on Earth and the few that existed (last I'd heard, the count was nine, total) lived together in a Dryad convent. It was known as "The Valley of the Trees," and supposedly located in the center of the Netherworld, deep in the Oslanian Forest. Dryads were all females and devoted themselves to the preservation of nature. They specifically presided over forests and the flora and fauna residing therein.

While growing up, my mother had told me many stories about the Dryads. They were the guardians of the trees and each Dryad had a special relationship to a particular tree, which they termed "the kinship." If one of these kinship trees were ever destroyed, the Dryad associated with that tree would also perish. And the death of a Dryad was not a good thing. Mom told me stories of famine, hurricanes and drought resulting from a Dryad's death. But the one particular associated with Dryad lore that struck me the most was that Dryads could never be removed from the forest. Doing so was extremely detrimental to their health. I wasn't sure if that meant they would die, get sick, or just become unbearably irritable. At any rate, there weren't any forests in Splendor or the surrounding cities, so I figured I'd soon find out.

When I asked Quill about taking the Dryads out of their natural habitat and if they could quite possibly die in the process, he had no answer for me ... and what was more, he didn't seem like he was interested in furthering the discussion. I could tell he was uncomfortable with the subject but I could also tell he'd convinced himself there was no way around it. All it proved to me was that my father placed far more importance in the successful marketing of the *Draoidheil* than he did on the lives of the Dryads. What was more, I had a feeling the Dryads were a good example of a magical ecosystem, and one I was worried about disrupting. One ecosystem's failure could lead to the destruction of many others which could ultimately mean devastation for the Netherworld as a whole. Not that my greedy father would care. It seemed the only green that interested him was money.

And why did I think that? Because I now knew that this shipment of *Draoidheil* wasn't just another street potion trafficking. No, the *Draoidheil* represented far more than that. It was the vehicle by which my father planned to seal his definitive tyranny. His ultimate hope was to ensure that all creatures of the Netherworld would become dependent on the *Draoidheil* and, therefore, dependent on him for distribution. The Netherworld creatures would then become like a race of automatons, all obeying the whims of one man.

That was why Melchior didn't want the *Draoidheil* to fall into the hands of the ANC. He couldn't afford to let the addictive power of the *Draoidheil* be known. As Regulators, if we busted a shipment of an unknown potion, the first thing we would do was send the potion to a lab in order to trace all of its components. In doing so, we could have the means to manufacture an antidote to the *Draoidheil* ourselves, something that would throw a monkey wrench into Melchior's campaign.

Fearing the ANC would discover his plans, Melchior made certain to dot all of his i's and cross all of his t's. Not only were Dryads scheduled to be present at each shipment station, thereby scrambling the psychic reception of any other sensitives, but Melchior also hired witches. They were tasked with charming each of the potion deliveries prior to the shipment to Earth. In other words, as soon as the *Draoidheil* came through the portal, and was received on the other end, one of the vials would detonate. The powder would blast out into the air, a wind of charmed intoxication suddenly spreading the *Draoidheil* far and wide. Of course, anyone working for Melchior would have already taken the antidote, leaving only the staff of the ANC to fall under its influence. And if that happened, the Regulators would be about as threatening as infants.

Given the previous example, it would only be a matter of weeks before all the creatures of the Netherworld came into contact with the *Draoidheil* and fell under its addictive power. Why was I so certain of this? Because one of the very convenient facts about the *Draoidheil* (which my father had failed to report when he first introduced us to it) was that there was a trigger in the potion. It made the person under its influence feel magnanimous and want to share his or her feelings of bliss with someone else. Consequently, the addicts would spread the drug themselves, addicting one creature at a time. And the only reason I'd found that out was because Quill had told me.

Now fully aware of my father's finely orchestrated and well-planned strategy, you can imagine how nervous I was about it actually succeeding. As far as I was concerned, it couldn't succeed ... I couldn't allow it to happen because it would destroy the balance between the Earth and the Netherworld as well as the lifestyle to which we were accustomed.

After Quill finished briefing us on what was supposed to happen and we wore him out with our questions, he adjourned the meeting. I waited until Christina left before asking Quill how he could follow my father's plan in good conscience, knowing what it would mean for all Netherworld creatures.

I don't know what I expected from him, considering my father had basically browbeaten him into submission a long time ago, but still, I expected more than I received. All I got from Quill was his acknowledgement that my father's plan would certainly enable his absolute tyranny and supremacy over the Netherworld. But when Quill discussed the subject, there was no fear in his eyes. Actually, I hadn't seen anything in his eyes, but a hollow void, a deep chasm, which made me realize that Quill had given up. And he'd done so years ago. There was no fight left in him. The fires of hope that burn in each and every one of us were nothing but smoldering embers in Quill, mere wisps of smoke, flapping their white flags of surrender. With no resistance left in him, he was useless to me.

The thought saddened me because I always thought of Quillan as a smart, strong person. He'd been a fair and good boss (well, at least until I caught him with his hand in the illegal potions jar). Now he was just a weak, vacillating, ineffective toady to my father. But having said all that, I felt sorry for him, more than ever before. I mean, despite the shit I was in, at least, I still had hope … And the ability to challenge Melchior's agenda. But as for Quill, he wasn't strong enough to support me anymore. No, he was a lame duck. And I couldn't rely on a lame duck.

As far as who could support me, Knight was the first person to pop into my head. Of course, I couldn't involve him in any way, knowing my father still ransomed his life over my head. And, furthermore, I'd have to figure out a way to protect Knight if I was going to breach my agreement with my father. And as far as I knew, I had to breach that agreement—I had no other choice.

With Knight out of the picture, there was only one other person I could turn to, one person with the position and morality to help me—Caressa Brandenburg.

For the remainder of my evening, I schemed and plotted until an idea began to construct itself in my mind, laying the building blocks of a solid foundation. Now that I had a fairly decent plan in place, it was time to get to work. The unfortunate part of my plan was that I couldn't use magic for any of it. I was too afraid that whatever I magicked for myself wouldn't work in the Netherworld, where my magic was ineffectual. Instead, I relied on commonplace conveniences such as the Rite Aid drugstore right around the corner.

Needing to "un-Dulcify" myself, I purchased the darkest semi-permanent hair dye I could find, even though I was incredibly bummed to have to use it. But c'est la vie ... Sometimes you have to sacrifice your naturally gorgeous hair in order to save the Netherworld.

Once I located the hair dye, my thoughts turned to makeup. I found the lightest liquid makeup I could in the Cover Girl aisle, along with four compacts of extra loud eye shadow, with colors ranging from fuchsia to electric blue, a bright red lip liner and matching lipstick, and a coral pink blush. The idea was to make myself look as unlike myself as possible. I was going for camouflage, disguise and incognito. I was going for Cyndi Lauper meets Boy George with a bit of RuPaul thrown in for good measure.

When I got home, I quickly dyed my hair. While it was wrapped up in a towel on top of my head, I searched through my closet for my white jeans and a white T-shirt. Once I located them both, I left the jeans on my bed and carried the v-necked T-shirt into the living room. I pulled out the ironing board and the iron, plugged it in and set it for "high steam." Then I ransacked the first two drawers beside my kitchen sink until I found the iron-on alphabet decals I'd purchased for Halloween last year when Sam and I had dressed up like Tweedle-Dee and Tweedle-Dum.

Our costumes had sucked so bad that we hadn't looked a thing like either Tweedle, so in a last ditch attempt to salvage our dignity, we opted to spell out our characters with iron-on alphabet letters. I couldn't help smiling as I remembered how much fun we'd had while cutting out the letters and arranging them just so. I was in charge of cutting while Sam did the ironing. After a few glasses of wine and too many laughs to count, my "Dee" ended up off center and Sam's "Dum" looked like it was falling downhill, which only made us laugh all the more.

I suddenly was overcome with feelings of depression as I cut out the letters to spell: "Flowertime." I promised myself, then and there, to prove Quill wrong. Nothing could ever get in the way of my friendship with my best friend. Whatever crimes I committed with regards to Melchior would soon be wiped clean from my slate. I promised myself that I would come up with a plan to stop my father and this was just the first step. I had to ensure that the *Draoidheil* never made it to the black market. Because if it did, my father's sovereignty would be guaranteed.

Once I finished ironing the letters onto my shirt, I turned the iron off and set the T-shirt aside to check on my hair. I unwrapped the towel and combed out the long tresses, noticing they looked sort of purple. Either way, purple-black was less Dulcie than honey-gold. I started for the living room again and turned on my computer, opening Microsoft Word as soon as the computer booted up. When I was greeted with the blank page, I started typing:

Caressa,

There is a shipment of illegal narcotics coming from the Netherworld scheduled to hit Splendor, Moon, Estuary, Haven and Sanctity. The narcotic is called Draoidheil and it's like nothing you've ever seen before. Immediate addiction. The only way to avoid it is an antidote (I will include two vials of the antidote with this letter for you to distribute to any ANC members involved in busting it). It is very important that you find someone who can recreate the antidote exactly. Once you are able to duplicate it, make as much as you can. Again, this is the ONLY way to avoid the addictive effects of the Draoidheil). The potion is airborne and anyone unlucky enough to inhale it will immediately become addicted. The narcotics will be arriving on May 10th at the following ports and at the following times:

8 pm Splendor: The Loading Docks and The Abandoned Railway Station on the Upper East Side

8:15 pm Moon: The old asylum off Grover St.
8:30 pm Sanctity: The train tracks where Green St.
crosses Blue St.
    8:45 pm Estuary: The Henderson Tomb in the
Briarwood Cemetery
    9:00 pm Haven: The abandoned Highgate Theater

I finished the letter by naming all of Melchior's thugs
who would be receiving the *Druvidheil* at each portal
station. I also mentioned the Dryads. I thought about telling
her that Melchior was behind it all, but then worried that if
Caressa didn't already know my father was in charge of the
trafficking, she might not act on the information; especially
if she thought it could mean her own personal safety. I
ended the note with:
    As soon as you finish reading this letter, please
destroy it.
    I stood up from my computer and stretched my arms
above my head. There wasn't anything more I could do
tonight. Tomorrow, I would stop by the florist in downtown
Splendor and purchase a bouquet, paying for it with cash so
I could remain anonymous. Then I planned to hop through
the portal to the Netherworld where I would pretend to be a
flower delivery person with an arrangement for Caressa.
    I was nervous, the anxiety pumping through my veins
ever since I'd devised this plan in the first place. But there
was no turning back now. I was stuck between a rock and a
hard place and Caressa was the only person I could turn to. I
knew she'd eventually recognize me under my blackish
purple hair and overdone makeup. I was betting on it
because I needed her to believe the information I told her
was accurate and true. And I had to imagine that she would
trust me, given the relationship she and I had already built.
It wasn't much of a relationship but it had definitely been
built on trust. It was everyone else in the Netherworld who I

was attempting to hide from, not wanting to be recognized on video surveillance, etcetera.

I was interrupted by the sound of the phone ringing. I glanced at the caller ID and recognized No Regrets, Bram's nightclub.

"Hello?" I asked.

"Sweet," Bram's English accent seemed especially thick tonight. "Are you engaged this evening?"

I figured he was going to make good on the promise I'd made him to allow him to take me to dinner five times in return for serving as my guide in the Netherworld. Unfortunately for me, I still owed him all five dinner dates. More unfortunately for me, Bram had also stipulated that on every date, I was to wear a short dress which was also low cut. If nothing else, Bram was persistent. And as much as I didn't want to have to fend off the advances of the three-hundred-year-old vampire all night, I had nothing else to do.

"No, I'm free," I said, sounding less than thrilled.

"Very good," Bram answered, but seemed to be weighing his words. "I would like you to meet me at No Regrets, sweet."

"We're going to have dinner there?" I asked, surprised because Bram usually seemed only interested in dining in five star restaurants, even though he, himself, never ate a thing.

"No, no, sweet. I am not interested in supper this eve. My request for your companionship has nothing to do with my list of demands; although I do hope you still plan to hold up your end of the bargain?"

"I do," I grumbled.

"Very good, sweet, very good."

It struck me as odd that Bram was requesting my company when there didn't appear to be anything in it for him ...Well, nothing that I could immediately see anyway. "What is this about then?"

He paused for a few seconds, which had to mean something was on his mind. "I prefer to discuss the specifics in person, sweet Dulcie. I will send a vehicle for you."

"I have my bike," I started.

"No," he interrupted. "I prefer your visit be clandestine, sweet."

I was surprised and intrigued, I couldn't help it. "Okay, I'll see you soon then, I guess."

FOURTEEN

It was only twenty minutes later when Bram's black limo arrived in front of my apartment, chauffeured by a long-haired, bearded werewolf. The were was even dressed in a black suit, white-collared shirt, black tie and a funny little hat that made him look like he just stepped off the Newsies lot. I'd seen the guy previously around No Regrets a few times. I think he also moonlighted as Bram's bodyguard. Why would a vampire need a bodyguard? I had no clue—I think it was mostly for show. It seemed everything Bram did was merely for the sake of doing it.

"Thanks," I said as the were opened the door for me and I seated myself in the plush black leather interior of the limo. I was immediately enveloped by Bram's smell— something slightly exotic and foreign, but captivating all the same.

The ride to No Regrets was quick and silent, which was just as well because I wasn't in the mood for small talk. Instead, I found my thoughts centered on why Bram requested the pleasure of my company this evening and more importantly, why was he being so secretive about it?

I lost track of time and when I felt the limo come to a stop, it didn't even seem like ten minutes had gone by. I smiled my thanks to the were when he opened the door for me and helped me out of the limo. Then he escorted me to the back entrance of No Regrets. So Bram hadn't been fibbing when he'd said he wanted my visit to remain secret. And I couldn't even say that it offended me … Nope, I was getting used to skulking in shadows.

I'd used the back entrance of No Regrets a few times when I'd visited Bram in the past (basically when I needed information from him and he wanted me kept on the down low) so when the chauffeur bypassed the door and started down the alley abutting Bram's nightclub, I was instantly on high alert.

"Um, isn't it this way?" I asked, motioning to the back door.

The were shook his head and his voice was deep when he spoke. "Bram insisted you enter through the alleyway." Figuring I was relatively safe with the werewolf, since he was in Bram's employ, I followed him into the alley where he paused at the top of a flight of stairs. He glanced back at me as if to make sure I was keeping up and then started down the stairs, which terminated in a nondescript white door. He knocked and the door opened maybe three inches, at which time the were announced Bram had a visitor. Then he turned to face me, gesturing for me to approach. The person on the other side of the door held it open twelve inches wider, expecting me to squeeze my way through. Good thing for me that I was both small in stature and thin, otherwise I wouldn't have made it through.

Once on the other side, it took my eyes a few seconds to get used to the darkness of the room. Although it was nighttime outside, the moon was incredibly bright and now I felt like I'd just been thrown into a pitch-black cave. After a few seconds, my eyes adjusted and I found myself at the end of a long hallway. I could hear the sounds of Rihanna's "Rude Boy" in the distance, raucous laughter punctuating the song.

"This way," the person at the entrance said gruffly. I didn't recognize the thuggish looking guy although I could tell he was a troll of some sort—whether from the Netherworlds of Scandinavia or Britain, I had no clue. He encompassed an enormous amount of space with his head nearly touching the ceiling. It would have, if not for the exaggerated hump on his back that caused him to hunch over to support its massive weight. He looked like a giant with osteoporosis. As if the hump on his back weren't enough to ensure he wouldn't win any beauty contests, he also walked with a limp. It was as if his left side had suffered from a stroke, his foot dragging behind him. All in all, I felt like I was on my way to visit Victor Frankenstein and his lab of horrors, Igor leading the way.

I followed the troll down the darkly lit hallway which T-boned into another corridor. Not only had I never been in this section of No Regrets, I never even knew it existed. Yep, Bram was a sneaky one. We took a left and continued down the passage until we came to a door. The troll whipped out a key ring, which was maybe ten inches wide, and gripping the longest key out of the bunch, unlocked the door, motioning for me to enter. When I did, I found myself in the midst of yet another corridor. I followed the troll when he made a right, suddenly feeling like I was in a maze. I definitely had no idea how to get back out again. The music from the main section of the club now sounded distant and muffled.

"How much farther?" I asked. "I forgot my walking shoes."

The troll just "humphed" as if laughing at a joke, stupid though mine might have been, was entirely beyond him. He said nothing, but paused in front of another door before rapping his beefy knuckles against it, panting as he tried to catch his breath.

"Announce yourself," came Bram's voice from the other side.

"Your visitor is here," the troll breathed back, his tone of voice reminding me of Rensfield, Dracula's servant. Hmmm, how fitting.

"You may enter," Bram responded and the troll groaned as he turned the doorknob and opened the door, leaning against it for support. Immediately, I recognized Bram's office—the white, red and black motif being hard to forget. Twin red velvet armchairs sat atop the plush white carpet in the middle of the room. Both the walls and ceiling were painted black, making it feel like I was actually standing outside, under the night sky. The only things missing were some twinkling lights to act the part of the stars.

Bram was sitting on one of the red velvet armchairs, his right leg crossed over his left knee and his hands clasped beneath his chin as if he were Madonna, striking a pose.

I walked through the door and turned around to watch the troll close and lock it behind me. Only then did I realize the reason I'd never noticed this door before—it was conveniently disguised as a bookcase. Clever, Bram, really clever.

"If you're going for Rodin's Thinker, your posture is a little off," I said as I glanced over at him again, my hands on my hips. He was always predictable in his attempts to appear important.

He stood up and approached me, frowning as he observed my newly dyed hair. "Dulcie, sweet, you have done this to yourself again?" Then he shook his head as if he thought it was a damn pity. "It is not a good look."

"I didn't do it for looks, dumbass," I grumbled back, not wanting to get into a long, drawn-out explanation. He ran a strand of my hair through his fingers, "tsking" at it with obvious displeasure. I didn't pull away.

"Then why did you do it?" he asked glumly, maybe taking offense to being called a "dumbass."

"It's all part of the game," I said simply.

"I do not care for it," Bram replied as he arched his eyebrows as if to further emphasize his disapproval.

"Well I don't care that you don't care so I guess we're even."

Bram threw his head back and chuckled heartily, not making any attempt to maintain personal space between the two of us. Instead, he looked at me with amused eyes, a smile pulling at his plump lips. "I believe it must be your distinctive scent that so intoxicates me."

167

I shook my head with a deep sigh, desperately searching for the patience to deal with him, but coming up short. "Bram, why is it that every time I see you, we have to go through this song and dance? Haven't we been through it enough times now that we can just bypass it?"

"I am always hopeful, my sweet," he started, while circling me as if he were inspecting a horse to purchase. He stopped walking when he was directly behind me and I could feel his gaze on my ass. I never encouraged this behavior and tonight was no different. I wasn't dressed up for the occasion, wearing fitted blue jeans and a v-necked, long-sleeved white T-shirt.

"Hopeful for what?" I snapped, even though I really wasn't looking forward to his answer. Things with Bram never seemed to change. I always had to play his little game of cat and mouse before he'd open up and tell me what I really needed to know.

Patience, Dulcie, patience.

I felt him grab a handful of my hair tightly at first, then loosening his grip, he draped it over my shoulder. At the touch of his fingertips along the sensitive skin of my shoulders, I got goose bumps.

"Hopeful that you will give in to me," he whispered into my ear, his fingertips following the line of my T-shirt to my front, before trailing down to the cleavage of my breasts. I grabbed his fingers once it seemed they were intent on further exploration.

"A for your effort, Bram," I said, turning around to face him. "Whatever acting classes you've been taking, they're paying off. I bet you could even outdo Brando in *A Streetcar Named Desire*."

He frowned and sighed loudly to show his lack of amusement. "One night with you, sweet, would cure me of this insatiable hunger." His gaze moved from my eyes to my bust and back up to my eyes again as he smiled broadly. "Of that I am certain."

It almost sounded worthwhile. Just one night of sex (which would probably result in a wham, bam, thank you, Bram) and he'd no doubt get over me, relegating me to all his other conquests he grew bored with. Yes, it all sounded fine and good until I got to the sex part. "Sorry, can't help you there," I said with an apologetic smile. "Now how about you tell me why you wanted to see me? And what's with that maze of hallways?"

Bram pouted but at the steely expression in my eyes, he dropped the pout. "I have been thinking about you, sweet," he said as he led us to the red chairs in the center of the room again. He sat in the one he'd previously occupied and motioned for me to take the other. I did and faced him expectantly.

"And what's with all the secretive stuff?"

He shrugged as if it should be obvious. "I didn't want your presence here known." Then he nodded as if he were seeking more time to say whatever he intended to say. "I have been quite worried about you."

I frowned, not buying this story for one second. Emotions like worry and caring had no place in Bram's world. "Well, you couldn't have been that worried, considering you're just broaching this subject now," I said as I arched one brow at him skeptically. I'd been up to my eyes in chaos for at least the last two weeks, so Bram's timing was definitely tardy.

He nodded as if I had a point. "Yes, sweet, I was quite overcome by the fact that I was experiencing any human emotion at all. It took a few days for me to come to terms with it."

I just shook my head and rolled my eyes. "You are truly one of a kind, Bram." He smiled with fangs and I couldn't help shrinking back into my seat. Sometimes Bram could be ... slightly intimidating. But it was never wise to reveal one's fear to a vampire, especially this one. I sat up straight and glared at him. "Why did you want me to come here?"

Bram nodded and eyed me narrowly, his jaw tight. "I have been battling myself over whether or not to reach out to you ... dare I say it? To help you."

"Really? Let me guess, you looked inward and discovered you actually had a heart, after all."

He frowned as if he didn't find my comment amusing and looked down his nose at me. "I do care for you, more than I prefer to say."

"Well, I care for you too, Bram," I said, feeling a little forced to reciprocate. I mean, it was obvious he had information for me and the best way to obtain it was by being nice and appreciative. I had to admit that a part of me, (albeit a very small part), actually felt sorry for Bram because he seemed so helplessly infatuated with me. Furthermore, it wasn't like him to go out on a limb like he always did for me, especially since he was the most narcissistic, self-centered, egomaniacal person I'd ever met.

He smiled broadly at that, and almost looked innocent. Almost. Then the smile on his lips dropped and he inhaled dramatically, which was ridiculous, considering he had no respiratory system. "All hope is not lost," he said simply.

It was my turn to take a deep breath and count to ten before I lost my temper. "What does that mean?"

"Last we spoke, you intimated that you were 'in deep,' is how I believe you termed it, with your father's business?" he asked as I nodded, eager for him to continue, which he did. "There is a way out."

I felt my eyes go wide as my heart sped up. "A way out ... of what?"

"Your situation with Melchior O'Neil."

I didn't say anything for a few seconds, my surprise overwhelming me. "And what is the way out?" I asked finally.

Bram arched a brow, but remained quiet as if he were still debating over whether or not to tell me what was on his mind. "It is called The Resistance," he said simply. His silence told me if I sought any more information, he wanted me to dig for it. It was like trying to have a serious conversation with the Sphinx, who only offered riddles.

I reminded myself to keep my cool since I should have expected this. Conversations with Bram amounted to playing the game of Twenty Questions—me asking the questions and his answers amounting to no more than tidbits of what basically seemed like nonsense. "What is The Resistance?"

"An underground movement," he started, and when I hoped he'd expound, he simply stopped talking again. Yep, my work was cut out for me and this was going to be tiring.

I sighed. "What underground?"

He shook his head, as if irritated that he had to go back to the beginning. "There is an underground ..."

"Where?"

"It does not exist anywhere," he snapped. "The underground is termed so because it is a hush-hush society. And in this underground, there has arisen a group who call themselves The Resistance."

"And what are they resisting?" I asked, although I had a pretty good guess where Bram was going with this explanation.

"They resist your father's rule," he said simply. "They resist servitude, dictatorship and tyranny." All the things my father advocated.

Although I sort of had been half expecting to hear the words from his lips, I still couldn't conceal the shock that made me inhale sharply. "How many are there?"

Bram shook his head. "I do not know."

"Are you part of The Resistance, Bram?"

He eyed me hungrily, arching one of his brows. "No, although I have their ear."

That was how Bram did most things in his life—he was always on the periphery, never quite involved enough to get his hands dirty, and far enough away to avoid reprisals.

"Then who is the leader?"

Bram shook his head. "I am not at liberty to say."

"Okay then, what can The Resistance do about my father? Are they actually a legitimate threat?" Bram studied me for a moment or two, and it was almost as if he were sizing me up, trying to judge whether or not he could trust me. "Bram, I want nothing more than to put this lifestyle and the tyranny of my father behind me. You should know me well enough by now to realize that."

He dropped his suspicious expression and merely nodded, apparently convinced of my loyalty.

"Are they a real threat to my father?" I repeated. "Can they take him down?"

Bram simply nodded. "They continue to recruit sympathizers to the cause daily. The Resistance is stronger now than it has ever been and, yes, I consider them a compelling threat."

And that was when I realized Bram was right—there was a way out of this mess and I had a feeling this Resistance was just the ticket. As to Knight's safety? I'd already worked that one out. When I met with Caressa, that would be the first topic I discussed. And once Knight's safety was secured, I believed The Resistance would be the best force to dethrone my father and strip him of his power permanently. Well, that is, as long as their army was large enough to take on my father's.

"I need to meet with them," I said urgently. "I need to tell them everything I know so we can stop my father together."

Bram held up his hands to quiet me down. "It is a secret society, sweet, and if they knew I had broken their trust by relaying this information to you, they would never forgive me and my relationship with them would be destroyed."

I frowned and hunched back into my seat. "So what should I do then? How am I supposed to get into touch with them?"

"They will call for you when the time is right," he said simply. "Until then, I have their ear."

I suddenly realized what he was getting at. He wanted me to spill the beans, and like playing a game of telephone, he would pass the information on. At this point, I had to seriously weigh my options and more specifically, my trust in Bram. Because just as Bram lived on the periphery of doing good, he also lived on the periphery of doing not so good. It wouldn't have come as an enormous surprise, consequently, to learn that Bram was employed by my father. I doubted he was, but how could I really be sure?

I eyed him speculatively as the conflict of whether or not to trust him continued to rage inside my head.

"Shall I provide you with some information to prove that all I have said is true?" he asked as I realized my emotions were as visible as the nose on my face.

I just nodded and watched him smile and study me for a few moments before he opened his mouth to speak again. "Were you notified of a certain letter to the ANC which warned ..."

But he never was able to finish his sentence. Instead, my mouth dropped open and I interrupted him. "That was you?" I asked, dawning realization instantly replacing the shock on my face. "You left the note with the ANC?"

Bram simply nodded. "Although there was no need to."

"Why?"

He leaned back against his chair and stretched like a cat. "The Resistance has eyes and ears everywhere, Dulcie sweet."

"In the ANC?" I asked, stunned, as I tried to imagine who could be the eyes and ears in our office. Trey? Elsie? Lottie, the super annoying pixie? Sam? I gulped. Knight?

"Everywhere," Bram said simply while buffing his nails against his lapel. "The note was a mere test."

I swallowed hard, disliking the sound of that. "A test?"

He nodded and glanced at me, his eyes suddenly harsh. "A test to evaluate what happened to the highly valuable information."

I realized then that I'd failed the so-called test. I sat back in Bram's chair and felt like I might pass out because my heart was beating so quickly. My stomach dropped to the floor. "I told Quillan, Bram," I said in a small voice, shaking my head as I realized the extent of my mistake. "I did exactly what I shouldn't have."

Bram nodded, but there was no sign of disappointment or blame in his eyes. They were uncannily hollow, devoid of emotion. "It will be difficult for you to gain their trust," he said while raising his brows to emphasize the sentiment. "You cannot play both sides of the coin."

"I had no choice!" I railed back at him, my voice sounding slightly hysterical. "I have to do what my father says because Knight's life is on the line!"

But Bram's lips were tight as he studied me. "The choices we make are ultimately our own responsibility," he said, adding, "Eleanor Roosevelt."

I nodded, because he was right. I couldn't play both sides. If I wanted The Resistance to trust me, I couldn't feed their information to Melchior. "What do I do, Bram?" I asked, in a flat tone.

"You make your decision and then stick with it," he answered.

I decided then to tell him everything I knew—everything about the *Draoidheil*, my father's dreams for

absolute rule, my plan to visit Caressa, everything. If Bram
had the "ear of The Resistance" even though they weren't
yet prepared to trust me, he could be my vehicle to reach
them. That's all there was to it. So I spilled my guts about
everything, naming names, places, events. I must have
blabbed for a good ten minutes straight before I had to come
up for air.

"I see," Bram said at last. With a single nod, he let it
be known that he'd digested everything I'd just regurgitated.

"Can you tell them everything for me?" I asked,
perched on the edge of my seat.

But he shook his head. "There is no guarantee that
they would trust me with such information."

My heart dropped and I clenched my eyes shut tightly
as I rubbed my temples, wondering why I'd bothered
explaining everything if he wasn't going to do anything with
the information.

"You must stick to your plan and visit Caressa," Bram
said firmly.

"Is Caressa in The Resistance?" I asked, my eyes
going wide.

Bram simply shook his head. "No, but her word is
valued much more highly than mine. If I were to deliver
your information, it would only be as good as an
anonymous note."

"They would doubt its validity?" I asked, although I
saw the truth in his words. Anything that came from
Caressa, a highly ranked officer of the ANC, would never
be questioned. And I was sure whoever comprised this
Resistance was well aware that Caressa detested my father.
Even though she'd never said as much, it was obvious.
Which meant she must have a friend in The Resistance.
Yep, I was spot on when I'd decided to talk to Caressa. She
really was the only person left capable of preventing the
Draoidheil delivery from going as Melchior planned.

"Very good, Dulcie sweet," Bram said as he stood up, indicating that our meeting was over.

"Thanks," I said, eyeing the bookshelf, trying to decipher where the doorway was. "How the hell am I supposed to find my way out of here?"

Bram smiled and then shook his head. "You may use the front entrance. I was unaware of your altered appearance," he finished, with a dismayed glance at my hair again. "You look nothing like Dulcie O'Neil."

I just shook my head and rolled my eyes, inwardly pleased that I wouldn't have to retrace my steps through the maze again with Igor. "I'll be swift and discreet," I said.

"I will instruct Harper to pick you up at the front door," Bram continued.

"Harper?" I couldn't help but laugh.

Bram didn't share my amusement as he held the door to his office open for me. Before I could take a step forward, I suddenly felt Bram right next to me, his arms around me. He leaned over and placed a kiss on my cheek, dangerously close to my lips.

"We shall be in touch," he said with a suggestive smile.

I raised my brows, lacking the energy to bitch at him for stealing a kiss. Instead, I turned around to face No Regrets, only to find Knight sitting at the end of the bar, staring at me.

FIFTEEN

I must have stopped breathing for at least a few seconds; and in those seconds, I simply watched Knight glare at me and shake his head angrily, his jaw so tight it looked like it might snap right off his face. He glanced from me to Bram, who I guessed was still standing behind me, and then simply downed his drink, dropping a twenty on the bar before standing up and leaving.

I didn't go after him because I knew better. There wasn't anything I could say—I mean, yes, I could have run after him and sworn it wasn't what I was sure he thought it was. But to what end? It wasn't like I could get back together with Knight, well, not anytime soon anyway. I still had to figure out everything with my father and Caressa, not to mention The Resistance. I could only hope that once the dust settled (if it ever did settle), Knight and I could work things out because the truth of the matter was that I was absolutely in love with him and hated every second of this game I had to play.

But saving his life was worth playing it, I had to remind myself.

After leaving Bram, I went home, but I couldn't sleep all night. I just tossed and turned as I imagined what Knight must be thinking. With me leaving Bram's office, him leaning down and kissing me and me not attempting to bitch slap him, it had to look like there was something between us. Throw in the fact that I wasn't currently working on any cases at the ANC which meant I really had no reason to visit Bram and I must have looked guilty as charged. And the icing on the cake? The Rolex my father had given me, which I'd failed to convince Knight had been my purchase. If anyone had the kind of money for such an extravagant gift, it was Bram. Yep, I could only imagine Knight thought there was a whole lot more going on between Bram and me than there was. And that made me sick to my stomach.

I tried to push the thoughts from my mind in favor of sleeping. I even downed two Tylenol PMs around one a.m., but by the time eight a.m. rolled by, I was still wide awake and hadn't managed to get a wink of sleep all night. Finally abandoning it as a lost cause, I got up, fed Blue and started the coffee. I thought I should eat something, but my nerves were on full speed ahead and food would only disagree with my stomach. Instead, I started fretting over my plan to visit Caressa today—well, Hades willing, anyway. I'd already rehearsed the plan repeatedly through my mind, trying to imagine any and every obstacle that might possibly arise as well as a solution to them.

By the time nine o'clock rolled by, I'd dressed in my flower delivery costume, curled my hair into a frizzy mess and painted my face full of makeup, even indulging myself with a beauty mark just below my right nostril. I definitely didn't look like me, which was exactly the point.

Glancing down at my portal compass watch for the tenth time since getting up this morning, I made sure I remembered Quill's instructions on how to use it, and outlined each step in my head. After that little task, I looked at the vials of antidote that stood on my kitchen table, where I'd placed them the previous night with the express purpose of not forgetting them this morning. Next to the vials was a long piece of white ribbon and a pair of scissors, which would come in handy later on.

Checking the clock, I realized it was nearly nine thirty and time for me to go. The flower shop opened at ten a.m. and was located in the city center so it would take me a good twenty minutes to get there. I'd already called in sick this morning to the ANC, even though I didn't expect Knight to care. He'd probably be glad not to have to see me, if he were even there today.

Pushing thoughts of Knight from my mind, I grabbed my helmet and the keys to my bike, throwing the vials, ribbon, scissors and the letter to Caressa into my backpack. I supposed I could have taken the Mercedes, but the truth of the matter was that I wanted nothing to do with my father. Not when I was about to rat his ass out. Instead, I took a deep breath, remembered that in two days time, the *Draoidheil* was scheduled for delivery, and headed for the door.

The drive to the florist took exactly twenty minutes, just according to plan. And because I was their first customer of the day, I was in and out in another thirty minutes, sans forty dollars, but with a large bouquet of Casablanca lilies and red roses. I crammed the arrangement in my backpack, making sure it fit snugly and only zipped it up on one side, allowing the lilies and roses to poke out of the top. Then I started for the freeway that would take me out of Splendor toward Estuary.

I was going after the most remote portal, one which was located off an old, single lane, fire road with nothing but cows and trees nearby. Once I hit the street, aptly titled FireHouse Road, I searched for the telltale sign of a white picket fence on one side, denoting a nearby farm, and an open lake on the other. I found it without issue and pulled to the side of the road, steering the Ducati behind a large tree beside the lake. After I felt confident I was alone, I looked down at my portal watch.

The dial was spinning in circles, which meant it had picked up on the portal's energy. Now it was just a matter of dialing into the right location and then specifying the area in the Netherworld in which I wanted to arrive. I took a few steps toward the lake and noticed the dial starting to slow down, still making large loops around the face of the watch, but not nearly as quickly as it had before. I was on the right track. I continued forward, and the dial on my watch continued to slow. Once it stopped, so did I as I found myself facing the lake, the water's edge only about two feet from mine.

The portal I wanted to connect with in the Netherworld was located on the third floor of the ANC building, down the hallway from Caressa's office. It was supposed to be located in the women's restroom, which seemed the perfect site, considering I'd have to adjust my wardrobe before delivering the arrangement.

I checked my watch again and took a step to the right, noticing the hour hand moving from twelve o'clock to one o'clock. I was almost there. It needed to be aligned with two o'clock. I took another step and the hand paused as the minute hand indicated thirty minutes. One-thirty. Another mini step brought the placement to one-forty-five. Another mini step and I was at two o'clock.

I reached my hand forward and felt the difference in the air immediately. The air in the portal was viscous, gel-like to the touch and balmy. Now was the moment of reckoning. I put my backpack on the ground, pulled my T-shirt over my head until I was standing in just my jeans, sneakers and bra. Then clutching the backpack in one hand and my T-shirt in the other, I leaped forward.

I was starting to get used to the feeling of portal travel, sort of like landing in a gigantic, warm gummy bear. But only a second later, you get shot out into a much colder atmosphere and have to take a deep breath to get your bearings straight. After experiencing exactly that, I took another big breath and found myself standing in the middle of a restroom.

Portal travel? No problem.

I could feel my idiotic wings sprouting from my back, only to begin frantically beating as I started to rise into the air. I lurched forward and grabbed hold of the sink with the hand that was also still clutching onto my T-shirt. I managed to station myself in place as I put the backpack in the basin before me. Then, while holding onto the sink with my other hand, I unzipped my backpack all the way and pulled out the bouquet. I propped it between the mirror and the faucet. Then I unzipped the backpack, taking out the scissors and the ribbon. My wings had started to calm down so I carefully released the sink, testing myself to see if I was going to start floating again. Luckily for me, it seemed I was finally earthbound, my wings only beating every few seconds.

I continued to breathe in and breathe out slowly, trying to calm my wings to make them stop flapping entirely. After a few minutes, it seemed they got the point and lay dormant against my back. That was my cue. I picked up the ribbon and holding each end between my fingers, draped it over my neck, and pulled it down until it rested against my back at chest level. I pulled the ribbon tight against my wings, then I looped it over my neck again and tightened it a bit lower, making a crisscross sort of pattern along my back. Once I was convinced my wings couldn't break free of the pseudo prison, I tied the ribbon in a knot right above my breasts and trimmed the excess with the scissors. Then I pulled my T-shirt back over my head and carefully smoothed it down over my wings. Turning to glance at my profile in the mirror, my wings were small enough that they folded nicely beneath my shirt. Granted, they still appeared slightly lumpy, but lumpy I could handle. It was the flying I couldn't.

I grabbed the bouquet and retrieved the note from the backpack, folding it in half and then half again so it just fit in my palm. Then I wadded my backpack up into as tight a bundle as I could and jammed it into the corner of the restroom, pulling the silver trash bin in front to conceal it. Yes, I was concerned about leaving the vials of antidote in the restroom unattended, but I was more concerned with being caught and as part of that, being questioned and detained. I mean, I had bypassed the whole front desk, sign-in procedure so it wasn't a stretch to imagine someone might have questions for me if I were caught.

Steeling my courage with a big breath, I pulled the restroom door open and started down the hallway, pleased that no one else seemed to be out and about. I held the bouquet up high, so that it partially concealed my face and started scouting the nameplates along the walls outside each office. I wasn't sure if Caressa's assistant, Alex, would be stationed outside Caressa's office, but I hoped she wasn't. I was afraid that Alex might recognize me, even through my clown makeup. And if Alex did recognize me, I wasn't sure what she'd do.

When I was halfway down the hall, I noticed Caressa's nameplate on the wall, outside of an undersized office, the walls made of glass. She was sitting at her desk, eating lunch as far as I could tell. No one else was with her. I felt my heart start beating hopefully.

You're going to be fine, Dulcie, I told myself. *It's now or never.*

I knocked on the glass door and when Caressa glanced up from where she'd been poring over a magazine, she nodded her head, giving me silent affirmation to enter. I did and swallowed hard as I closed the door behind me.

"I've gotta delivery for Caressa Brandenburg," I said, making my voice sound high pitched and nasally. "Are you she?"

She placed what looked like a PB&J sandwich back on the brown paper sack beside the magazine and studied me suspiciously. "No one from the lobby alerted me that I had any deliveries. They just let you up here?"

"No one was there," I said, shrinking beneath her stringent gaze. "So I just let myself in." I frowned and offered her an apologetic smile. "Maybe whoever was manning the desk had to go to the bathroom," I added.

She shrugged and eyed the bouquet with unconcealed interest as I watched her. Caressa was a shape-shifter; she could shift into a cheetah, and overall had the look of a cat; it was evident in her eyes and high cheekbones. She was tall, probably five foot eight, with long brown, wavy hair and blond highlights. Her eyes were nearly the same shade of blue as Knight's. All told, Caressa Brandenburg was beautiful and intimidating as shit.

"Who are the flowers from?" she demanded, suspiciously.

I shook my head to say I didn't know and walked right up to her, handing her the arrangement. She studied me for a second or two and I could see recognition in her eyes, although it was clouded with confusion. She was trying to place me.

"I'm not at liberty to say," I replied, sounding like Mickey Mouse. Then I handed her the note.

She watched me curiously, but accepted the letter and unfolded it, honing in on the words. Her eyes twitched as she read it. Immediately, her expression dropped and she gulped hard. Then she suddenly seemed to recognize me. She said nothing, but simply looked down at the letter again and her expression changed from one of shock to appreciation. A huge smile plastered itself across her lips and she shook her head in apparent amusement.

"Wow, how sweet of him," she said, smiling up at me. "They're from the guy I'm seeing."

Immediately, I caught on to her. Obviously, it wasn't safe to talk in her office and she was playing into my game to throw off anyone who could be listening or watching us via a surveillance system. She apparently finished reading the letter because in a matter of seconds, she reached over and fed it into a paper shredder below her desk, destroying it per my request.

"Thank you for the delivery, they are lovely," she said, with an artificial smile. "I need to get some water for them," she added as she reached for a vase in the hutch behind her desk. When she stood up, I noticed the cast on her foot and then the crutches leaning against the wall behind her.

"Allow me," I said, reaching for the bouquet, but with my eyes, I asked her: *Where can we talk in private?*

She handed me the vase and smiled appreciatively. "Thank you, we can fill it in the restroom just down the hall."

I simply nodded, figuring it made sense that the only place where cameras wouldn't be allowed would be the restroom. Apparently, there was a certain level of respect for privacy even in the Netherworld. I turned around, and with Caressa by my side, headed back down the hallway. When we reached the restroom, I held the door open for her and followed her inside. Before either of us said a word, I bent over and scanned under each stall for feet. There weren't any. We were alone.

Caressa reached over and turned on the water.

"Did you memorize the drop-off locations and times?" I asked, my voice barely a whisper.

She simply nodded. "I made sure I had everything stored in my mind before I destroyed your letter. Lucky for you I've got a photographic memory." She paused and took a deep breath, obviously displeased with the information. "Where did you get ..." she started.

I shook my head. "We don't have time, and even if we did, I can't tell you. All I can tell you is that this is a dire situation. You need to get every ANC person you have in the know and at least three in each of the locations I specified in that letter. And ..." I reached for the backpack which was still behind the trashcan. I fished inside it until I found the two vials of antidote and handed them to her. "Make sure everyone takes one of these prior to arriving at each destination. Otherwise they'll become addicts within seconds of the stuff being released into the air."

"How long will the antidote last?" she asked.

I wasn't exactly sure, so I just answered, "Long enough."

She nodded and accepted both vials, opening her jacket and placing them in a pocket beside her Op 6 which was holstered across her chest. "Are you sure that's the extent of the traffickers who will be at each location?" she asked. "I don't want to set my people up to be outmanned."

I shook my head. "As far as I know, but it would probably behoove you to plan for more, rather than less."

"And the Dryads? They can't survive for more than a few hours outside of the forest."

I nodded and sighed deeply. "That will also have to be part of the ANC's job —to get the Dryads back safely."

She said nothing, but breathed in deeply and then nodded, as if approving of my plan to ensure the safety of the Dryads. Thank God. "He's responsible for this, isn't he?" she asked. It didn't take a genius to figure out she was referring to Melchior.

I didn't deny it, but neither did I confirm it; instead, I raised a subject far more important. "I need you to make sure Knight is as far away from Splendor as possible," I continued. "Once the *Draoidheil* comes through, his life will be in danger."

She glanced down at me with concern in her eyes. "Why?"

I shook my head. "I can't get into it. I've already stayed here too long. You just need to ensure that Knight is elsewhere—wherever he's least likely to be found. And give him orders to leave Splendor today." After all, there were only two days remaining before the *Draoidheil* was scheduled to arrive, only two days remaining before the shit was really going to hit the fan.

"Okay," she said and then paused, studying me intently. "Are you in trouble?"

"Up to my ears." I took a deep breath. "That's the other thing, do NOT tell anyone that I came here or that I gave you this information. If it gets out that it was me, Knight will be the one to suffer, do you understand?"

She frowned. "Crystal clear."

SIXTEEN

The days leading up to the *Draoidheil* delivery passed by in a blur while the moments before we were due at the docks seemed to go by at a snail's pace. For the last twenty-four hours, I was on autopilot, just going through the motions of living my life (including magicking my purple-black hair back to my natural honey gold), fully aware that everything I knew was about to change drastically

After tonight, when Melchior's plan went awry, my father would be fully aware that something *was* rotten in the state of Splendor. I had to imagine it wouldn't be a stretch to realize I was the one with the loose lips. As soon as Melchior discovered that Knight was no longer in Splendor and unaccounted for, it would be obvious that I was the mastermind. Yep, I would be the one to destroy my father's dreams of despotism. And what did that mean for me? Well, honestly, I hadn't even thought that far ahead. But considering it now, en route to the loading docks, with Quillan as my only companion, I realized my neck would soon be on the chopping block.

"Are you okay, Dulce?" Quill asked. He was driving the red Mercedes my father lent me. With my current state of nerves and anxiety, I didn't think driving myself was a good idea.

According to plan, it was just going to be Quill and me working on the loading docks. We were supposed to meet up with Baron and Horatio to receive six shipments of *Draoidheil*. After securing the crates in the Mercedes, we would take them to Ink, where we would store them in the cellar until further word from Melchior. Christina was supposed to do the same at the abandoned railway station, also in Splendor, with three sidekicks provided by my father.

"Yeah, I'm okay," I said with a sigh when I noticed the concerned smile on his handsome face. As I took in the sweet expression in his eyes and the fullness of his lips, I suddenly wished things were completely different. I wished I could rewind time to how things were a year ago, before I discovered my so-called friends were illegal potions importers. And before I'd become one too.

"Do you ever think about how things used to be?" I asked him in a small, wistful voice, the seatbelt across my chest suddenly binding and tight.

He nodded and chewed on his lower lip for a second or two as his eyes seemed to glaze over with something that resembled nostalgia. "I live in my memories, Dulcie," he said softly. "The only way I've been able to survive is to relive the memories I once found so much enjoyment in."

My lips went tight. "You realize that's not living, right, Quill?" When he didn't respond, I continued. "He's reduced us to this." I shook my head, hating my father with every cell in my body.

"We don't have to endure this alone," Quill said, reaching over to pat my knee consolingly. I eyed him with surprise, and when he didn't move his hand, I moved it for him. "You used to care about me, Dulcie," he said, apologetically, his eyes boring into mine.

"Yeah, a long time ago."

"Once you called me your hero," he continued and I couldn't swallow the frog that lodged in my throat. He was referring to the protagonist of a romance novel I'd been writing who had been modeled after him. And, to be fair, once upon a time he had been my hero. But if I'd learned anything in the last year or so, it was that "once upon a time" didn't exist. Fairy tales depicting happily ever afters were just that: tales ... lies ... crocks of total shit.

"I could be your hero again, Dulcie."

"Quill," I began, unhappy with the direction this conversation seemed to be headed. Things were as different now as night and day; and the feelings I'd once felt for him had changed.

But Quill shook his head. "I think about you constantly, about us, about what could have been." He hit a red light and used it to his advantage, turning to face me as he spilled the contents of his heart. It made me feel like a total asshole because I didn't want to hear any of it. "I've felt your passion for me, Dulcie. I've kissed you and I know you enjoyed it. I want to know what it means to taste you again."

I took a deep breath and riveted my attention out the window, knowing that tonight I would not only betray my father but Quillan as well. And what was more, he would remember this exact moment, this conversation, and he'd probably hate me for it.

"We could be happy together," he said, breaking the silence in the car that was now suffocating me. The light changed to green and he started forward. The docks loomed into view.

I faced him, my eyes harsh. "We'll never find happiness doing this," I said acidly. "This is no way to live and you know it."

"I would live my life around you. You're the only thing that brings me any joy anyway."

"You have to stop talking to me like this," I said, diverting my eyes, not able to stomach the expression of pain in his gaze.

Quill laughed an ugly sound as he took a right on the road that led down to the docks. We were twenty minutes early and there was no sign of Baron or Horatio anywhere. Neither was there a sign of anyone from the ANC. As far as I could tell, Quill and I were the first to arrive.

"Things will never be the same between you and Vander," Quill said, seemingly enjoying holding my tattered relationship with Knight over my head. "You occupy opposite worlds now and the sooner you realize that, the better. You need to move on."

"Move on with you?" I snapped, turning to glare at him, even as I told myself to cool it but I couldn't seem to keep my anger in check. I was so overwhelmed with rage and fear about the unfolding events that I felt like a ticking time bomb.

"You cared for me once," he said simply.

I shook my head. "We are not having this conversation right now."

Quill said nothing more, but parked the Mercedes in the lot just beside the docks. Faced with the silence between us, I undid my seatbelt, opened the car door and stepped out into the dark night. I stared up at the stars, feeling the cold, salty air dance with my hair, shifting it this way and that. Watching the stars twinkle back at me, I suddenly yearned to be anywhere but here. For once I actually wished my fairy wings would sprout from my back and carry me away with the gentle winds.

"Where the fuck you been?" I heard Baron's voice and turned around, feeling dismay fill my gut as my heart dropped. He stood maybe six feet from me, leering at me as if I were naked. And I was far from naked—clad in my yoga pants, tennies and a long-sleeved black T-shirt. I'd strapped daggers to my upper arms and my Op 6 was snugly holstered around my waist and hidden beneath my zippered sweatshirt.

"We didn't see you," Quill said as he stepped out of the car and came up behind me. Horatio appeared out of the darkness, standing beside Baron. I checked my watch and noticed it was five minutes from show time.

As soon as I brought my eyes back up to face Baron, I heard what sounded like paper tearing, only much louder. It resounded in the air, somewhere off to my right. I felt like I was in slow motion as I turned and saw four men, dressed in grey and black uniforms, suddenly materializing from thin

air. It was as if the sky had just spat them out. Clutched in
their hands were firearms—some long-barreled, like rifles,
and others small and short, like my Op 6. Obviously, they'd
just come through a portal. But as to who they were, I had
no clue. As soon as they got their bearings, they faced us
and I recognized their Netherworld uniforms.

They began to fan out, forming an arc in front of what
I assumed was the same portal they'd just come through.

"Who the hell are you?" Baron spat out.

"Security," the man nearest me answered, with a
frown aimed at Baron before settling his gaze on me.

"And who sent you?" Baron continued, visibly
affronted that whoever it was obviously didn't trust us
enough to handle things on our own. Yep, must have been
good ol' Dad.

"The Head of the Netherworld," the same man
responded. My heart sped up as I realized what this meant
for the ANC. I'd already told Caressa it would just be Baron,
Horatio, and Quill to contend with. I could only hope she'd
decided to beef up the ANC numbers, like I'd suggested
when we spoke, or this could have a very bad outcome.

"When's the delivery?" the uniformed guard that
spoke to us earlier piped up.

I glanced at my watch and realized the *Draoidheil* was
due to hit any second. So where the hell was the ANC? I got
the sinking feeling that maybe Caressa had failed to
remember all the destination points or maybe she simply
hadn't believed me?

A few seconds later, there was another sound of the
air ripping apart and the night sky suddenly produced two
women. They fell against the asphalt, although one quickly
regained her senses and assisted the other, who seemed
completely out of it, with a panic-stricken expression. They
were dressed in outdated, empire-waisted gowns, the hems
of which touched the ground. Their sleeves were also long,
so long that they obscured their fingers. Their hair was

191

gossamer and delicate—cascading down to their elbows and giving them an ethereal look. Not exactly like angels, but more like the girls from Little House on the Prairie. I had to assume they were Dryads.

Both Dryads stared at their surroundings as if trying to understand where they were, both becoming anxious when they saw the guards in uniform, along with Quill, Baron and then Horatio. When they spotted me, they instantly made a beeline in my direction, only to cower behind me. I imagined they weren't comfortable around men, seeing as how they'd come' from a convent and all. I could hear soft whimpering and when I turned around, I realized the situation wasn't getting any better. The one with dark hair was leaning against the blond, her breathing shallow and coming in spurts. Both of them looked petrified, their eyes wide. They clung to one another, obviously in terror.

"Is she okay?" I asked the blond, then turned to face her friend whose eyes were clamped tightly shut, her face pale, and sweat beading on her forehead.

The blond looked at me and shook her head. When she opened her mouth, words didn't come out, but sounds did. Sounds that I can only compare to the voice of Charlie Brown's teacher. So the Dryads were unable to communicate? Fantastic.

I couldn't concentrate on the Dryads much longer because what sounded like thunder crashed into my ears and I turned to see another man come forth from nowhere, accompanied by the same sound of ripping paper. He wasn't dressed in the garb of the guards, but he was one of my father's, all the same. He stretched his arms forward and then his torso, half of him disappearing back into the portal. When he managed to pull himself out again, he was holding a large, plastic crate.

The crate was maybe three feet wide and two feet tall, with over one hundred vials of *Draoidheil* inside it. As soon as the crate made contact with the air on this side of the portal, one small vial flew up into the air, as if carried by invisible hands. Then the particles inside of it began swirling around, like the vortex of a tornado. The particles sped faster and faster until the cork seal flew off the top and the *Draoidheil* exploded into a mass of what looked like glitter. The sea breeze suddenly picked up the particles, scattering and lifting them even higher, and sprinkling them all around us.

Meanwhile, the man holding the crate passed it off to Quill as he leaned into the portal for the next one. I watched Quill take the crate and head for the Mercedes. He loaded it into the trunk and then jogged back to us again. The man pulled out the second crate and handed it to me. It only weighed about fifteen pounds, so wasn't a big deal. I carried it to the Mercedes, and slid it in next to the other one. When I stood up, I watched as the man in charge of delivering the crates handed another off to Baron. As soon as Baron touched it, the crate suddenly exploded in a mass of glass and *Draoidheil*. With a throaty scream, Baron dropped the crate, destroying the remaining vials. Before any of us could respond, the crate suddenly ignited in an array of orange and yellow flames. Both the Dryads began shrieking as they ran from the commotion, cringing in the hollows beneath the trees on the hillside next to the docks.

Obviously, the ANC had arrived to run interference. I slammed the trunk of the Mercedes and pulled my Op 6 from around my waist, holding it in low ready. Of course, I had no intentions of harming anyone on the ANC side, but I wanted to make sure I was armed and able to protect myself if and when I needed to. Anyone on the ANC side would naturally assume I was working with the bad guys.

With a swift look around me, I jogged away from the Mercedes, and away from the spotlights of streetlamps until I reached the line of shadows offered by the hillside trees. As soon as I touched the grass, an enormous blast issued from the direction I'd just come. With a gasp, I craned my neck toward the Mercedes and watched it jump a few feet in the air, suddenly exploding into a fireball of shrapnel and flames. I threw my arms over my head and fell forward, my face hitting the grass as I sought cover. When I sat up, the blond Dryad was sobbing. The other one lay still on the grass.

I didn't have the opportunity to inquire after her condition because chaos immediately enveloped us. The Regulators from the ANC must have made their move when the Mercedes exploded because they were now in hand-to-hand combat with Melchior's men. The cacophony of screaming, fists pounding flesh and gunfire filled my ears. I scurried to the top of the hill, taking shelter behind the crest of it. With my Op 6 in my hands, I searched for any sign of Quill, to make sure he was okay. I didn't know what I'd do if he wasn't. Could I shoot one of my own people if it meant saving Quill's life? I knew the answer to that was yes, especially given the fact that I didn't recognize anyone on the ANC side. But I wouldn't shoot to kill. I would shoot to debilitate only because I couldn't allow Quill to die. Not on my watch.

My plan was to retreat back into the shadows offered by the trees on the hilltop. Once I could hightail it across the street, I would to take cover in the lushness of overgrown bushes and pepper trees alongside the road. With the help of some of my fairy dust, I could shrink myself down to a mere sprite. Then I'd hide out in the branches of the pepper trees and wait until everyone cleared the scene. My life as a renegade had already begun because I obviously wasn't working for my father now. But it wasn't like I could just pick up the pieces and return to my previous life.

From my perspective, the ANC outnumbered Melchior's men and were increasingly gaining the advantage. Horatio and two of the guards had been apprehended, and all three were cuffed and under the surveillance of two ANC men. I could also make out the bodies of two other guards on the ground, obviously dead. As I continued to watch, another crate of *Draoidheil,* which was sitting beside one of the deceased guards, suddenly erupted in flames when what looked like a Molotov cocktail made contact with it. The ANC had employed a witch or some other kind of creature that was capable of sophisticated magic, because blowing the *Draoidheil* to Kingdom Come was no easy feat.

When the smoke dissipated, I could make out Quill's figure, also in cuffs and sitting beside Horatio. He was searching for me, his eyes scanning the horizon. When his gaze met mine, I could see the shock in their amber depths. It felt like minutes ticked by, but it was really only seconds that we stared at one another. And in his expression, it was obvious he knew that I'd ratted everyone out. Instead of throwing daggers and tightly fierce lips, he smiled at me. It was a proud smile —although I didn't understand why. Apparently, Quill was proud of what I'd done.

I didn't have the opportunity to further consider it as two ANC Regulators suddenly appeared at the base of the hill, each lifting a Dryad in his arms. I ducked down so I wouldn't be seen and when I looked again, they'd already disappeared through a portal, on their way to the forest where the Dryads dwelled.

It was time for me to make my move. Reholstering my Op 6, I crawled down the embankment and once I knew I was out of sight, stood up and turned around. I was about to dart across the street and take shelter behind the scraggily bushes beside the road when I found myself face-to-face with an enraged Baron.

We glared at one another for maybe three seconds as I'm sure the weight of my actions registered with him. His eyes narrowed as he growled and came for me, running full bore and plowing into me. He knocked me off my feet but when I fell, I didn't feel the bite of asphalt beneath me. Instead, it felt like I'd merely landed on an air pillow. I glanced down, shocked to find myself on the asphalt. Feeling a buzzing around my wrist, I pulled my sleeve up to find Sam's Viking Bracelet vibrating. So it *had* managed to protect me from harm. I couldn't help my smile but it was short lived as Baron, apparently realizing I was wearing an enchanted bracelet, lurched for it and ripped it off my wrist in a split second. He threw it on the ground and stomped on it, the chain weave collapsing beneath his immense weight. The beautiful stone broke in half as did my hopes of escaping Baron. Realizing he now had the upper hand, he grasped me around the neck and lifted me into the air, my feet lashing out as I gripped his forearms, digging my nails into his skin as I struggled to breathe. He released me while I was still in the air and I fell onto my back, the breath completely expelled from my lungs. I hit the ground hard and had to blink back the stars from my vision.

"You little back-stabbing bitch!" he railed as he slammed his enormous fist into my face. I felt my head snap back in response and bit my cheek hard. Suddenly feeling dizzy, I tried to force my eyes open, already feeling the blood trailing from my mouth down to my neck. I shook my palm until a mound of fairy dust appeared, but before I could throw it at him, he slammed my wrist against the ground, and the magical dust disappeared between my fingers. I forced my bleary vision on Baron's face and caught his ugly smile immediately.

"Yer not gittin' away from me this time," he said, reaching for my sweatshirt, he ripped it off me and then went for my T-shirt, shredding it in two. The tattered pieces fell on either side of me, revealing the daggers strapped to my upper arms. Baron shook his head but the smile on his mouth hinted to his elation as he pulled the daggers from their makeshift straps. He flung one down the hillside and held the other one at the base of my neck, the sharp point slightly piercing my skin.

"I could end you right now," he breathed and I gulped as the point pressed harder, cutting into me.

I felt my chest began to rise and fall as my heart rate increased. I was in full panic mode, and worse, Baron knew it. He lowered the blade and placed it between my breasts, his eyes suddenly feasting on the cleavage offered by my push-up bra.

Reaching for my gun, Baron quickly grabbed my wrist, pinning it to the ground painfully. Then, realizing he needed to have at least one free hand to molest me, he replaced his hands with his knees, thrusting his lower body directly into my face. This new position appeared to amuse him because he chuckled heartily. Holding the dagger above my right eye, he suddenly tossed it aside. It landed nearby, within twenty feet, but I had little interest in it. Instead, my immediate concern was Baron, who reached down to unzip his fly. I thrashed against him, kicking out and trying to nail him with my legs, but I was unsuccessful.

Before I could think of another strategy, he pulled himself free of his pants. I slammed my eyes shut tightly, trying to avoid what I imagined would be a hideous and traumatizing sight. Then, realizing his intentions, I clamped my jaws shut, telling myself not to open my mouth for anything, not even air, knowing what it might mean if I did.

"Open your mouth and take it," Baron demanded, slapping me across the face when I refused. I bucked beneath him and felt tears starting in my eyes, leaking down each side of my face.

"You filthy son of a bitch!" It was Knight's voice. I opened my eyes and watched Knight ram his Op 7 at the back of Baron's head. I brought my eyes to Knight's as I wondered if he would shoot. Before I could comprehend what was happening, Knight squeezed the trigger. I shut my eyes as the sound of gunfire assaulted my eardrums. Screaming out in shock, I opened my eyes, focusing on Baron's face as it came nearer to mine, complete with a bloody hole in the center of his forehead. His enormous body slumped on top of me, twitching in death. I tried to push him away from me, but Titans are an enormously heavy race, and Baron was no exception. A second or so later, Knight rolled Baron off me and offered me his hand.

I took it, not even knowing what to say as I realized he'd just killed Baron in cold blood. It was against ANC protocol one hundred percent. But when I looked into Knight's eyes, they were glowing eerily. It was the same glow they revealed whenever another man was near me, whenever another man hungered after me sexually. And then I understood. Knight realized I'd just come incredibly close to being raped and in his rage, he hadn't been able to stop himself from pulling the trigger.

"Knight," I started, as questions suddenly raced through my mind. *What was he doing here? Had he been here all along?*

I felt him yank me to my feet only to turn me around so my back was to him. Then he pushed me up against a nearby tree, and the bark scratched roughly against my cheek. He grabbed my arms, securing them behind my back as confusion clouded my mind.

"Dulcie O'Neil, you are under arrest. You have the right to remain silent. Anything you say or do can and will be held against you in a court of law."

"Knight," I repeated, completely unaware of what was happening. *I was being arrested?* For what? I was the one who'd ratted out the bad guys and in the process, stopped a potentially devastating situation from happening ...

"You have the right to speak with an attorney. If you can't afford an attorney, one will be appointed for you. Do you understand your rights as I have recited them to you?"

"Why are you doing this?" I demanded angrily when he pulled me away from the tree. I searched his face, looking directly into his eyes as I tried to understand.

198

His face was livid and his lips were sealed tight. "Do you understand your rights as I have recited them to you?" he said again, his tone one of indifference and apathy.

SEVENTEEN

"How long have you been working for your father?" Knight demanded finally, after not speaking to me for at least ten minutes. He'd placed me into the passenger seat of a black Yukon Denali, my arms still cuffed behind my back so I had to lean forward slightly to obtain any semblance of comfort.

The only thing he'd admitted to me thus far was that I was being arrested for my involvement with the illegal potions trade; and specifically, for participating in the aid and distribution of the *Draoidheil*. Apparently the ANC had been able to salvage one crate of the stuff which was being transported with us in the Denali. The other ANC officials had taken Quill, Horatio and the surviving guards to Hades only knew where. Knight hadn't admitted that much to me yet.

At the mention of Melchior, I felt my heart drop, even though it was pretty obvious that Knight already knew about the relationship between my father and me. Even so, I still couldn't help the shock that warred through me. "You know?" I asked in a hollow tone as I looked at him, and felt my stomach sour.

He refused to look at me, keeping his attention focused on the road as he left the loading docks and headed for the freeway. "Of course," he spat back. "I've always known." He said it like I was stupid for even asking, like he was so accomplished as an ANC detective, by all rights, he would know.

"I ... Why didn't you ever mention it? If you knew he was my father, why didn't you ever tell me?"

He looked at me then and laughed, but there was no levity in the sound. He shook his head like I just didn't get it, like the joke was on me. "I never mentioned it because you obviously already knew and, furthermore, it would have given too much away."

I closed my eyes, wondering if this whole thing was a dream. Maybe it was merely a fabrication from my muddled mind, arising from the fact that Baron had hit me too hard. But even after blinking several times, when I opened my eyes, I found that Knight was still driving and I was still sitting beside him. I glanced down at myself, realizing I was dressed in only my bra and yoga pants. With my hands firmly locked behind my back, my arms went numb, and when I tried to move them, they stung like pins and needles. "I don't understand," I said simply, wishing the headache behind my eyes would fade away. "You would have given too much of what away?"

Knight expelled a breath and didn't appear to be in the mood for a lengthy explanation. "How long have you been working for Melchior, Dulcie?" he demanded again.

I shook my head and tried to focus on the question, tried to remember, tried to look past the pain that was throbbing between my eyes. "I don't know, maybe two weeks."

"You're lying." Knight snapped, glaring at me before returning his attention to the road, apparently remembering he was behind the wheel. "Don't play this innocent fucking game with me, Dulcie. I don't have the patience for it."

And that was when I lost it. I craned my neck in his direction and felt my eyebrows furrowing because I honestly didn't understand what was going on and my headache was only making my temper that much shorter. "I have no idea what you're talking about! So why don't you drop your shitty attitude and tell me what the hell is going on?!"

Knight failed to reply, but seemed to focus entirely on driving, refusing to look at me. I could see his ears tinged red with anger. When he finally spoke, his voice was hollow and pained. "Your father and I always had our differences," he started and his hands tightened around the steering wheel, making his knuckles go white. "I was at the top of my game in the ANC, getting accolades and rewards left and right. Of course, Melchior not only respected my position, but realized he could use me to his advantage. He approached me about becoming his top potions smuggler and, in the process, had to put everything on the table. He had to show his hand. When I refused, he banished me to Earth, telling me I would never be allowed to return to the Netherworld. I was basically exiled to live the rest of my life beneath the radar." He looked at me and frowned as I thought about the fact that Knight's story was very similar to Quillan's. It was like my father had searched out the best Regulators in the ANC to call his own.

"Obviously he didn't know me very well," Knight continued. Then he took a deep breath. "He would have had me killed, but by that time, I'd gained so much notoriety in the ANC, knocking me off would have created too much suspicion. Instead, he banished me to Earth, and permitted me to work in any ANC location of my choosing. What he wasn't aware of, though, was that I kept a close eye on him, even from afar. When he pronounced my sentence, I promised myself, he would be taken down, that I would personally see to it ..."

I felt my jaw drop as something dawned on me. "You're part of The Resistance?" I asked as my mouth formed a perfect "O."

He said nothing, merely inhaled deeply. But he didn't have to say anything because his lack of a response was answer enough. He was definitely part of The Resistance and probably always had been. I studied him, as the pieces of the puzzle titled, "Why Melchior O'Neil wanted Knightley Vander dead" were quickly falling into place. "Melchior wanted to wipe you out in order to end The Resistance," I said, watching as he exited the freeway. We were on Coconut Street, which led to Splendor's city center. I thought we were en route to the ANC, where I'd be kept in custody for Hades only knew how long. Obviously I didn't imagine Knight would return me to the Netherworld for sentencing because, in his mind, it wasn't as though I'd actually be sentenced since Melchior was my father. The truth of the matter was that I'd probably be dealt with in the harshest possible way given my involvement in destroying my father's immediate chances at tyranny.

Knight glanced at me and shrugged. "Most recently, yes, but at the time he exiled me, he wasn't aware of my ties to The Resistance. However, I was more than aware of his ties to the illegal potions industry and after doing a little recon of my own, I learned he had a daughter." Then he frowned at me.

"You came to Splendor because of me?" I asked, feeling nauseous at the realization that Knight assumed I'd been serving my father during the entire course of his and my association.

"Yes," he snarled back at me. "I knew there was a mole in the ANC ranks in Splendor, and at the time, I figured it was you. So given my hatred of your father and my determination to see him dethroned, I transferred to Splendor so I could beat you at your own game."

"But you knew the mole was Quill," I said, wishing I could press my fingers to my temples, to try to assuage the pain between my eyes. I had to wonder if I had a small concussion. "You were there when I let Quill go."

He glanced at me and shook his head. "I wasn't with you, I took you on your word that you let him go. Quillan might never have been there, for all I know." Then he laughed cynically. "At the time, I might have bought into your little charade where Quill was concerned, but now I know better. Now I know the truth."

"The truth?" I repeated, starting to become pissed off with this whole situation.

"Quill was the fall guy for you. Your father knew it was wiser to ensure your place in the ANC than Quillan's so he told Quillan to take the fall for you, with the knowledge that having you in the ANC would be a far greater advantage to him." He looked over at me then, taking me in from face to breasts. "Your father is no idiot. He realized you were the best weapon in his arsenal. He knew you were every fucking man's dream."

I shook my head, feeling panic stirring within me. Looking at things from Knight's perspective, I could understand how he'd come to this conclusion, even though he was completely wrong. But the evidence seemed to support his theory. "That isn't true, Knight. None of that is true. I met my father for the first time two weeks ago, I swear it."

"I'm not finished," he interrupted in an irate tone. "So I figured you got word back to Melchior about Knightley Vander and how he was now working in Splendor; and I'm sure Melchior had a field day with that one." He slammed his fist into the steering wheel, making the horn blare as I jumped a few inches out of my seat. Knight came to a stop sign and inhaled deeply before looking over at me. "So, Dulcie, you tell me, what did your father tell you to do? Did he ask you to target me? To make me want you? Did he tell you to make me fall in love with you? To wrap me around your finger?"

Glaring at him, I was no longer okay with having to defend myself against false accusations. "So you think you have this whole thing figured out, don't you?" I asked icily. "And it all fits into a tiny, neat little box called Dulcie's guilty, right? None of it's true—it's just a load of bullshit!"

"Disprove it then, Dulcie," he raged back at me. "Prove that it's false. Go on, I'm curious to hear you try and back pedal your way out of this."

But there wasn't anything that immediately came to mind on how I could disprove it. Instead, I opted for simply

telling the truth. "I started working for my father two weeks
ago because he forced me to do it."

"And how did he manage that?" Knight asked, his
tone facetious.

"He held your life as ransom," I snapped at him. "I
made the deal with him that I would be his eyes and ears in
the ANC, as long as he agreed to leave you alone."

Knight shook his head and laughed acidly. "I don't
believe that for one second, Dulcie," he said, facing me, his
lips tight. "I fell for your bullshit once, and told myself that
everything I'd previously thought about you wasn't true, that
you really had no idea who your father was, and you really
were the girl for me." He shook his head and bashed his
hand into the steering wheel again. "You were pretty good,
Dulcie, I'll give you that. You even had my body convinced
that you were the one."

He was referring to the fact that as a Loki, only his
body could choose his mate, a woman strong enough to
handle his powerful seed, and the one woman to whom he
would be dedicated for life. When his eyes first glowed in
my presence, it was his body's announcement that I was his
woman.

"Knight, that is the truth! I didn't know who my fa ..."

"I don't want to hear it!" he railed at me.

I swallowed hard, suddenly intimidated by the anger
and pain in his eyes. But there was also a fire in me that
refused to be extinguished, a fire that wouldn't stop burning
until Knight learned the truth and realized I was innocent of
all of his accusations. "And what about everything we said
to each other while we were in High Prison?" I demanded.
"What about the fact that I came back to the Netherworld to
save your ass? And how do you explain my being
imprisoned with you and nearly raped by that Cyclops thug?
How the hell have you talked yourself out of the legitimacy
of all that?"

He shook his head. "You being imprisoned was just part of the overall act, something that was just a façade but meant for me to drop my defenses and trust you wholeheartedly. Looking back, to your credit, it worked … but now I can see right through it ... and you."

"And that bit about Cyclops?" I persisted, my lips tight.

"Bad luck. Wrong place at the wrong time. Your father should have known better than to lump you, a fairy, in with the likes of the goblin and a Cyclops. Just goes to show how much he truly loves you."

I couldn't argue with him about that because he was correct—my father didn't care about me. Not a damn.

"Besides," he continued, "Caressa said she never took you to the portal. Remember how I caught you in that lie?" Without allowing me to respond, he continued, "Of course, she never took you to the portal because your father released you from High Prison, something which in and of itself was highly problematic, considering you skipped any trial and simply got released. It's good to have a big daddy up high in the ranks, isn't it?"

"I never knew why I was released," I admitted. "But it's true that Caressa never took me to the portal. Instead, I told her what my plan was where you were concerned and she allowed me to escape." Knight shot me a disingenuous glance, but I wasn't about to let him deny me my explanation. "Then I went to my father's office and I demanded that he release you. And of course, once he realized he had me right where he wanted me, I ended up in this mess."

Knight shook his head. "Do you really expect me to believe that trite shit? Fuck, Dulcie, I'm not going to buy into your soap opera."

"Yes, I expect you to believe it because it's true!" I screamed at him, trying to find some way that I could prove I wasn't lying. But as much as I racked my brain, I couldn't think of anything that would clear me of this blame. Nothing tangible, anyway. I glanced outside my window, realizing that Knight had driven straight through Splendor and was now merging onto the freeway, headed toward Haven. As I stared out at the darkness, something occurred to me. "Knight, if my father wanted you dead so badly, and I was his liaison, why would I have fought so hard to spare your life? If he really wanted you dead, he had you exactly where he wanted you when you were in the Netherworld. You admitted as much yourself."

Knight inhaled deeply and frowned at me, clearly not convinced with this fact. "Because he realized my connections to The Resistance, something you've already demonstrated you also knew about. So he informed you to sink your claws into me even deeper than you already had, in order to find out all you could about The Resistance so Melchior could shut it down."

I realized I'd made a big mistake in admitting I knew about The Resistance. I ransacked my mind, trying to think of something else that didn't ring true, of something else that could help me in my quest to prove my innocence. "If nothing I've said is true, why did you just catch Baron trying to kill me?" I asked. I knew I was reaching, but I had to go for it anyway. "If I was really working for my father, do you think Baron would have come after me, calling me a back-stabbing bitch?"

Knight frowned. "I didn't hear him call you anything and furthermore, he wasn't trying to kill you," he said. Then he shook his head like I was a great big idiot. "And I think it's pretty obvious what he was after, just seizing a good opportunity to go for it."

"Okay, then what of Trey?" I demanded, playing every card I could.

"What of Trey?" Knight repeated.

"Don't you think if I'd been working for my father this entire time, that Trey would have picked up on it since he's a sensitive?"

Knight shook his head. "Your father's obviously creative, exemplified by the fact that he forced the Dryads on this little *Draoidheil* mission to throw off Trey and others like him. It's not a stretch to imagine he'd been doing something similar all along where you're concerned."

I felt like crying as I realized all my defenses were failing. There really wasn't anything concrete that I could use to prove to Knight that he totally had me pegged incorrectly.

"And speaking of coworkers, is Sam in on this too or did you pull the wool over her eyes also?"

I glared at him. "Sam has nothing to do with this! She's completely innocent!"

He shook his head. "Nice that you're even lying to your best friend."

I sighed, long and hard, trying to salvage a shred of something that would prove my innocence but my mind was a blank. "Everything you believe about me isn't true, Knight," I whispered, my voice sounding grainy as tears filled my eyes. "And everything I said to you while we were in prison was the truth. Every last word."

Knight chuckled humorlessly. "The only one of us who was telling the truth was me ... Something which was blatantly demonstrated when you broke up with me as soon as we returned to Splendor. And then to really rub salt in my wounds, you started dating Bram."

"I did that to protect you, Knight," I threw back at him. "And I'm not dating Bram and never have been. I broke things off with you because I didn't want you to find out that I was working for my father." I briefly considered telling him about my visit to Bram's and how I'd told Bram everything I was now telling Knight but I didn't imagine that would hold any weight because there wasn't any solid proof in it. And, furthermore, I didn't imagine Knight would appreciate the reminder of Bram when the vampire was obviously a sore subject. "I broke up with you only because I wanted to put some distance between us to keep you safe, Knight. That was my only intention."

He gave me a look which I'll never forget—his eyes had never appeared so furious, so livid. His nostrils flared as he breathed in and out and I could see his racing heart rate in the pulse thumping in his neck. "I don't want to hear another fucking word from you, got it?"

I shook my head, refusing to be shut down. "I'm the one who told the ANC about this whole thing to begin with," I yelled at him, my voice shaking. "I went to Caressa and I told her everything about the *Draoidheil* delivery, as well as every drop-off location. The only reason you aren't addicted to the shit now is because I gave her vials of antidote and told her to make sure all of you took it." I didn't even want to think about Caressa not delivering on her promise to ensure that Knight was kept far away from Splendor. Somehow, I didn't blame Caressa for it, as much as I did Knight's iron will, and his insistence on doing whatever the hell he chose to.

He shook his head and glared at me. "Funny, but when Caressa notified the ANC about the deliveries happening tonight, she failed to mention that any of it had come from you."

And that was because she'd kept her word to me by not associating my name with the information. I was tired and at the point now where I'd exhausted any further means to prove my innocence in all of this. I didn't know how to prove Knight wrong anymore. I suddenly felt my fatigue gaining on me and gazed out the window, watching the scenery blur by, wishing things were drastically different.

"Where are you taking me, anyway?" I asked, in a defeated tone.

"To jail," he answered quickly.

I felt my stomach drop at the thought, but I knew he wasn't taking me to the holding cells in the ANC of Splendor because we'd passed them already. "What jail?" I demanded.

He didn't spare me a glance. "One you don't know about, and one where I can ensure your father will never find you."

Something which was fine by me because I wasn't sure what would happen if or when my father found me. I had to imagine, though, that it wouldn't be a happy homecoming. I said nothing else, as I tried to find a comfortable position. Having my hands clasped behind my back, it seemed comfort was too much to ask. Instead, I focused on the confusion of my own thoughts. I just couldn't understand how things had turned ugly so quickly between Knight and me. Only weeks ago, we'd confessed our undying love for one another, and now he seemed to hate me.

From the corner of my eye, I watched Knight reach for the CD player as he turned the volume up and Pearl Jam's "Deep" filled the SUV in a rich harmony of guitar and drums. The fury of the song seemed to match my mood and I would have bet it matched Knight's as well, only for different reasons. I turned my head even farther away from him, not wanting him to see the tears that were sliding down my cheeks.

I closed my eyes, and scolded myself, telling myself to stop crying. I would find a way out of this and my vehicle was Caressa. Somehow I had to get in touch with her because I knew she'd set Knight straight. Only she could tell him about my release from prison and how she'd been charged with escorting me to the portal. Only she could admit that she really released me to go after my father in order to ensure Knight's safety. And, after that, she could tell Knight that I really was the one who'd spilled the beans about the *Draoidheil* delivery.

I heard Knight turn up the volume as the words of the song sunk into me: *And she doesn't like the view, she doesn't like the view but he sinks himself deep ...*

"Tell me one thing," Knight started, suddenly turning to face me, his voice almost lost in the song. I looked up at him expectantly, hoping the tears were no longer visible on my cheeks. "When Bram's inside you, is it my face you imagine?"

"You son of a bitch," I spat out at him, shaking my head, and forcing my gaze away from his. I slammed my eyes shut, not wanting to lose control of my tears. I would not cry in front of him!

I'd just never seen this side of Knight before— an icy cold, calculating side. And I wanted to hate him for believing I was ever capable of something so horrendous and awful. I wanted to hate him for not being able to see clearly, for obstructing his own vision. But there was something within me that refused to allow me to hate him, something that wouldn't permit me to throw in the towel.

I would make him see the truth. I would make him realize the picture he was trying to paint of me was entirely wrong.

And I would make him eat his words.

EIGHTEEN

Knight suddenly pulled the Denali over to the side of the road and I had to balance myself against my seat to keep the side of my head from hitting the window. The uneven ground caused my teeth to chatter in my head, and when he hit the brakes to keep us from plowing into an enormous oak tree, I was grateful he'd seat-belted me in.

"What the hell are you doing?" I asked with a confused frown.

He didn't respond, but put the Denali in park, not even bothering to look at me. Instead, he threw his door open, leaving the engine on and jumped down to the ground. The SUV beeped angrily at him, warning him the door was open. I couldn't say I was really paying much attention to the incessant beeping though. Instead, I watched as Knight jogged around the front of the Denali. The headlights illuminated his incredibly broad build and the ample swell of his biceps. I was suddenly overcome with fear, remembering the time when Knight and I first met and I tried to fight him. I lost because fairy magic was useless against Lokis. Taking in his impressive physique now, I found myself hoping I wouldn't have to go up against him again.

He yanked my door open and released my seat belt, refusing to so much as look at me. Instead, his lips were a tight line as he grabbed me by my waist and lifted me down. I shivered in the cold night air and worried for a minute that he was going to leave me out here. I glanced around to figure out just where "here" was. I couldn't say I'd been keeping track of where we'd been going because my mind was so consumed by our most recent conversation. As I looked around myself now, I realized we were in the middle of nowhere with rolling fields of untouched land on either side of us, brightened by the beams of the full moon A few gnarled oak trees dotted the horizon, the lights of the nearest city far in the distance. The only sound to interrupt the otherwise still air was the chirping of the crickets.

All alone with an enraged Loki, a creature created by Hades, the god of the Netherworld, and in his own image, Knight was a soldier by all accounts and well trained in the art of combat, committed to destroy and win. Nearly two feet taller than I, and much larger in both breadth and brawn, (well, triple my size where the girth of his chest was concerned), my magic was utterly useless against him. In essence, I was about as threatening as a little butterfly. I felt myself instinctively avoiding him, trying to seek shelter in the warmth and the light of the Denali. Knight gripped me by my upper arms and jerked me forward, slamming the door behind me. I jumped at the loud sound and felt my heartbeat racing through me, every fiber of my being on high awareness.

"Why are we stopping here?" I asked, my voice teetering with my own anxiety. I was tense and I couldn't hide it. Knight's eyes narrowed and bored into mine with heated fury.

"Why? Are you scared, Dulcie?" he asked. Suddenly, his mask of anger lifted and he smiled, but it was a smile that said he was enjoying every ounce of my disquietude.

I gulped down my trepidation, but refused to respond.

"Are you afraid I'm going to hurt you?" he persisted, leaning into me until less than two inches separated us. I forced myself not to break his eye contact, straining to hold my own ground. "Kind of like the way you hurt me?" he continued and then shook his head, forcing his face up close and personal with mine. Now no space existed between us and I could feel the kiss of his breath against my mouth. "No, kind of like the way you devastated me?"

He pulled back as I shook my head and opened my mouth, about to deny everything again, while begging him to believe me, to allow me to prove my innocence. Apparently disconcerted at where the conversation was headed, he gripped my cheeks between his large fingers, forcing my mouth into a fish kiss expression. He released my cheeks, his hand then finding purchase around my neck as he pressed me against the Denali, forcing the back of my head against the glass.

"Please don't hurt me," I whispered, honestly frightened by his wild expression.

He just stared at me for a second or two. His eyes began to glow, that same glow that said I was his and always would be. In that moment, I realized that Knight was as much in love with me now as he always had been.

"Knight," I said softly, my heart breaking for both of us. If he would just listen to me, just put aside his anger and injured pride, maybe we could get somewhere. "Please just let me explain. I can make you understand how wrong you are about everything."

"No," he said and slammed his hand against the door beside my head, dropping his face so I couldn't see the glow of his eyes. He clenched his eyes shut tightly, trying to compel the radiance of his gaze to subside, trying to force himself to believe that I wasn't the woman he thought I was.

When he looked up at me again, the glow disappeared from his eyes. He shifted my hair, half of which had fallen into my face, behind my neck, his fingertips brushing against my skin. I couldn't help remembering how those same fingers once touched me so tenderly, exploring my body in the most loving and gentle manner. I knew my eyes were wide with fright, my body still on high alert, but he just stared at me, appearing hesitant in whatever he was planning to do to me. He rested his hand against my collarbone as he honed in on my neck, his eyes narrowing. I glanced down and saw the line of golden blood that trailed from the gash at the bottom of my neck, the blood disappearing into my cleavage. Apparently Baron had sliced my skin when he threatened me with my dagger. The bastard.

Knight shook his head and took a deep breath as he reached forward and ran the pad of his thumb over the cut, healing it instantly. It was one of his many Loki abilities. "Fuck me for still caring," he whispered and sighed as his eyes found mine.

Before I could respond, he gripped the back of my neck, wrenching me forward. A single breath later and his mouth was on mine as he snagged a fistful of my hair at the nape of my neck almost painfully. His kiss was hard and impulsive, his tongue plunging into my mouth as he pushed his body against mine. It was as if he were trying to devour me, thrusting his tongue into my mouth, regardless if I wanted it or not. And although I loved his kiss, and loved him, this wasn't how I wanted him. Not with all this unresolved anger and baggage between us.

I tried to pull my head back to break the seal of our lips, but his fist at the nape of my neck held me firmly in place. Trying to extricate my body from his, I felt the cold steel of the Denali against my naked back as I turned my head to the side. He pulled away from me and I faced him, glaring at him all the while. "I want you to stop," I said in a small voice, my eyes begging him to keep away from me.

"Why, Dulcie? Would it upset Bram?" he asked in a lascivious tone, his eyes dancing with ire. "Have you sworn loyalty to him, just like you did to me?" Then he shook his head and chuckled. "The poor, stupid son of a bitch."

I felt something inside me break at the thought that he actually believed there was something between Bram and me. "You know that's a lie."

He shook his head, but said nothing, his gaze traveling from my face down to my breasts. He stared at me unabashedly, as if wanting to make me as uncomfortable as

possible. It was almost as though he wanted to make me feel
like nothing more than a vehicle for his desire, rather than a
person. I felt myself inhale deeply. "Please don't do this," I
whispered but I couldn't deny the fact that something was
heating within me, something fueled by the expression in
his eyes when they'd feasted on my cleavage.

He brought his eyes, which were now alight with
desire, up to mine and smiled, but it was a smile of victory.
"You know you want me to."

I swallowed hard because I couldn't argue. It was true
that I wanted his hands all over me, his lips on mine, his
tongue in my mouth and his penis inside me, but I also
knew now was not the right time nor the right place. Not
when things weren't good between us. I dropped my gaze to
the ground, angry with myself for my own duplicitous
feelings. But Knight wasn't going to allow me to hide.
Instead, he tilted my chin up, forcing me to look at him.

"Please," I said again, my voice husky with desire.

Saying nothing, he stared down at me and I was sure
he realized I wanted nothing more than to feel him inside
me, to have him claim me again. I just watched him, my
eyes wide as I tried to guess at his thoughts. He continued to
stare at me, finally releasing my hair. When I thought he'd
back away, he held his ground. I shrank beneath his
rigorous gaze.

"Knight," I said, but lost my train of thought when he
touched his index finger to my stomach and traced the waist
of my yoga pants. While keeping his gaze fixed on mine, he
looped his fingers beneath my pants and tugged, dragging
them down my legs, exposing every inch of me, because I
wasn't wearing panties beneath them. He kneeled down
until his hamstrings rested on his heels and he was exactly
eye level with my navel. Of course, his eyes traveled
downward, resting on the triangle between my legs. I tried
to shimmy my hips away from him, but his hold on my
pants was tight and he simply reached down, slipping my

sneaker off and pulled one pant leg free. With my arms cuffed behind my back, I was helpless to stop him.

"Knight, please stop," I said again, realizing he was lapping up the sight of my nude body, his eyes transfixed. "This isn't the right place for this," I started. "I don't want ..."

"You don't want me?" he asked, suddenly looking at me, but obviously not believing such was the case, because a smile turned up the corners of his mouth and his eyes were vibrant and alive. He knew I wanted him.

"I don't want to do this right now," I stammered, even as something inside me firmly planted its heels in the dirt, invalidating my words. No, the truth was that I wanted to feel him inside me now more than ever before. "Not when things are this bad between us," I added, my tone of voice so soft that it nearly disappeared on the slight breeze that wafted between us.

Knight chuckled acidly. "Things will never be good between us again, but that doesn't change the fact that I still want this." With that, he grabbed my ass, pulling me into him, until my lower body was maybe four inches from his face ... and his mouth.

I tried to step away from him, but didn't get far, considering he'd taken hold of my thigh with his vise-like grip. With my arms behind my back, I was basically his for the taking. He stood up and pushed me against the Denali again, studying me, his fingers now beneath my bra. "I don't want to do this," I whispered, the tone of my voice in complete contradiction to my words.

Knight didn't respond but gripped the cups of my bra and with the strength inherent in his species, simply tore it in half as I gasped out in shock. My breasts bounced with the attack as my heart thundered in my chest. Knight's eyes narrowed as he stared at me, watching my breathing shorten into shallow gasps. His eyes traveled down my face and rested on my bare breasts, my nipples alert and standing at

217

attention. He brought his fingers to one of them and pinched it softly, rolling it between his fingers. I dropped my head back and moaned. I was helpless to his touch.

"Tell me you don't want it," he whispered, his breath causing goose bumps to dance across my skin. I didn't respond. "Tell me … you … don't ... want ... it," he demanded much more slowly, pronouncing every syllable of every word in a steely tone. Before I could stop him, I felt his fingers slip between my thighs. I jumped at the invasion as he started rubbing me in gentle circles. Then I threw my head back, unable to stifle another moan from escaping my lips, only this one was much louder.

"Open your eyes and look at me," he demanded, his fingers suddenly going still. I did and found him staring at me with a hungry gaze. "Funny that you say you don't want it," he said archly, "when you're soaking wet."

I couldn't respond because his fingers had resumed rubbing me back and forth, playing with me, torturing me, stealing my ability to form words. "Why," I started, but when he increased the pressure on my sensitive nub, I had to fight the need to arch against him. "Why are you doing this?" I breathed out finally, insisting my logical side regain control.

He chuckled at that. "Why am I doing this?" he repeated, shaking his head as the smile dropped right off his lips. "I'm doing this because I can." And then he thrust his fingers inside me as if to prove his point. There was no warning, no warming me up with one finger and then adding another. He simply forced his fingers in me and I could feel myself growing wetter. I was on the brink of an orgasm as he pulled his fingers out and rammed them back into me again, nothing tender about it. I screamed and clenched my eyes shut as I felt myself give in to the tremors that were starting to quake inside me.

"Come on, Dulcie," Knight taunted me. "Show me what you're feeling."

And so I let go. I allowed my hips to gyrate against him as I threw my head back and let the orgasm seize me. Allowing it to take hold of me, I screamed until my voice was hoarse. A few crows squawked their protest and flapped away from the tree they'd been resting on, but I was elsewhere. When I opened my eyes, I found Knight's glowing. This time, he did nothing to conceal them. He pulled his fingers out of me and dropped to his knees, grabbing me by the ass as he brought my pelvis forward. He glanced up at me, his expression daring me to stop him and then buried his face between my thighs, lifting my leg up slightly and dropping it over his shoulder so he could slip his tongue deep inside me. I started to whimper with pleasure, my hips undulating as another orgasm gripped me and caused my legs to shake uncontrollably.

My knees were becoming the consistency of jelly, and when I felt like they were going to buckle, he lifted me against the Denali and I wrapped them snugly around his middle. Balancing me against the SUV, he reached down and unzipped his pants, staring at me as he freed himself and rubbed his hardness against me, sighing at the wetness he was about to enter.

"Tell me," he demanded, his lips tight. "Tell me again that you don't want this."

He gripped each of my thighs, spreading me wide. Teasingly, he entered me with the very tip of his penis. I felt myself stretching to accommodate him, preparing for his entry.

"Answer me," he demanded gruffly.

There was no way I could deny that I wanted him. "I want it," I said softly. "I want you."

Knight chuckled, and gripping my thighs, stuffed himself into me, as deeply as he could. I screamed out against the intrusion and bucked against him as he started to drive himself in and out mercilessly. He grasped a fistful of my hair and held it tightly as I opened my eyes and found his on me.

"Lie to me, Dulcie," he said, his eyes narrowed. "Lie to me and tell me you love me."

I felt my brows knot in the middle as I focused on his beautiful blue eyes, his face so chiseled and perfect I'd never seen another to equal its beauty. Feeling his body inside mine, there was no one else—there never had been anyone else. "I love you," I said softly, about to add that it wasn't a lie, but Knight didn't allow me the chance. Instead, he thrust inside me so hard, I felt like I needed to brace myself, which, of course, wasn't possible since my hands were bound behind me. Knight lifted me up higher and slammed me against the Denali, pushing into me as deeply and quickly as he could. We'd never had sex like this before—never anything this bestial and furious.

It was suddenly very obvious that Knight hated himself because he still loved me.

His thrusts were gaining momentum as he bit his lower lip, driving himself into me as hard as he could. He clenched his eyes shut and moaned loudly as he climaxed inside me, grinding his pelvis into mine.

When he opened his eyes again, he didn't say anything, but pulled out of me and lifting me by my waist, brought me to the ground. He reached down and gripped my pants, pulling them up my legs. Glancing at my breasts, he sighed and took hold of his T-shirt, pulling it up and over his head. I couldn't help my gaze, which was fastened onto his chiseled upper body, so broad with sinuous muscle. He draped his shirt over my head, then realizing I was helpless to dress myself, yanked it down to cover me. Grabbing my arm and opening the passenger door of the Denali, he lifted me up and placed me back into my seat. When I looked down at him, his eyes were even angrier than they had been earlier, as if now he was berating himself for not resisting the need to be inside me.

"This changes nothing between us," he said.

The remainder of the ride was silent except for Pearl Jam's album, "Ten," which was still blasting through the speakers, so loud it was obvious that Knight didn't want any conversation. When we pulled off the two-lane highway and onto a dirt road, I had to summon the interest to pay attention to my surroundings. The terrain hadn't changed much and looked the same as when we'd pulled over. Unrecognizable.

"What are you going to do with me?" I asked loudly, fighting the volume and the silence between us.

"You'll find out soon enough, won't you?" he responded, glaring at me and making no motion to turn the volume down.

I didn't say anything more, but watched a small structure as it came into view. It was a rectangular shaped, one-story building without windows. It looked so small from the outside that I didn't imagine it could have more than four rooms inside. Knight pulled up in front of it and stopped the Denali, putting it into park. I assumed this building was the jail he'd mentioned earlier.

He turned off the engine and sighed, not making any motion to move. He just sat in his seat, staring straight ahead for another few seconds before he opened his door and jumped down. He walked around the Denali and then opened my door, hoisting me into his arms, only to set me on the ground. Gripping my upper arm, he forced me up the gravel entryway to the nondescript building.

He unlocked the front door and pushed me over the threshold none-too-gently. It was dark inside, but moments later, he turned on a light switch and the fluorescent bulbs overhead flickered as they lit the place in a sickly yellow. The jail amounted to one enormous room with four holding cells, two on each side. The front of the room boasted a table with a phone on it, a small television and a case of bottled waters. There were three fold-up chairs arranged around the table.

When I slowed, not sure where I should go or what I should do, Knight pushed me forward. "Watch it," I ordered when I nearly tripped over my own feet. He said nothing, but gripped my arm and turning to the first cell, unlocked it, shoving me inside. There was a cot on one side and a toilet on the other, with a small sink beside it. I turned around at the sound of him closing the barred door and locking it.

Then he simply disappeared down the hallway. I could hear him sitting in one of the chairs and throwing his legs up on the table. He turned the television on and the volume blared out. Seconds later, the volume dropped to a mere hum.

I'd fallen asleep. I'm not sure how long I was out, but I awoke to the sound of loud voices and heavy footfalls. I stood up and approached the bars of my cell, watching as two men I didn't recognize escorted Horatio into the room. He cursed them left and right, but they just laughed in response and showed him to the cell at the end of the hallway, on the opposite side of mine.

At the sound of more voices, I watched as Quillan walked through the front door, another ANC man behind him. Quill was silent as he stepped into the hallway. The man behind him gripped his arms and pulled him to a stop, making it known that he didn't want Quill to venture any farther. The man holding Quill glanced at Knight and I tried to make out their exchange, but their voices were too muffled. Instead, I watched as Knight took hold of Quill's arms, which were cuffed behind his back, and the other man disappeared through the front door. Then I watched Knight push him forward as Quill glanced in my direction, recognizing me immediately.

"Dulcie!" he said, his voice sounding relieved. Relieved probably because I wasn't dead. Then he looked over his shoulder at Knight, and his eyebrows furrowed in the middle. "If you so much as laid one finger on her," he started.

Knight glared at him. "You'll do what?"

"If you hurt her," he started again, a new fire burning in his eyes.

"I didn't hurt her," Knight responded stonily, his tone implying the hurt was the other way around. Neither of them said anything more as Knight showed Quill to his cell, which was right beside Horatio's. After locking the cell door behind Quill, Knight started back up the hall, refusing to even spare a glance in my direction.

I retired back to my cot and laid down, the fluorescence of the lights suddenly going dim as Knight turned them off. Well, in my part of the jail anyway. It was still bright in the front of the room, the gentle droning of the television supplying the only sound.

"Are you okay, Dulce?" Quill asked, his tone hopeful.

"Yeah, I'm fine," I said softly, even as I thought I was far from being fine.

"Everything is going to be okay, Dulce," Quill said, his tone sounding sweet, but defeated. 'Course, I couldn't say I believed him. Instead, I closed my eyes and fell back to sleep.

When I woke up, again to the sound of voices, I was pretty sure I'd been asleep for at least a few hours. I had that feeling of dreariness you get when waking up from a deep, REM sleep. I sighed and tried to hone in on the sounds of the voices coming from the front of the room. I recognized

Knight's, but couldn't place the other one. It was a woman's, the resonance and tone seeming somehow familiar to me. Yawning and rubbing the sleep from my eyes, I sat up, trying to decipher what they were saying.

"Are you sure?" I heard Knight's baritone.

"Yes, Vander, I'm more than sure. I heard it from Caressa herself. Now stop being an obstinate ape and let me see her."

Then the sound of heavy steps—Knight's—and he suddenly came into view. His expression was unreadable. He actually wouldn't even look at me. But seeing as how he was holding the key to my cell, I had to imagine something was up. I didn't get the chance to further consider what the hell was going on because I suddenly noticed the woman with the long, dark hair who couldn't have been more than five feet tall coming up behind him.

"Christina?" I asked, absolutely shocked.

She smiled broadly. "We meet again."

I glanced at Knight, wondering why he didn't have her in custody, why her hands weren't cuffed behind her back and, furthermore, why he wasn't escorting her to her own cell. But he just stood there, making no motion to do anything aside from unlocking my cell door and holding it wide open. I stayed put, staring at Christina's pretty face. "But, you ... you work for my father?"

She beamed then and nodded eagerly, as if about to tell me an incredibly exciting story. She stepped inside my cell as my gaze returned to Knight, who just stood there, austere in his silence.

"Yep, I do work for your father, well, that is, I did," Christina said with a soft laugh as if the whole thing were one big joke. Then the laugh died on her lips and she eyed me speculatively. "I'm also the leader of The Resistance."

H. P. Mallory is the author of the Jolie Wilkins series as well as the Dulcie O'Neil series.

She began her writing career as a self-published author and after reaching a tremendous amount of success, decided to become a traditionally published author and hasn't looked back since.

H. P. Mallory lives in Southern California with her husband and son, where she is at work on her next book.

If you are interested in receiving emails when she releases new books, please sign up for her email distribution list by visiting her website and clicking the "contact" tab:
www.hpmallory.com

Be sure to join HP's online Facebook community where you will find pictures of the characters from both series and lots of other fun stuff including an online book club!

Facebook: https://www.facebook.com/hpmallory

Find H.P. Mallory Online:
www.hpmallory.com
http://twitter.com/hpmallory
https://www.facebook.com/hpmallory